Praise for *New York Times* bestselling author Diana Palmer

"Palmer proves that love and passion can be found even in the most dangerous situations."
—*Publishers Weekly* on *Untamed*

"You just can't do better than a Diana Palmer story to make your heart lighter and smile brighter."
—*Fresh Fiction* on *Wyoming Rugged*

"Diana Palmer is a mesmerizing storyteller who captures the essence of what a romance should be."
—*Affaire de Coeur*

"The popular Palmer has penned another winning novel, a perfect blend of romance and suspense."
—*Booklist* on *Lawman*

"Diana Palmer's characters leap off the page. She captures their emotions and scars beautifully and makes them come alive for readers."
—*RT Book Reviews* on *Lawless*

Dear Reader,

I can't believe that it has been thirty years since my first Long, Tall Texans book, *Calhoun*, debuted! The series was suggested by my former editor Tara Gavin, who asked if I might like to set stories in a fictional town of my own design. Would I! And the rest is history.

As the years went by, I found more and more sexy ranchers and cowboys to add to the collection. My readers (especially Amy!) found time to gift me with a notebook listing every single one of them, wives and kids and connections to other families in my own Texas town of Jacobsville. Eventually the town got a little too big for me, so I added another smaller town called Comanche Wells and began to fill it up, too.

You can't imagine how much pleasure this series has given me. I continue to add to the population of Jacobs County, Texas, and I have no plans to stop. Ever.

I hope all of you enjoy reading the Long, Tall Texans as much as I enjoy writing them. Thank you all for your kindness and loyalty and friendship. I am your biggest fan!

Love,

Diana Palmer

NEW YORK TIMES BESTSELLING AUTHOR

DIANA PALMER

TAMING A TEXAN

4 Heartfelt Stories

Christopher, Luke, Guy and
Hank (previously published as *Redbird*)

 HARLEQUIN SPECIAL RELEASE

HARLEQUIN® SPECIAL RELEASE

ISBN-13: 978-1-335-51719-7

Taming a Texan

Copyright © 2022 by Harlequin Enterprises ULC.

Christopher
First published in 1999. This edition published in 2022.
Copyright © 1999 by Diana Palmer

Luke
First published in 1999. This edition published in 2022.
Copyright © 1999 by Diana Palmer

Guy
First published in 1999. This edition published in 2022.
Copyright © 1999 by Diana Palmer

Hank
First published as Redbird in 1995. This edition published in 2022.
Copyright © 1995 by Diana Palmer

Recycling programs
for this product may
not exist in your area.

For questions and comments about the quality of this book,
please contact us at CustomerService@Harlequin.com.

Harlequin Enterprises ULC
22 Adelaide St. West, 41st Floor
Toronto, Ontario M5H 4E3, Canada
www.Harlequin.com

Printed in U.S.A.

CONTENTS

A prolific author of more than one hundred books, **Diana Palmer** got her start as a newspaper reporter. A *New York Times* bestselling author and voted one of the top ten romance writers in America, she has a gift for telling the most sensual tales with charm and humor. Diana lives with her family in Cornelia, Georgia. Visit her website at dianapalmer.com.

Books by Diana Palmer

Long, Tall Texans

Fearless
Heartless
Dangerous
Merciless
Courageous
Protector
Invincible
Untamed
Defender
Undaunted

The Wyoming Men

Wyoming Tough
Wyoming Fierce
Wyoming Bold
Wyoming Strong
Wyoming Rugged
Wyoming Brave

Visit the Author Profile page
at Harlequin.com for more titles.

CHRISTOPHER

CHAPTER ONE

TANSY DEVERELL WAS missing again. In fact, she'd been missing for a week. It disturbed Christopher Deverell when he couldn't find his mother, who was in her seventies. More particularly, it disturbed him when the famous Lassiter Detective Agency of Houston, Texas, couldn't find her. Chris had come home from a trip to Spain to find the family in an uproar over the matriarch's disappearance. Tansy was known for her madcap lifestyle, and she tended to cause scandals wherever she went.

Chris's older brother, Logan, lived in Houston with his wife, Kit, and their new son, Bryce. Since Logan's marriage, Tansy had become even wilder than usual. She was a diabetic who was on insulin and had to watch her diet very carefully, and Chris worried that she might indulge too much in her travels. For a woman in her early seventies, Tandy was adventurous indeed. Old age, she often said, would have to run very fast in order to catch up with her. She wasn't kidding.

On a whim, Chris had traveled to Jacobsville, Texas, to see his cousin Emmett Deverell. In the past, nobody visited Emmett unless they were nuts, but now that Emmett had married Melody and they'd settled down nicely with his three children from his first marriage, Emmett had mellowed. He managed a ranch for Ted Regan, in which he now had a partnership. Things were looking prosperous there, and Tansy might have detoured to visit them. But she hadn't. Chris met with disappointment. Emmett hadn't seen nor heard from Tansy in months.

Chris drove into town and had lunch at the local high-class restaurant, sitting alone at a corner table with his steak and salad while he brooded about his mother. Logan hadn't been overly concerned. It was amusing how the brothers had changed over the years. In the past, Logan was the straitlaced, worrying one. Now, he was more relaxed and less anxious, especially since his marriage. On the other hand, Chris had been almost as madcap as their mother when he was younger, and women had passed through his life like butterflies. He was thirty-three, and a devastating automobile accident had left him with a different view of the world. His once-handsome face was now less pleasing to the eye, two long furrows having been carved into one lean cheek by shattered glass. He'd lost the sight in one eye, although plastic surgery had spared him deformity. But nothing seemed to erase the scars completely, and he was too weary of hospitals and skin grafts to pursue them further.

He wasn't repulsive by any stretch of the imagination. His smooth olive complexion was enhanced by liquid black eyes with thick black lashes and eyebrows, and a chiseled mouth that was more sardonic than amused most of the time. He had a lean face and a tall, lean, muscular body that was more attractive than ever since his weeks of sailing near the coast of Spain with an old friend. He enjoyed the challenge of the sea, where he could pit his muscle against the waves and wind. A man with as much money as he'd inherited from his father could do whatever pleased him. Unlike Logan, who enjoyed working at the family investment firm, Chris had invested his inheritance in multinational corporations and tripled it in less than ten years. He could live comfortably off the interest, and he'd never found an adequate reason to work a routine job. He dabbled in designing yachts with the friend with whom he'd been sailing in Spain. His ideas were innovative, and one of his designs had taken its owner into the finals of the America's Cup race. He was paid for that idea, and for several others that had sold well.

He watched his investments like a hawk. But increasing his means no longer satisfied him. The carefree bachelor's existence that was such fun in his early twenties was distasteful to him now. He no longer sized up women as potential conquests or enjoyed the attention of pretty fortune-hunters. He felt jaded and life was suddenly empty.

He fingered his coffee cup absently, the motion bringing the waitress with a refill.

"Can I get you anything else?" she asked pleasantly, sizing up his expensive suit and shoes with practiced expertise.

He shook his head. "Thanks. I'm fine."

He didn't encourage her to stay and chat. She was young and pretty, but so were dozens of other women. He envied Logan his family life. Maybe marriage wasn't so bad a thing. Certainly that baby was a delightful little bundle. Chris had never been around children much, but he adored his new nephew and spent a lot of time shopping for educational toys to bring him. That had amused Tansy, who'd suggested that Chris get married and have children of his own.

He'd only shrugged it off with a smile. He'd never had a serious relationship with a woman. His romantic encounters over the years had been light and pleasant and brief. Now he felt as if he'd missed something. Except for his friend who built yachts, he had no one who was close to him. Most of his old girlfriends were married. He traveled alone, ate alone, slept alone. He felt ancient, especially since the wreck.

"Excuse me, but aren't you Christopher Dev-er-ell?"

The voice was quiet, unhurried, with a pleasant huskiness. He turned his head to find the face that went with it. Not bad, he thought. Pale gray eyes, pretty complexion, rounded chin, bow mouth, short blond hair with a wave over the pencil-thin eyebrow.

She looked like something out of the thirties, he mused.

"How would you know who I am?" he asked indifferently.

"It's my job." She produced a pad and pen. "I work for the Weatherby News Service. We're not as big as the Associated Press, but we're working hard to catch up," she added with a faint smile. The smile faded quickly. "We're trying to locate your mother, as it happens."

He lifted his hot coffee to his mouth. "Join the club."

"She's gone into hiding," she continued. "Not that I blame her, under the circumstances, but—"

"Sit down," he said curtly. "You're on my blind side."

"Your...what?"

He turned his head and looked fully at her, so that she could see the extent of the damage the accident had done to his once-handsome face. The black eye in the socket above the two deep scars and just below a smaller one stared straight ahead, but without sight. The nerve damage had been extensive.

She caught her breath audibly and sat down, visibly flustered. "I'm sorry!" she said. "I didn't realize..."

"Most people don't, until they look at me for a while," he added with a mocking smile. He leaned back in the chair, pulling his jacket away from the thin white shirt that covered his broad, hair-roughened chest. In the position, the muscles were visible, and the woman quickly averted her eyes, as if looking at him that way embarrassed her.

"About your mother," she continued.

"First things first. Who are you?"

She hesitated. "I'm Della Larson."

He nodded. "Do you have some idea where my mother might be?"

"Of course." She turned back a few pages in the

small flip notebook. "When last seen, she was in a little town just outside London, called Back Wallop." She glanced at him. "That's a village."

"And what would she be doing there?"

"That's where *he* lives," she replied, surprised.

"He, who?" he asked with a broad scowl.

"Look here, she's your mother," she returned. "Don't you know that she was involved with an MP?"

"A Member of Parliament?" he exclaimed.

"Oh, yes, Lord Cecil Harvey. He belonged to the House of Lords and was a relative of the Windsors." She shook her head. "I can't believe you don't know this!"

"I've been on holiday in Spain," he said.

"It's been all over the tabloids," she continued.

His face hardened. "I don't read the scandal sheets," he said tersely.

"Considering how many times you're featured in them, I guess not," she agreed pleasantly. "You had the front page of most of them for two weeks when that Italian countess accused you of fathering her child—"

"We were discussing my mother," he interrupted curtly.

She grimaced. "Sorry. I guess that hit a nerve. Anyway, Mrs. Deverell was photographed coming out of a London hotel with Lord Harvey. There were rumors that he was going to divorce his wife and marry her."

He put the coffee cup down audibly. "My mother?"

"Your mother." She studied him curiously. "You

don't look at all like her," she commented. "She has blue eyes and a very fair complexion, almost girlishly pretty."

"My brother and I take after our father. He was Spanish."

"Spanish?" She frowned and flipped quickly through the notebook. "That's not what I was told. They said your father was French, a member of the nobility."

"Our stepfather was French," he returned, and refused to even think of the man, despite the many years it had been since he'd seen him. "Our father died when I was pretty young. Tansy remarried. Several times," he added drolly and picked up his coffee cup again.

"Oh, I see." She was watching him closely. "Why isn't your father mentioned?"

He chuckled. "He was a minor businessman until he bought a few cheap shares of stock and put them away in a safe-deposit box. Long after his death, the box was discovered and opened, and Logan and I inherited a small fortune."

"What was the stock?" she asked suspiciously.

He lifted the coffee cup to his chiseled mouth. "Standard Oil."

She grinned at him. "Amazing foresight."

He shook his head. "Sheer, damned luck. He didn't know beans about investments."

"They say your brother does. And so do you."

He chuckled. "I dabble. Not much." His dark

eyes narrowed. "Why are you trying to track down Tansy?"

"Why do you call her Tansy instead of 'Mother'?"

"She isn't old enough emotionally to be anyone's mother," he said simply. "Logan and I grew up trying to keep her out of trouble, with occasional and brief assistance from her five husbands."

"Five?" She glanced at her notes. "I only found four."

"You haven't answered my question."

She fingered the notebook and stared at it instead of him. "I blew a story, a really big one. I'm going to get fired unless I can make amends somehow. I can't lose my job. I have…responsibilities." She lifted her pale eyes to his. "I want to find your mother before the rest of the media can. I want an exclusive interview."

"Ask her for one."

"I can't find her. She's left Back Wallop and nobody knows where she went."

He finished his coffee. "Don't look at me. I can't find her, either, not even with the help of the best detective agency in the state."

She gnawed her lower lip worriedly. "I guess it's understandable that she wouldn't want to be found."

"Thank you for noticing," he said in a tone that dripped sarcasm. "A woman being accused of breaking up a marriage wouldn't rush to find the media."

Her eyebrows went up. They were pencil thin, very dark despite her blond hair, and quite interesting. "That's not why she's running, of course."

"It isn't?"

She sighed heavily. "Mr. Deverell, I already know the truth. There's no sense in pretending you don't know what's going on."

"I'm not pretending."

"Have it your own way." She put the pad into her large purse and stood up, slinging it over her shoulder.

"Giving up so soon?" he taunted.

"I've got to get to England before somebody beats me to the story. It will make my career if I can get it before the others do."

He stared at her with something like contempt. "By all means, ruin a life. You and your colleagues put a high price on your own careers, don't you? Nobody else's pain or suffering is too much to ask."

She flushed. "You make us sound perverted."

"I don't, actually." His eyes darkened. "You are perverted. All of you."

She stiffened. "We don't make the news."

"No, you just spread it around, with as many embellishments and enhancements as your editors see fit." He got to his feet, too, and looked down at her. She barely came to his chin. She noticed the discrepancy in their heights and stepped back a few inches.

"Frightened?" he chided, his black eyes glittering as he smiled down at her. "I'm not much of a threat these days."

"You'd be a threat if you were missing both legs," she muttered uncomfortably. The proximity was making her legs wobble. She backed up again. "I'm not responsible for what a few renegade reporters do."

"I know several families, including one royal one, who could give a chilling response to that remark."

Her fingers clutched the strap of her shoulder bag tightly. He noticed her nails, short and rounded and unpolished. The suit she was wearing was of the chain-store variety, and not new. Her shoes were scuffed, vinyl instead of leather, like her purse. He stared at her with new interest. She wasn't a successful professional, judging by her looks.

"As unfair as it seems, we are judged by the company we keep," he said quietly. "Some of your colleagues have no scruples and no conscience."

"I'm not like that."

"Yes, you are," he said simply. "Otherwise, why would you be chasing my mother over an indiscretion?"

"That's a rather weak thing to call it," she pointed out.

"What, a would-be affair?"

Her lips parted. "Mr. Deverell, Lord Harvey's body was found just this morning floating naked in the Thames. Your mother is Scotland Yard's number one suspect."

He caught his breath. The shock and terror he felt were in his stiff expression, his clenched jaw.

"You really didn't know, did you?" she asked worriedly. "I'm most dreadfully sorry. I thought…"

He caught her by the upper arm long enough to look at his check and lay a wad of bills down with it before he propelled her out the door.

"What you ordered doesn't cost that much," she murmured as he took her out through the doorway.

"I know how little waiters and waitresses get paid. What business is it of yours?" he asked curtly.

"Could you let me go?"

"Not on your life. You're not making my mother front page news. I've got you and I'm keeping you until I get to the bottom of this."

"You can't! It's kidnapping. It's against the law!"

"Big deal," he muttered. "Come on."

He put her into his big Lincoln on the driver's side and got right in beside her, quickly pressing the master lock switch on his door so that she couldn't open hers. She fumed and pushed, but she was trapped.

"Put on your seat belt," he said.

She did, only because when he put the car into gear and took off, she didn't want to go into the backseat the hard way.

"You drive like a maniac!" she exclaimed.

"So I've been told."

"Listen here, I'm not going anywhere with you. Let me out!"

"When we get to the airport," he assured her.

Her eyebrows lifted. "The airport?"

"We're going to London. You're resourceful and you have contacts that I lack." He glanced at her formidably. "You're going to help me find Tansy."

"Oh, am I, now?" she returned haughtily. "And what am I going to get out of it?"

"A front page scoop when we clear her name."

"You're nuts!"

He nodded. "Apparently."

"But I can't leave the country. Not like this. I told you, I have responsibilities."

"So have I. They'll wait until you get back."

"But I must stay," she persisted.

He lifted the cell phone from its cradle in the floorboard and handed it to her. "Call somebody and make arrangements."

She hesitated, but only for a minute. She couldn't afford to miss the opportunity of a lifetime, which this certainly was. Once she got the story, she'd file it no matter what he tried to do. If she didn't go with him, he might find some way to block her, to keep her from finding his mother. That wouldn't do at all.

She punched in the number and then the button that would send the call along the airways. It rang once, twice, three times.

"Hello?"

She smiled at the pepper in that sweet old voice. "Hi. It's me. I just wanted to tell you that I'm going to be out of town for a day or two. You let Mrs. Harris come over and cook for you. I'll make it right when I get home."

"Chasing after that mad old lady, are you?" A deep chuckle came from the other end of the line. "Just like me, when I was younger."

"Not just like you," she replied, smiling. "You used to hang out in bars with the Lafayette Escadrille and the SAS. I just walk in your shadow."

"Flatterer!"

"Don't forget to put the chain latch on at night," she added worriedly. "And if you need me…"

Chris already had the picture, from the brief snatches of conversation he overheard. "Give him this number," he told her without taking his eyes from the road—a good thing, at the speed they were going. He recited the cell phone number, and then added one with a foreign exchange. "That's in London. He can call anytime if he needs you. I'll make sure the call is forwarded immediately."

She relayed the information.

"Sounds young," the old man cackled. "Is he?"

"Sort of," she replied warily. "Stay warm, too. Don't worry about turning up the heat. Okay?"

"Okay. Now stop worrying about me and get the job done. Don't shame us."

"I wouldn't dare!" she chuckled. "I'll see you when I get back, Grandad."

"You take care, too. You're the only family I got left."

"Same here." She smiled as she put the receiver down. She glanced at the taciturn man beside her warily. "Thanks."

He shrugged. "You'll do better sleuthing if you're not worried. Your grandfather sounds like a character."

"He was, and still is. He was a reporter during the gang wars in Chicago, during Prohibition, and after that he was a war correspondent." She laughed. "He can tell some stories. I followed in his footsteps, but not very well. I'm not sure I'm cut out for investigative reporting after all."

"What did you do before?"

"I did political news and features." She grimaced. "I was good at it, too, but Grandad said I was wilting on the vine and wasting away. He wanted me to do something exciting and risky while I was still young enough."

"Don't you have any other family?"

She shook her head. "My parents died overseas. They were touring the Middle East when the plane they were in was shot down accidentally. Grandad took me in when I was just ten and raised me."

"Tough luck," he said. "No brothers, sisters, uncles or aunts?"

"An aunt," she replied. "She lives in California and never writes." She glanced at him. "At least you have a brother."

"A brother and a mother," he replied.

"What's she like?"

"She's a hell-raiser," he returned amusedly. "I've never known her when she wasn't in trouble. But she doesn't kill people," he added firmly.

"I hope you're right," she replied.

"I know I am." But there was the faintest doubt in his voice. He turned the car onto the highway that led to the Jacobsville airport, new lines in his worried face.

CHAPTER TWO

HEATHROW AIRPORT WAS BUSY, especially for the time of year. Summer was high season for most tourists, and as Chris passed along the crowded path to the customs line, he heard accents from countries all over the world. He glanced at Della, surprised by the look on her face. She seemed overly affected by her surroundings, by the people around her. Some were wearing exotic dress, and she seemed to find those fascinating.

He had a sudden thought. "You have your passport, but you've never been out of the States before, have you?" he asked.

She glanced at him with a shy smile. "Actually, I haven't. I always wanted to travel like my grandfather did, so I applied for my passport, but I couldn't afford to go anywhere until I landed this latest job. Now that I can, I've been too afraid to leave him on his own. He's diabetic, you see, and he won't leave sweets alone. He's been in a coma twice in the past three years, because he's too stubborn to admit there's anything wrong with him."

"That sounds familiar," Chris murmured under his breath. He glanced at the line beside them, which had thinned considerably. He took Della's arm and steered her and her wheeled suitcase to the shorter line.

"You know how to do this, don't you?" she asked, impressed.

"I spend a lot of time overseas," he commented. "Got your ticket?"

"Right here." She held it up.

They passed through customs and baggage control with a minimum of fuss, and Chris went right to the rental car agency to hire a vehicle. Minutes later, they were on the way to their hotel to check in. He seemed to find driving on the left-hand side of the road very easy. It made Della nervous, but after the first few minutes, she relaxed and began to pay attention to the sights.

"We'll leave the luggage, get a bite to eat and head out for Back Wallop," he said.

"I'm glad to see you aren't planning to let jet lag hold you back," she commented dryly.

He lifted an eyebrow and smiled. "What do you know about jet lag?"

"I've read lots of travel books. Besides, my grandfather is an authority. As I mentioned before, he was a war correspondent."

"In which war?"

"World War II, Korea, Vietnam and several other little wars in Hispanic countries."

"I'm impressed."

"He can tell some stories," she mused. "It's killing him that he can't do it anymore. He's seventy-three, and he's got arthritis as well as diabetes. It's like he's given up on life because he's been slowed down."

"Tansy has the same problem," he confided. "She thinks like a sixteen-year-old, but her body can't do what her mind wants it to."

"She must be a fascinating person."

"I've always thought so," he said. "My earliest memories of my mother are flamboyant, colorful images. She was always going somewhere, hosting parties, dragging us to cultural events like opera and the theater." He shook his head. "She used to be just a little less reckless." His face sobered. "I can't believe she'd get herself mixed up in a murder. It's not like her."

"Anyone can get in a circumstance where violence becomes the only answer," she said, glancing out the window at the crowded streets. "Are we downtown?"

"Yes. And here's our hotel." He pulled off the road into an elegant courtyard, where a man dressed like something out of medieval times was opening and closing car doors for guests.

"It's very elegant," she commented.

"When I travel, I always go first-class," he said carelessly. "I find it's less wearing to be pampered, especially if you've been to more than one or two countries on business."

"I thought you didn't work," she said.

He gave her an incredulous glance. "I inherited money, but I have to work at keeping it," he said. "I own interests in businesses all over the world, in several multinational corporations. I like to know where my money's going, and how it's being spent."

"So that's how it's done," she murmured.

He chuckled. "Stick with me, kid. I'll make an entrepreneur of you in no time."

"That would be nice," she said. "I think I'd like making a fortune." She shrugged. "Well, I'd like the challenge of making it," she added thoughtfully. "Money's not really very important to me, except that I'd like to spoil Grandad a little while I've still got him. He sacrificed a lot to bring me up."

The uniformed man opened the door for Della and helped her out, while he signaled for a porter to take the luggage from the boot, which Christopher had already opened automatically from the driver's side.

Chris escorted Della to the front desk and registered them, in separate double rooms. He handed her the encoded card key and led the way into the elevator.

"You look embarrassed," he commented.

She was. The clerk had asked if they were sharing a room. She felt uncomfortable. "Sorry," she murmured. "I'm not used to sophisticated circles. I guess they get a lot of unmarried couples here and nobody thinks anything about it. I'm a little out of step with the rest of the world."

He was gaping at her. She was an anachronism, all right. It probably came from being raised by a man from a different generation.

"No love life?" he teased.

She didn't rise to the bait. "Not now," she replied.

He paused while they got off on the fifth floor. He showed her how to work the card key.

"The bellhop will bring the luggage up shortly," he promised. "Meanwhile, I'll freshen up and drop by to pick you up on the way out of the hotel." He hesitated. "Ever eaten fish and chips?"

"Not real English ones," she said.

He grinned. "You've got a treat in store."

THEY STOPPED AT a roadside stand and gobbled down fish and chips and strong tea to the foreign sound of proper English being spoken all around them. Della was delighted with the new experience.

"Later, we'll have a proper, sit-down meal," he promised. "But there isn't time now. I want to find Tansy."

"Oh, this is lovely," she protested. "I'm enjoying it!"

He chuckled. "So I see."

She was standing on his right side, so that he could see her and vice versa. He looked very worried, and she wondered how she'd feel if it was her grandfather the police and the press were chasing.

She put down her cup of tea, frowning.

"What's wrong?" he asked.

"I was thinking how I'd feel, in your place," she said, looking up at him with darkened gray eyes. "Grandad is my whole life."

He searched her face and nodded slowly. "Tansy and Logan are the only close family I have. I didn't worry so much about them several years ago. Since

I've had the wreck, my perspective has changed." He looked grim.

"Life is short, and you hadn't realized how short before," she speculated.

His eyebrows jerked. "That's it, exactly. I had a concussion, internal and external injuries, as well as the damage to my left eye. It took months for me to get back on my feet, and I'll never regain the sight in my eye. It woke me up."

"I remember reading about you in the tabloids, when you were younger," she recalled. "You were like your mother, forever in and out of scrapes and scandals."

"Not anymore," he said. "It isn't worth the risk."

"What is?" she asked solemnly.

He turned and looked down at her pensively. "Leaving the world a little better than we found it," he said simply.

She smiled. "I like that."

He touched his finger to the tip of her small nose and smiled. "I like you," he said genuinely, and chuckled when she flushed prettily.

"Are you sure? I thought I was at the top of your enemies list."

He shook his head. "You don't fit the image of a hardened newshound," he said simply. He frowned slightly. "In fact, I don't think you have what it takes to do the job properly. You've got too much heart. Eventually, you'll be wrung out like a damp cloth."

She stiffened. "I've been a reporter for several years and I can do this job," she asserted stubbornly.

"Grandad says I just have to put aside my hang-ups and concentrate on the process of gathering information."

"Your grandad can probably eat lunch while he watches war footage," he replied. "I expect he's grown such a hard shell over the years that nothing much affects him."

He was right. She hated admitting it. "He said he was sensitive when he started out, too."

"Bull. He'd have gotten over that the first day in the field." His eyes narrowed. "Can you really see yourself printing everything you find out about peoples' intimate lives behind the social masks they wear? Can you destroy a marriage by turning in stories on unfaithful spouses or headline-making news about their private sexual perversions? That sort of news destroys lives, Della. Are you really hard enough to hurt people deliberately for the sake of making headlines?"

He was asking the same questions she'd asked herself. He made her uncertain, unsure of herself. He made her ashamed. She didn't answer him. Instead, she wiped her mouth on the napkin and put it on her plate.

He glanced at his watch. "Are you finished? We need to get started."

"Yes. I'm through." She finished her last swallow of tea and didn't look at him as she got up from the counter and left him to pay the bill. She started down the road toward the thick of the commercial district, thinking how ancient this country was and how many empires had embraced it. The history of Great Britain had always fascinated her, and now here she was in London itself, and she was too sick at heart to pay much attention to sights she'd always dreamed of seeing.

She felt Chris's hard fingers close around her elbow as he escorted her back to the car and put her in what would be, in the United States, the driver's side of the car. The steering wheel was on the right side, here.

"Curious feeling, isn't it?" he asked with a smile.

"Very."

He got in and cranked the engine. "Tell me everything you know about the murder," he asked.

"Well, honestly, I don't know a lot," she had to confess. "I was told that the late member of parliament was found floating in the river with a blunt-force injury to the right temple. The official cause of death was drowning, though."

"The right temple? You're sure?"

"I'm sure."

He looked a little relieved, oddly, but he pulled out into traffic again and the moment for questions passed.

Della was enchanted with the English countryside. She was full of questions, to which Chris seemed to know most of the answers. She was surprised to find him something of an authority on Tudor history.

"I'll bet you watch every British drama special on Henry VIII that comes on television," she said with a chuckle.

"I do. And pick holes in most of them," he added. "History isn't exciting enough for visual displays, because it happens over such a long period of time. In order for it to be palatable for the masses, it has to be compressed, and that distorts it. But I take fiction for what it is, simply entertainment, and I enjoy it just the same."

"I like Native American history," she said. "The Indians got a raw deal."

"Everybody got a raw deal," he countered. "What about the Irish who starved by the thousands during the great potato famine and received no outside help? How about the political prisoners who died in concentration camps in Nazi Germany, or the Russian people that Stalin purged? In fact, what about the French Huguenots who had to flee Europe or be slaughtered?"

"Good grief," she exclaimed.

"That's not a fraction of the whole," he continued. "Civilizations long gone had their own vicious persecutions and slavery. Our own ancestors were probably among that number. Otherwise why would they have come to America in the first place? They were looking for something they didn't have in their own countries."

She smiled at him. "You're very interesting to talk to," she said unexpectedly.

He burst out laughing. "That's new," he murmured. He didn't glance toward her; she was on his blind side, and it would have been dangerous to turn his head far enough to see her face. But she was already becoming a vivid portrait deep in his mind.

"I don't understand."

He gave a turn signal and pulled out onto a long highway. "In my younger days, I was what most people refer to as a rake," he commented. "And I only dated a certain type of woman, very sophisticated and modern, if you get my meaning."

She did. She cleared her throat. "I see."

He smiled reflectively. "How I've changed," he murmured.

The wry comment caught her attention. "Why have you changed?"

"Perhaps I'm not as confident as I was," he said thoughtfully. "The scars depress me sometimes, when I look in a mirror. They could probably get rid of the rest of them, but I am so tired of hospitals and doctors."

She studied him covertly for a moment before she shifted her eyes back to the road ahead of them. "The scars look rakish, you know," she murmured.

"Do they?"

He didn't sound amused. "I know it must have been terribly painful," she added quickly.

"I'm not offended. I've gotten used to it, I guess. But I miss having the sight in both eyes."

"Of course you do. I only meant that you aren't disfigured."

"So I've been told." He stopped at a signpost that indicated the way to Back Wallop. "Well, something's gone right today," he said, indicating the sign. "From

the map, I'd say we're about ten minutes away. I hope
we can trace her," he added uneasily. "England's a
big country."

"You've always found her before, haven't you?"

"Yes. But we had private detectives on the case,"
he corrected. "And I don't dare involve them again
now, under the circumstances. Dane Lassiter, who
does investigative work for our family, was a Texas
Ranger. Regardless of his sympathies, he'd follow
the law all the way and make no apologies for doing
it."

"In other words, he'd turn your mother in," she
decided. "Is he really that hard-nosed?"

"Less so since he married and had a family, but
he's still a law-and-order man. I didn't want to put
him on the spot." He smiled grimly. "I wish I'd paid
more attention to those lectures on criminal justice
in college."

"Did you graduate?" she asked.

He shook his head. "I was too busy drinking and
carousing to pay much attention in class. I dropped
out in my sophomore year. It's no great loss," he assured her. "I inherited more than most college graduates make in a lifetime."

"So you just have fun."

He shrugged. "Up until the wreck, I didn't know
another way to live." He turned fully toward her, so
that he could see her face. "Things are more complicated now. I'm rather sorry that I wasted so much of
my life on trivial things." He searched her soft eyes
and smiled warmly. "You're a pretty little thing," he

murmured, liking the way she flushed. "I'd have had you for breakfast a few years ago. But you'd lie on my conscience like lead."

"You'd be lucky," she murmured coolly. "I don't think much of casual affairs or people who have them."

"I noticed."

She shifted uncomfortably. "Shouldn't we be going?"

"We should."

He turned the car toward Back Wallop. He was glad he'd insisted that Della come along on this trip, although he wasn't quite sure why. She appealed to him as none of his casual conquests ever had; probably because she was a unique commodity in his carefree life. Logan would say he was losing his grip on reality, but Chris thought he was only just finding a handhold. He realized as he drove down the narrow road that he'd never really thought ahead very far. Della made him think about houses in the country and flower gardens. He scowled, because they were unfamiliar feelings. He'd never felt them with other women. Not that his sort of woman would waste her time planting flowers, he mused. He wondered how Della would look in a blue silk gown, sprawled on black silk sheets....

The direction of his thoughts brought him crashing back to the present. He couldn't afford that sort of lapse, not with this woman. She was the wedding-ring sort. He'd better remember it, too.

THEY ARRIVED IN the small village of Back Wallop fifteen minutes later and parked beside a news agent's shop.

"Best place to ask questions, if we aren't too obvious," he pointed out, as he opened the door for her and helped her out of the small car.

"With our accents, we'll blend right in," she said, tongue-in-cheek.

He chuckled softly. "Never mind that. Just follow my lead." He curled her fingers into his, tightening his grip when she pulled back, and walked her into the store.

"Mornin'," the proprietor greeted them with a speculative glance. "Need help, guv?"

"Just directions, thanks," Chris said with a warm smile. "The wife and I are over here to visit my cousins, the Duke of Marlboro and his wife, Lady Gail, but we just heard about Lord Harvey and thought we'd swing through Back Wallop on the way and pay our respects to Lady Harvey. Could you direct us?"

"Your cousin is the Duke of Marlboro, you say?" The man was impressed.

"Yes. Do you know Georgie?"

He cleared his throat. No, he didn't, and even if he had he wouldn't presume to call his lordship the duke "Georgie."

"Lady Harvey lives just down the road in Carstairs Manor. It's to the left just across the bridge as you round the curve. Can't miss it. Sad about the old man."

"Yes, it is. Thank you," Chris said. "Ready to go, darling?" he added, pulling Della close to his side and looking down at her with an expression on his face that made her knees wobble. She colored again and nodded, not trusting her voice.

"Newlyweds, aren't yer?" the shopkeeper said with a grin. "Anyone could see it. You're in luck, there, guv, she's a beauty."

"Don't I know it?" Chris murmured, with a wink in her direction. "Let's get going, old girl. Thanks for the help," he added over his shoulder.

"Sure thing." The shopkeeper chuckled to himself, watching them go. Chris had put his arm around Della and pulled her close, so that she fit nicely under his arm. They looked good together, the tall dark man and the pretty little blonde woman. He sighed, remembering his own youthful marriage. He did miss his wife, he thought, and looking at the couple before him made the ache even deeper. How lucky they were, to have a whole lifetime together to look forward to.

Chris, unaware of the shopkeeper's thoughts, pulled Della even closer as they paused at the passenger side of the automobile.

He tilted her soft round chin up with his fingertips and searched her confused gray eyes. They were soft as summer rain, he thought, oblivious to everything around them. She had a heart the size of the whole world, and she felt so right in his arms. He looked down at her bow of a mouth, pink and pretty and just slightly parted. It would be stupid to do what he was thinking. He realized that, even as his head bent and his mouth fastened gently onto those lovely pink lips. They were every bit as soft as he'd imagined, and they were just faintly unsteady under the gentle pressure. He hesitated, lifting a breath away to see what she wanted. Her fingers were against his thin shirt, barely touching, and then opening, pressing against his chest. The tiny movement was all the encouragement he needed. He bent again, and this time the pressure was neither tender nor brief.

Della felt her heart stop in her chest as his arm contracted and brought her much too close to his tall, fit body. His mouth was warm and hard and devastatingly expert. He did things to her lips that she'd never experienced with anyone else, arousing things that made her moan.

The sound brought him out of the trance he'd fallen into. He lifted his head, breathing a little roughly, and looked into her turbulent, shocked eyes.

"You don't know much about kissing for a woman your age," he said, with no expression whatsoever in his lean, handsome face.

She swallowed and tried to steady her breath. "I told you…"

"Kissing won't get you pregnant," he continued relentlessly. "Not even openmouthed kissing. You don't like it at all, do you?"

She felt all too much on the defensive, gauche and untried. She glared up at him from eyes that were still half shocked. "It's a public street!" she said on a nervous laugh.

"Yes, I know, and on a private one, you'd have fought me," he said flatly. He eased her away, inch by inch. He was scowling, quiet, almost grim. There was a look in her eyes, in her face, that disturbed him.

"Shouldn't we…go?" she asked breathlessly.

"Probably," he agreed. He opened the door and seated her before he went around the bonnet and got in beside her. His lean hand hesitated on the switch. "Someone forced you," he commented, staring at her. Her eyelids flinched. "Were you raped?"

She shivered. "Please…"

"Were you raped?"

She lowered her eyes to her lap. "Not…quite."

"Someone you knew?"

"My fiancé," she said dully. "When I broke the engagement two days before the wedding, because I caught him with one of my bridesmaids at the wedding rehearsal supper. He was missing during the toast. I stepped outside to look for him, and I found him, and her, in the backseat of his car." She sighed. It felt good, somehow, to tell someone the truth. She hadn't been able to talk about it with her grandfather. "He took me home. Grandad was out that evening, and when I told Bruce I wouldn't marry him, he was furious and tried to have his way with me. Luckily, he backed down. He said I wouldn't give out, so he found somebody who would, and it was just as well that I was breaking the engagement because he didn't want to spend his life trying to get me aroused."

The pain in her voice softened him. He stared at her quietly. After a minute, his fingers lifted to her short hair and touched it, lightly. "Sometimes people fall into relationships because they're lonely, or frightened. But marriage has to have a physical as well as an emotional foundation. Did you ever want him?"

She shifted nervously. "Not…that way."

"Then it would have been a disaster if you'd married him. Surely you know that now?"

She turned her head and looked at him. She seemed unusually vulnerable. "All that…is wrong," she said. "Isn't it? I mean, after marriage you're supposed to, but outside marriage you…"

His hand stilled. "Don't tell me. You were raised by missionaries."

He was being facetious, but he didn't know how close to the truth he was.

"Yes, my parents were missionaries," she agreed, wide-eyed. "How did you know?"

CHAPTER THREE

CHRIS SMILED RUEFULLY after the surprise wore off. "Well, well," he murmured. "So that's it."

"I guess you've forgotten more about love than I'll ever learn," she mused. She shrugged. "I told you I was a dead bust as a modern woman."

"No, you're not," he argued. "You've got potential," he added in a deep, sensuous tone. "All it needs is developing."

"Are you volunteering?" she asked with a wry smile.

He tugged on a lock of her hair. "Don't tempt me. We've got enough complications without adding that to them. Tansy, remember?"

She grimaced. "Sorry."

"No harm done," he said with a chuckle. He let go of her hair and cranked the car. "First we'll find Tansy and solve her problems. Then we'll have time to devote to our own."

"I don't have a problem."

He gave her a look of mild astonishment. "You don't like French kisses, and you don't think that's a problem?"

She glared at him. "It isn't!"

He smiled slowly. "See what I mean?"

She decided that it would be best if she ignored him, so she tried it for the five minutes it took to get to the manor house.

"This is where things get a little sticky," he said thoughtfully, as they sat at the closed gates where three carloads of reporters were camped out.

"Can't you use the phone over there and tell her we're lost and need directions?" she suggested.

"That wouldn't work. I'll guarantee every one of these newshounds has already tried that angle. I suppose the direct approach is always the best one." He got out of the car, smiled genially at the reporters as he worked his way past them, and picked up the telephone at the gate. He spoke softly so that the reporters couldn't hear him. After a minute he nodded, put the phone down and got back in the car with Della.

"She's sending a man down for us. I described the car I'm driving," Chris told her.

"What did you say that got her to open the gates?" she asked, astonished.

"I said that I was a relation of the Duke of Marlboro and I needed to speak to her urgently about her late husband."

"And she believed you?"

He chuckled. "As it happens, we know each other," he admitted. "I didn't realize she'd married, which is why I didn't recognize her as Lady Harvey. I knew her as just plain Clothilde Elmore."

Della was immediately jealous and uncomfortable. He didn't say that the woman was an old lover, but she probably was. She hated the thought of those other women, and that was dangerous. She had to remember that she was here on a job, and not to try to catch the eye of this reformed rake—if he was reformed, which she doubted.

"What are you going to tell her when we get to the house?" she persisted.

He stared at her amusedly. "You're the reporter. Hadn't you better start formulating some hard-nosed questions?"

"I guess I had," she agreed, and pulled out her pad.

He covered her hand with his before the other reporters got a look at it. "Not here," he said softly. "They can't know we're infiltrating."

"Oh. Sure." She put the pad up. "I'll just do it mentally."

He looked as if he had doubts about that, but he didn't say another word. In a few minutes, a small car with two passengers shot down the driveway. One man came to Chris's car and climbed in the back. The other man opened the gate. Chris shot through the opening before the reporters could push their way through. The gate closed to a chorus of jeers and catcalls from the frustrated onlookers.

"Neat, that," Chris mused as he followed the other car up the long driveway.

"Damned vultures," the man in the backseat muttered in a thick Cockney accent. "Poor Lord Harvey not even buried, and all this going on. The poor old man. He did so hate publicity."

"Something I share with the late lord," Chris muttered.

The man in the backseat took a good look at the driver in the rearview mirror. "I know you," he said suddenly. "You're that Deverell from America, the one who was caught in bed with…"

"Never mind," Chris said icily. "That's past history."

"Well, sure it is, guv, but you must know how her ladyship feels now," he added.

"Indeed I do," Chris replied.

"She'll be glad of company. Had to live like a hermit these past two days, what with the inquisition from the Yard and all." He shook his head. "Poor old man, poor old lord," he said sadly, "naked as a jay-bird and floating in the river, all those people taking pictures of him. He was so stately, such a gentleman.… *Deverell*," he repeated suddenly, staring at Chris harder. "You're her son! It was your mother killed the poor old man!"

"My mother won't kill a fly on her salad," Chris said with utter disgust. "She may be a licensed lunatic, but she's no murderess."

The man looked vaguely placated. "You sure of that?"

"I'd stake my life on it. If Lord Harvey was murdered, my mother didn't do it."

"Had to be murder, don't you see," came the heavy reply. "Had a bruise the size of my fist on the side of his head. He drowned, but he was unconscious when he drowned they say."

"He was hit on the right side of his head, too, wasn't he?" Chris asked carelessly.

"Sure was. Right at the temple. The blow was so hard it broke the skull. Sorry, miss," he added when he saw Della go white.

Chris glanced at her. "I told you that you were too soft for the sort of work you do, didn't I?" he asked bluntly.

"What sort of work does she do, then?" the passenger asked.

"She's trying to make it as a crime novelist," Chris lied with a straight face. "But she gets sick at her stomach when she has to read about real crimes. I think she should write political thrillers, myself."

"That's my sort of book," the passenger said smugly. "Politics is the most interesting thing I know about. Not that most of what you read in the papers is the truth. No, sir."

"I'll agree with that, having been a victim of the gutter press myself," Chris said.

"It's not all gutter press," Della felt compelled to say.

"No, there are some good journalists," Chris agreed. "But then, they don't write for the tabloids!"

Which left Della without a comeback. She stared at the gray stone manor house with real interest. It was the closest she'd ever been to affluence on this scale. The place was surrounded by landscaped lawns and gardens, even a fountain where the driveway circled the house. There was an elegant porch with flower urns everywhere, and a huge garage and tennis court and swimming pool in the back.

"Nice gardens, aren't they?" the passenger said. "The late Lord Harvey was an avid gardener, always puttering out there, he was."

"My mother has the same passion," Chris said, "although she rarely stays home long enough to indulge it. She lived over here some years ago, when I was in boarding school."

"You have English ties, guv?"

"I'm a cousin to the Duke of Marlboro."

"Well, I'll be!"

"And a cousin to the ruling royal family, as well," he added on a chuckle. "So you see, Great Britain isn't so foreign to me, after all."

"I should say not, sir!"

They pulled up at the front door and the passenger got out quickly to help Della from the small automobile, smiling at her shy thanks.

"I'll put the car around back for you, sir," the passenger said, taking the keys. "Just give us a ring when you're ready to leave. Right-o, then."

A BUTLER ANSWERED the door and escorted Della and Chris into the elegant, antique-furnished living room, where the mourning Lady Harvey lay sprawled across the sofa in a gauzy rainbow-colored lounge dress that would have probably financed the entire annual budget of a Third World army.

Chris introduced himself, naming Della as his traveling companion with a finesse that made her blush. Lady Harvey extended her white arm and allowed Chris to kiss her knuckles with a continental air.

"So nice to meet you," the former Clothilde Elmore drawled in a cultured accent. "I'm in mourning, you know, but I look terrible in black. Do sit down."

"I'm sorry about your husband," Chris said.

She waved a hand. "He was in his early seventies, you know, and his health was failing," she said languidly. "Not that I won't miss him, of course, but he was so much older than I."

That was debatable, Della thought. The woman had obviously had several face-lifts, but her throat and hands showed her true age, and she was no spring chicken.

"I'm looking for my mother," Chris continued. "I understand that she's implicated in the homicide."

"*Homicide?* What homicide?" Lady Harvey exclaimed, sitting straight up with a hand to her throat.

"But the tabloids…" Della began.

Lady Harvey burst out laughing, although there was an odd flush in her face. "Good Lord, I had no idea they were spreading such drivel. Harvey was waterskiing in the lake day before yesterday. He came loose, hit his head on the stern of the boat your mother was driving, and drowned. That's all there is to it."

Chris almost fell over with relief. "Thank God!"

"I cannot imagine how anyone could construe this as anything other than a tragic accident," she continued curtly. "What motive would your mother have to murder him anyway? They were old friends through her late husband. The three of them were great pals, although they stopped corresponding when Cecil and I married, of course. I had nothing in common with such hijinks, quite honestly. Your mother was always in the middle of some outrageous circumstance."

"She doesn't know any other way to live," Chris agreed. He scowled. "But if there's no homicide, why is my mother being sought?"

Lady Harvey waved a hand. "I have no idea. The police questioned her, and myself, and went away. My attorney tells me that there is no evidence of foul play and no further investigation is warranted."

"Then I've made a trip for nothing," he said with a smile as he got to his feet. "I'm very grateful to you. But you say you have no idea where my mother might be?"

"None whatsoever, she left the country just after the police came, or so I heard. She didn't tell me where she was going." She thought for a minute. "Bainbridge might know. She and Cecil were friends with him, as well. Yes. You might try Lord Bainbridge. He lives just down the road, anyone can direct you."

"Thank you. You've been most gracious, and at such a trying time," Chris said, bending to kiss her hand again.

"Oh, not to worry, I'm grateful for the company. Those dreadful reporters won't go away, God knows why."

"They'll tire eventually and worry someone else," Chris assured her. "Good day."

The car was brought around by the same man who'd accompanied them to the manor house. He waved them off, the gates were opened, and Chris and Della drove through the massed press corps.

"Wait just a minute, please," Della asked as he started to pull out into the main road. She motioned to a woman journalist and rolled the window down.

"She says that there was no murder, and that Scotland Yard has determined that it was an accidental death," she told the brunette. "If that's so, why are you all still out here?"

"She said that?" the journalist asked. "It's news to us. We had word this morning that accidental death has been ruled out and murder charges are pending against a woman named…" She pulled out her pad and read, "Tansy Deverell, an American."

"She said that Lord Harvey was waterskiing, fell and hit his head on the boat's stern and drowned," Della persisted.

"He was knocked unconscious with a blunt object suspected to be a silver cane head," the woman replied. "Mrs. Deverell was known to possess such a cane. The police have it now. And Lord Harvey was found in the river, not in a lake, stark naked."

"I don't understand any of this," Della said heavily.

"Neither do we. But her ladyship up there stands to inherit ten million pounds, and even with inheritance tax, that's a bundle. Furthermore, she's mixed up with some bloke from a militant workers' party—" She stopped dead. "Who are you?"

"I'm an American journalist," Della said honestly.

"My paper sent me here to see what I could dig out. Well, you see, Mrs. Deverell *is* an American." She let the implication sink in.

"I see. Wouldn't know something about her, would you?" the woman asked cagily.

"Just that she has claimed to have been kidnapped by aliens once."

The woman journalist laughed delightedly. "Thanks! She doesn't sound like a murderess, does she? What a delightful old bird! I wish she was my mum."

"So do I," Della said. "Thanks."

"You, too!"

Chris drove off while Della was closing the window. "You didn't have to be so forthcoming!"

"Yes, I did. She gave me information, I gave her information. We're even." She glanced at him, saw the lines of strain. "I still don't think she did it, evidence or no evidence. I'd like to know more about this bloke from the worker's party."

"You looked relieved when they said the MP was hit on the right side of the head. Why?" she asked curiously.

He grinned. "Because Tansy is left-handed. Let's go see Bainbridge. Maybe he can clear some of the details up for us."

Lord Bainbridge could, and did. He was no friend of Lady Harvey, but he knew quite a bit about her.

He brushed back his thick white mustache and leaned his bulk back in his huge armchair by the fireplace. "Tramp, she is, begging your pardon, ma'am," he told Della. "Nothing but a tramp. I warned Cecil about her, but he was so obsessed with her beauty that he wouldn't rest until he'd married her. Face-lifts and tummy tucks and war paint and padding, that's all she was, with a mercenary eye. All of us could see it. Now she's killed him and she'll blame poor Tansy to save herself."

"Tansy isn't a killer," Chris said curtly.

"I know that. We all know that. But she's the prime suspect. It seems her ladyship has an ironclad alibi. She was giving a speech at a children's benefit at the time Cecil died."

"Nobody can be that precise about the time of death," Della said flatly. "Especially if his body was in the water for any length of time. The water temperature could distort the time of death by at least two or three hours."

He shook his head. "He was wearing a wristwatch and apparently lifted his arm to ward off the blow. His watch face was cracked and stopped at what they presume was exactly the time of death."

"How convenient," Chris muttered.

"Not convenient. Planned," Della countered. "And devilishly clever."

"If only Tansy hadn't run," Chris said heavily. "It's made her look guilty, even if she isn't."

"I don't think she ran," Lord Bainbridge confided. "I think she's been taken somewhere for safekeeping so she can't tell her side of the story. I think she saw the murder."

Two pairs of eyes widened. "By whom?"

"By her ladyship's boyfriend," the old man said. "Tony Cartwright. He's a young street tough with a loud mouth and a following. He heads one of the militant groups that wants to oust the ruling party. He's been tossing money around like corn flakes just lately, and he has no visible means of support. My guess is that Lady Harvey has been funding him and her husband found out and made the mistake of confronting her with it. Or maybe he even caught them together in a compromising situation. Cecil was never one to keep his mouth shut. He'd have gone in head-first."

"And died for it," Chris supposed. His eyes narrowed. "What can we do?"

"My suggestion would be to hire a private detective and have Tony and her ladyship watched," came the immediate reply. "In fact, I have just the man for you. He was with Interpol for a while, and before that, rumor has it, the SAS. He's costly, but he's worth every penny. I can put you in touch, if you like."

"What's his name?"

Lord Bainbridge smiled. "You can call him Seth."

"Does he have an office?"

Lord Bainbridge shook his head. "He does a lot of hush-hush government work, as a free agent. He takes the occasional private case, if it interests him. Frankly, he doesn't need the money anymore."

"You think he'll take this case?" Chris asked.

The old man nodded. "I think so. Let me have the name of your hotel and I'll ask him to contact you tonight."

Chris let out a long breath. "You've taken a load off my mind. My mother is a lunatic, but I love her."

"Many of us have, and lost her," the old man said wistfully. "Yes, even me. You have no idea what a beauty she was fifty years ago. I met her in Madrid one summer and never got over her. I'd do anything I could to help her."

"Does Lady Harvey know that?"

He shook his head and chuckled. "Doubt she'd have sent you to me if she had. She thinks I was best friends with her husband and might feel vengeful. I'm sure she thought I'd slam the door in your face. Tough luck for her," he added grimly.

Della and Chris thanked the old soldier and went back to their London hotel.

Chris was dejected as he left Della at her door. "I'll phone you if Seth gets in touch with me," he said. "Try to get some rest. I don't know where this will lead us, but I hope Lord Bainbridge was wrong about Tansy being held prisoner. This whole damned thing is crazy!"

"Most crimes are, but they make great sense to the perpetrators." She put a soft hand up to his lean cheek. "Try not to worry. It will be all right."

His teeth clenched. He caught her by the upper arms and pulled her to him. "I don't know how I'd have gotten through the day without you," he said huskily and bent to her mouth.

The words softened her as much as the slow, sweet kiss he pressed on her open lips. She gasped and his own lips opened, pressing deeper. He made a sound under his breath and his hands let go of her arms to catch her hips and pull them deliberately into his.

She pulled away, breathless. "It's…public," she stammered.

He was having trouble getting his own breath. She was delightful, pretty and sweet and intelligent. He'd looked at women as acquisitions until the wreck. Now he saw what he'd been missing for most of his life—a woman with a heart. Perhaps he had to grow old enough to appreciate what was inside instead of outside.

He caught both her hands in his and lifted them to his lips. "You're a treasure," he said quietly. "Thank you for coming to England with me."

"Well, I didn't have a lot of choice, remember," she stammered, because the kiss had shaken her.

He chuckled. "So you didn't." The smile faded. "Going to stay? I'll send you back home if you really want to go."

"Oh, no, not yet," she said quickly. "We have to clear your mother first!"

He was tracing the simple silver-and-turquoise ring she wore on her right middle finger. "Did you mean what you said, about liking Tansy for a mother?"

She nodded. "I barely remember my mom. She was always away with Dad somewhere. We never really knew each other. Not like I know Grandad, anyway. He's my best friend."

"I'd like to meet him when we go home," he said sincerely. "He must be one special guy."

"He is." She searched his eyes with her warm gray ones. "So are you," she added softly.

His eyes were smiling now, as well as his mouth. He looked up and down the hall and then bent and kissed her once more, briefly and tenderly. "I'll take you down to dinner when they open the restaurant," he said. "Wear something pretty."

She laughed uninhibitedly. "It'll have to be this," she indicated her beige pantsuit. "I didn't bring a dress."

He cocked an eyebrow. "Size ten?"

She gasped. "You roué!" she accused.

He shrugged. "What can I say? I spent a lot of years as a playboy. Guessing sizes is only one facet of my enormous store of knowledge." He gave her a wicked grin. "I'll have them send something over."

"Look here, you can't buy clothes for me," she said at once. "People will think I'm a kept woman!"

"Nobody, anywhere, could look at you and think that," he said flatly. "You don't have the hard edges of anybody's mistress."

"What hard edges?"

"Sophistication," he said. "It's not as alluring as the glossy magazines make it out to be. It's artificial and cold." He searched her eyes. "You're a warm, welcoming fire on a cold and rainy night."

Her eyebrows went up.

"Too corny?" he asked with a flash of white teeth. "I'll work on my approach before dinner. Consider the dress a loan, a stage prop. We wouldn't want people to think we were trailing a murderer, now would we?

After all, we have no credentials and no permission to interfere in the case."

"She's your mother," she said quietly. "You have every right."

He traced her small, straight nose. "Still going to smear her in the press?"

"Don't be silly," she replied. "I only want to tell the truth."

"Your editor won't like it."

"Some editor, somewhere, will," she said. "Integrity is and should be part of every journalist's makeup. I won't slander anyone for a story."

"No wonder I like you."

He kissed the tip of her nose and sauntered off down the hall.

She watched him go with mixed emotions. She knew he'd been a playboy, that he knew all too much about women. But he was attractive and sensitive and he had a wonderful sense of humor, even though he was worried about his mother. That concern was just as alluring as his smile and charm. He really cared about Tansy, and he was willing to take chances to save her. No wonder women fell over themselves to get to him. She was on the verge of it herself.

She unlocked her door with the card key and stepped inside. And just as she closed it back again, a shadowy figure rose from the sofa in the suite's sitting room and came toward her.

CHAPTER FOUR

"WHO ARE YOU?" Della asked at once, her hand still on the doorknob.

The man came closer. He had dark hair and eyes and a faintly foreign look. He tilted his head to one side and studied her, from her short, wavy blond hair to her small feet. "I'll ask the questions," he said. "Why are you looking for Tansy Deverell?"

She hesitated. "How did you know I was?"

"You arrived this morning with Christopher Deverell. I know of him, and I know his angle in this—she's his mother. I don't know yours."

"I'm a journalist," she said. "I get an exclusive interview if I can help find her."

He studied her narrowly for several seconds. "I did some research on you and Deverell before I came over. Tansy Deverell's husband—and the father of her two sons—was in Morocco during World War II," he said. "He saved the life of a young Arab who was spying for the French resistance."

"That's very interesting, but what does it have to do with Tansy?" she asked.

He moved into the light, and she could see the foreign look of him. "That young Arab was my grandfather," he said. "Ordinarily I don't get mixed up in high-profile cases, and Deverell wouldn't have had enough money to buy my help. But I'll take the case because of Deverell's father. I owe the family a favor."

"Who are you?" she asked belatedly.

"Oh, you can call me Seth," he replied carelessly.

Her eyebrows went up. "Lord Bainbridge told us about you."

"Not much, I'll wager." He moved back to the phone and with economical, graceful ease, lifted the phone and called Chris. "I'm in Della's room," he said when Chris answered. He hung up.

It didn't take Chris two minutes to sprint the distance from his room to hers. He was admitted at once, and he gave Seth a calculating scrutiny while he held on to Della's small hand.

Seth noted the protective attitude and smiled. "She was perfectly safe," he assured Chris. "I never hurt women."

"Why did you come to her, and not to me?" Chris wanted to know.

"I don't know you personally. But I know of you," he replied with a faint smile. "And I know of your father," he replied. "He saved my grandfather's life during World War II. Small world."

"Very," Chris agreed.

Seth moved back into the room and to a tray that was sitting on the table by the window. "I ordered high tea. Help yourselves."

They joined him at the table, warily.

He sat back with a scone in one hand and a cup of

tea in the other, studying them while they sugared their own tea.

"That's bad for you," he remarked. "Sugar is the curse of the twentieth century. Empty calories."

"Life without sugar is no life at all," Della said with a grin. "Sorry."

He glanced at Chris as he sipped tea. "Your mother is being held by some cronies of Tony Cartwright's," Seth said abruptly. "They've got her in a garage on the Manchester road, and they've just become desperate fugitives. Lady Harvey called a press conference twenty minutes ago to publicly blame the murder on Tony, via the press camped outside her manor house. Her story is that Tony killed and robbed the old man and then planned to say she did it because her husband was going to divorce her and she'd lose her inheritance. Tony got wind of it and snatched Tansy, who has friends in high circles in Great Britain, to use as a hostage. They plan to turn her over to the police in return for an airplane to fly them out of the country."

Chris cursed under his breath. "Do the police know about this?"

"Not yet," Seth said easily. "But they have access to the same sources I used to get the information and they'll find out what Tony's up to very shortly. Meanwhile, Lady Harvey, having freed herself from her husband and her greedy lover is busily making plans to stash her inheritance in Swiss bank accounts before it can be enjoined."

"What about the inheritance tax? Surely she uses banks," Chris protested.

"She does—banks in the Bahamas. A sharp little lady, indeed, no loose ends except Tansy, and she's arranged things so that Tony will be taking care of that one." He finished his scone and leaned forward abruptly with the cup in his hands. "You know they'll kill her when they get what they want, don't you? His sort doesn't take chances."

Chris had already guessed that. His face set in grim lines. "Damn them all," he said in a deep, low undertone. "I never cheated or threatened anyone to get where I am, and I didn't inherit all that much to begin with."

Seth nodded. "I know." He pursed his lips and studied the younger man quietly. He looked hard. His eyes were like black coals. "I can tell the police all this, including where to find Tansy, if that's what you want."

Chris stared at him levelly. "There's an alternative," he guessed.

Seth nodded. "Myself, two men, you and Della."

Chris glanced at Della. "I'll go. She shouldn't. This isn't her fight."

She gave him her best glare. "I go," she said shortly. "It would be the best story I ever wrote!"

"Maybe the last, too," Chris said. He didn't like to think of Della in danger.

"Tell him I can go," Della said to Seth.

Seth shrugged. "You can as far as I'm concerned.

You two will do my legwork for me while I set up the hit."

"You won't shoot anybody?" Della asked.

"That's up to the captors. If they shoot, we shoot back," he said with finality. "I'm not risking my men's lives."

"I thought people in England weren't allowed to carry guns," Della pointed out.

"Most people aren't. Some police and other agencies do." He met Chris's solemn gaze. "I'll clear it with the right people before I go in," he said. "I'm not an outlaw, in case that's what you were thinking. I always work within the law whenever possible. Especially in this country," he added with a smile.

"All right then. Della and I will do whatever you need. Name your price," Chris said. "I'll mortgage everything I own if that's what it takes to get Tansy back."

The other man studied him like a zoo specimen. "That's unusual these days, did you know?" he asked. "Most would rather have the money."

"Tansy's worth her weight in it," Chris said simply. "Even if she is a royal pain in the neck from time to time." He chuckled softly. "At least she's never boring."

Seth laughed. He put down his cup and stood up. "It's been a pleasure. I'll be in touch as soon as I've worked things out. Stick close to the hotel for the next day. I'll have to get a few things together and contact my men."

"Will do. But what about the payment?" Chris asked.

"The ransom, you mean?"

Chris frowned. "That, too, but I meant your fee."

"Oh, that. I'll settle for high tea at the Ritz, at your convenience," he said. "No skimping on the cream and butter, either," he added with a lifted finger. "First-class."

Chris looked at the man as if he were crazy. "High tea?"

Seth shrugged. "I love high tea. I can't get enough of it. I've already got more money than I like to have." He glanced at Della and smiled. "These days I take cases only when they interest me. You're a dish."

"Thank you," she said, flushing.

He sighed. "I love blondes," he murmured. He glanced at Chris wryly. "Pity she didn't see me first." He nodded and went out of the room as silently as a breath of air.

"What a very odd man," Della exclaimed when he was gone.

"I hope we can trust him," Chris murmured. "Although I don't really see that we have a choice. Tansy's safety has to be my first concern."

"What do you suppose he'll ask us to do?" she wondered.

He got up and went to the window to stare down at the busy street below. "At a guess, he'll want us to go to the hideout posing as a couple of lost tourists. It might just work. While we've got them distracted at the front door, he and his men can go in the back."

Della leaned forward with her forearms across her knees. "I just can't believe people would do something this vile for money."

"They might not, ordinarily. Lady Harvey seems to be playing both ends against the middle. No honor among thieves there, I'll wager." He turned back to her. "I hate to think of Tansy in such hands."

"I know." She got up and went to him, her gray eyes soft and compassionate as they met his. "But she's been in a lot of scrapes over the years. If anyone can come out on top, it's your mother. These guys are amateurs. Your mother is a professional troublemaker."

He forced a smile. "Yes, she is. But this is a new kind of situation, even for her. She's diabetic," he added worriedly. "I don't even know if she's got her insulin tablets with her."

"She doesn't take insulin shots?"

He shook his head. "For a while, she didn't even have to have pills, but she wouldn't leave sugar alone. Emotional upsets play havoc with her sugar levels, and she won't be eating properly as a captive." He slammed one fist into the palm of the other hand. "I'd love to get my hands on those guys for five minutes."

"We'll get her out," she said firmly. "You have to think positively."

He looked down at her through amused black eyes. "You're a tonic," he murmured. "A real tonic."

She smiled. "Thanks."

He reached out and touched her wavy blond hair lightly. "I haven't thanked you for letting me drag you into this." He was solemn all at once. "Listen, if this looks like being dangerous, I want you right out of it. I won't risk your life, even to save Tansy's."

She was taken aback by the unexpected, and touching, concern. She searched his face quietly. "You might not believe it, but I can handle myself."

"Not if you get in the way of a bullet," he assured her.

She lifted her thin eyebrows. "Have you ever been shot at?"

"Several times," he volunteered.

"In the army?"

He shook his head.

"How, then?"

"I did a brief stint as a mercenary," he confided. "Back in my wild youth, right after I got out of the service. I was in before Desert Storm. The only service I saw was in Germany, where I hit as many nightclubs as possible. After I got out, I met up with some career soldiers who were hired for a little job in Africa. I went along." He shook his head. "One taste of the life was enough to convince me it wasn't worth the price it exacted. I saw things I'll never be able to forget. When I came home, I went wild for a time. Life was suddenly short, and I was determined to squeeze every drop of pleasure out of each day."

That reminded her of the playboy he'd once been. "You didn't hold life very dear until then, did you?" she asked shrewdly.

He shrugged. "Not really," he agreed. "I didn't think very far ahead." His eyes were reflective as he stared out the window. "Looking back, it seems to me that I didn't have much grasp of the important things even after Africa. I lived from day to day and burned the candle at both ends. If it hadn't been for the wreck, I might never have strayed from that path."

"I'm sorry it took a wreck to wake you up."

He sighed. "That makes two of us." He put his hands in his pockets and jiggled his loose change. "Well, we seem to be stuck in the hotel tomorrow. What would you like to do to pass the time?"

"We could investigate the gym facilities," she offered. "I noticed on the way down in the elevator that they have a health club for visitors here."

"I had enough physical therapy after the wreck," he said. "I'll pass."

"They have a swimming pool," she said.

He looked uncomfortable. "I don't swim."

She glowered at him. "You're just making up excuses. I happen to know that you swim like a fish. You spent a month at that Italian actress's villa in Rome, and you swam with her every day."

His black eyes flashed. "Yes. I did. That was before the wreck."

"You mean you can't swim because of the injuries?" she asked, puzzled.

"I can't swim because of the scars," he said through his teeth. "The wreck was so bad, the car had to be cut apart to get me out." He added, "As I mentioned earlier, I had internal injuries as well as external ones, and there are gashes on my stomach and upper thigh that I don't want anyone to see."

She looked up at him quizzically. "Not even me?"

He hadn't thought about her seeing his wounds. Della wasn't like some women who would have turned away or averted her eyes. She wouldn't be intimidated by a few scars. When she looked at him, she wouldn't even see them.

"I haven't worn swimming trunks since the wreck," he murmured.

"It's time you did. A few laps in the pool will be good for you." She grinned at him. "You can teach me how to swim."

"You don't know?" he asked, aghast.

She shook her head. "There was never anyone who could teach me. Grandad can't swim, either."

"Didn't you take classes when you were in school?"

"Sure. All sorts. But not swimming."

"You should know how," he said seriously. "It might save your life one day."

"Then teach me how."

"I don't want to swim around people," he said doggedly.

"Okay. Let's wait until tonight, just at bedtime," she coaxed.

He stared at her uneasily. He didn't speak.

"Think about it," she added, and then let the subject drop.

THEY HAD A leisurely supper in the dining room. True to his word, Chris had bought her a lovely dress to wear. Della had a huge prawn cocktail, followed by Beef Wellington with exquisitely cooked vegetables and homemade breads. The dessert table was almost her undoing. She sat and stared at it for a long time before she decided what to order.

Chris watched her with undisguised delight. She ate the same way she did everything else, wholeheartedly and without inhibition. When coffee was served, she sat back with a long sigh.

"The food here is just delicious," she said fervently. "I can't remember when I've eaten anything so wonderful."

"I can't remember when I've enjoyed watching a woman eat," he murmured dryly. "Over the years, most of my dates have fancied rabbit food."

She glowered. "I'm not eating bean sprouts and tofu until I break a scale," she informed him. "Food should be a permissible vice."

"Especially at your age," he agreed with a chuckle.

"You aren't that much older than I am."

"Not chronologically," he said. "But you're a lifetime behind me in other things." He smiled with pure cynicism. "You still have illusions. I lost mine years ago."

"I hope I never do," she murmured as she toyed with her napkin. "I think that one person can make a difference in the world."

"And I know for a fact that several million people have tried and failed."

She looked up into his eyes. "How did you get so cynical?"

"I lived in the fast lane," he said with an unfamiliar hardness. "You grow up pretty fast."

She searched his black eyes curiously. "Tansy was married five times, you said?"

He nodded curtly. "Our father was much older than she was. But then, Tansy was about forty when I was born. Nobody thought she could get pregnant anymore—especially Tansy."

"Was she a good mother?" she asked.

He shrugged. "She wasn't around much. When Dad was alive, I have a faint recollection of how he took her with him most places he went on business. They spent a good deal of time in Spain with his rich relatives, or in England with hers. Logan and I were pretty much raised by a succession of housekeepers and governesses."

"Is your brother like you?"

"Oh, no," he said with a smile. "Logan's the solemn one. He was always responsible and mature. I was the gadfly. Maybe that's why Tansy and I got along so well. She saw herself in me." His eyes darkened. "After Dad died, she went wild. She'd always been outgoing and cheerful, but she collected and discarded men like paper napkins. After she divorced the last one, she seemed to enjoy creating scandals. Not that I can throw stones," he added in a soft, sensual tone. "I've done my share of headlining."

"She must have cared for your father a great deal," Della observed.

He frowned and then laughed hollowly. "Amazing that you knew that at once. It took me years to work it out."

It occurred to her belatedly that many of his stepfathers might not have liked a ready-made family. "Those stepfathers, were they very hard to take?"

He nodded. "For me, more than for Logan. By the time Tansy remarried, Logan was out on his own. I wasn't. Eventually Tansy decided that a military school would be just what the doctor ordered. I liked it, but I resented Tansy too much to stay there. I jumped ship after the first year and ended up in Spain with one of my father's brothers. Tansy let me alone. Eventually I wandered back to the States, just in time to register for the draft. By then, the military seemed as good a choice as any, so I enlisted."

"Nobody can say your life hasn't been interesting," she pointed out.

He chuckled. "It's been useless, for the most part," he replied. "Just lately, I've been feeling my age. Making money is nice, but I want to do something else." His eyes held a faraway look. "I want to build yachts. Racing yachts. It's been a dream of mine for years, but I've never had the commitment to try it. After spending time in Spain this summer, I've almost come to a decision. My friend who races in the America's Cup competitions has offered to go into partnership with me. I'm very tempted."

"You should follow your dreams," she said seriously.

He searched her face. "Do you know, I'm beginning to think I have a few of them left."

She smiled. "I'm glad."

THE POOL, AS Della had guessed, was deserted late at night. Since Chris didn't have swimming trunks, he had to buy a pair—but they were conservative, black with white stripes and as long as boxer shorts. Despite the scars that he was so self-conscious about, he looked good in trunks. His natural olive tan made his eyes and hair look even darker than they were, and his body was muscular without being exaggerated. Della found him exciting and had to force herself not to stare.

She was wearing a one-piece canary-yellow suit that outlined her hourglass figure very well.

"Not bad, Miss Larson," Chris drawled, giving her a sensual appraisal that made her knees feel weak. "Not bad at all."

"I could say the same thing," she murmured with a shy smile.

He moved closer, so that she could see the thin white scars that crisscrossed his abdomen and what she could see of his thighs. "Could you?" he asked with faint cynicism.

"If you think a few scars would put women off you, you're nuts," she said flatly. "You're devastating."

He chuckled. "Plain speaking, and here I thought you were shy."

"I am, mostly. But you're creating a problem that doesn't exist," she added. "The scars have faded so much that you have to look close to see them." She searched his eyes. "And it isn't noticeable that you only have vision in one eye," she murmured. "I'm sorry about the wreck. But you're still the man you were, aren't you?"

He moved even closer. "Am I? Let's see."

Before she could decide whether or not he was teasing, he bent and lifted her off the tile floor, holding her close to his warm body.

She gripped his shoulders hard. "You aren't going to toss me in?" she asked worriedly as he moved closer to the edge.

"I was thinking about it," he confessed.

"I'm afraid of deep water," she told him.

"Okay." He put her down at the steps that led into the shallow end of the pool. "Go at your own speed."

She smiled. "Thanks."

She eased down into the cool water, feeling it absorb her like wet silk. She sighed and spread her arms, enjoying the feel of it, but still on her feet.

Chris moved close to her and lifted her arms around his neck. "I won't let you drown," he promised, and struck off to the deeper water. "You're an elemental person, aren't you?" he asked quietly. "You're sensual."

She laughed nervously. "I've never been called that before!"

He didn't smile. His eyes were locked with hers as he paused at shoulder depth, holding her lightly by the waist so she didn't sink. "I'm sure you've never given yourself much opportunity to find out. It's pure loss of control to let your senses go free." He brought her close. "But it's time you learned how sweet it is."

"I don't…"

His mouth covered hers, stopping the words in the back of her throat. She'd been kissed before, but Chris was a totally new experience. He nibbled at her lips, teased them with his tongue, savored them until they parted and began to respond shyly to the lazy insistence of his warm, hard mouth.

She made a feeble effort to save herself, pushing gently at his broad shoulders, but he didn't stop. If anything, he became more demanding. On a soft, harsh groan, his hands went down to her hips and pressed them firmly into the aroused contours of his own. He held the kiss, built it into something devouring and exciting.

Della cried out softly as his hands became invasive, teasing under the elastic at her legs to find the soft skin of her thighs and hips.

He lifted his mouth. His eyes were black and his breathing wasn't quite normal. His hands lifted from her thighs, but they slid up and kept going until they found and caressed her high, firm breasts.

"Chris...!" she choked.

His thumb and forefinger tested the hardness of a small nipple while he searched her shocked eyes. He bent and kissed her at the same time that his hand slid inside the deep V of the bathing suit and found soft bare skin. His other arm impelled her even closer to his aroused body.

Della was flying. She knew that if she lived to be a hundred, there would never be another moment like this, another man like this. He was experienced, but it wasn't his way with women that attracted her. It was everything about him.

The sound of voices broke them reluctantly apart. He moved his hands back discreetly to her waist and held her there, fighting for breath, as a party of people came out to the pool area and put down towels and drinks on nearby tables.

"What will you do," he asked softly, "if I suggest that we go back to my room and finish what we started?"

She smiled. "I'd suggest that you teach me how to swim instead."

He chuckled. "As I suspected. Well, dash my dreams to bits, why don't you?" he murmured. "I'll never sleep."

"You will if you're tired enough," she assured him. She moved back a little. "Come on. Teach me."

"This isn't what I want to teach you, you little blonde witch," he muttered.

She grinned. "Sure it is! Just think, I might make it to the Olympics, and you could tell everyone that you taught me everything I know."

He let out a long, wistful sigh. "Okay, you win." He shook his head as he looked at her. "What raw potential."

She made a face at him. "Swimming. Teach me swimming."

"Would you believe that you're the first woman who ever turned me down flat?"

"There's a first time for everything," she assured him.

He shook his head and moved her into a position on her back. "We'll begin with floating," he said. "This will give you confidence in the water."

It didn't, at first. But as they went along, she began

to feel less intimidated by the deep water beneath her. The pool was lighted, and there were lamps on long poles all the way around it. Chris seemed both relaxed and pleased with her company. A gorgeous brunette in the party of people nearby found him attractive and tried to flirt with him. To Della's surprise, he cut her off abruptly and in such a way that she didn't try it again.

As they were going up in the elevator to their rooms, Della studied him from the folds of her beach robe with curious eyes.

"She was gorgeous, you know," she told him.

He searched her eyes. "You're gorgeous," he replied, and he wasn't teasing. "Inside and out. After you, I don't know that I could look at another woman."

She caught her breath. "Isn't this sudden?"

He nodded. "Like lightning striking. You never see it coming. Then it hits, and your life changes."

"Changes, how?" she asked hesitantly.

"I'm not sure yet." He studied her oval face quietly. "I wouldn't have gone into the water if you hadn't insisted," he said. "I'm glad you did. I don't look as bad as I thought, apparently."

"Of course you don't," she scoffed. "You're still devastating to women, scars and all."

"I noticed," he replied with a speaking glance at her body.

She felt uneasy. "You aren't angry?"

His eyebrows lifted. "At what?"

"At me, for not wanting to go back to your room with you."

He only smiled. "I'm disappointed. I'm not angry." The elevator stopped and he caught her hand in his and held it until they reached her door. He turned to face her after she'd inserted the card key and opened it. "I like you the way you are, Della," he said. "Old-fashioned hang-ups and all."

"I'm glad."

He bent and kissed her gently. "Get some sleep. I have a feeling we're going headfirst into the fire in the morning."

"You, too," she said. She reached up and brushed back a lock of unruly dark hair from his forehead. Her heart was in her eyes. "You need someone to take care of you," she said quietly. "You don't take care of yourself."

His fingers touched her cheek. "You might take on the job," he said softly. "There's a vacancy."

She smiled. "I'll think about it. Good night. Sleep well."

"You, too."

He gave her a long last look before he wandered off down the hall in his own beach robe, looking as elegant as he did in a suit. Della watched him until he was out of sight. It occurred to her that she was in love with him.

CHAPTER FIVE

THE DAY DAWNED rainy and dreary. Della ordered breakfast from room service and sat down by herself to eat it. She was still elated from the night before and anxious to see Chris, to see if he regretted how far things had gone between them.

He rang the bell just as she was drinking a second cup of coffee. She went to let him in. His dark eyes approved the soft yellow suit she was wearing with a lacy white blouse and white high heels.

"You look elegant," he mused.

She liked the way he looked in slacks and a navy jacket with a roll-neck sweater. "So do you," she replied.

He closed the door behind him and pulled her close, bending to kiss her with tender warmth. "Good morning," he whispered.

"Good morning." She pulled his head down and kissed him back, melting into his tall, hard body with obvious pleasure.

"Morning is always the best time," he murmured against her mouth.

"Is it, really?"

He wrapped her up against him, loving the smallness of her in his arms, the way she clung to him. "I've avoided commitment all my life," he said at her ear. "Trust me to let a gorgeous little blonde waltz up on my blind side."

"I'm not gorgeous."

"You're gorgeous." He held her closer. "Don't think you're going to get rid of me when this is all over," he remarked, feeling her heart jump at the statement. "I'll be tenacious."

"What a lovely thought," she purred.

He drew in a long breath. "I suppose it will have to be orange blossoms and white lace, after all," he said. "You'll be a vision in white."

"Are you proposing?" she squeaked.

"Of course."

She drew back. "We don't know each other!"

"We'll get married and go from there." He searched her soft eyes. "We like each other, we're attracted to each other, and we have mutual elderly headaches to take care of." He shrugged. "It's more than a lot of couples have to start with. Where's your sense of adventure? Don't you ever take risks?"

She was floored. She'd expected anything from him except a proposal. "You've had so many women in your life…"

"And now I only want one. You." He was dead serious. "We'll go at your pace. But at the end of the road, there's going to be orange blossoms and lace. Period."

She smiled slowly, feeling as if fountains of joy were rising up into her heart. "I can't believe it."

"Neither can I," he chuckled. "But there it is. All we have to do is rescue Tansy and get on with it."

Her face fell. "How can I possibly interview my future mother-in-law for a scoop?" she asked suddenly, horrified.

"You'll be kind to her," he said simply. "You're the very best person to do it." He sighed. "God, I hope she's all right. I hardly slept, worrying about her."

Just as he finished the statement, the telephone rang. He went past Della to pick it up. He listened carefully, murmured something, and hung up.

"Seth," he explained when she looked the question at him. "I've got an address. We're honeymooners, lost and looking for directions." He grinned. "I told you I know how mercenaries work." The smile faded. "You do exactly as I say. I won't risk you, not even for Tansy."

She nuzzled against him for a few sweet seconds. "I won't risk you, either," she said softly. "Let's hope Seth knows what he's doing."

"Amen!"

THE ADDRESS WAS on the outskirts of London in what looked to be a shabby apartment house. Chris took Della firmly by the hand and moved to the front door. There was a doorbell. He rang it. There was no answer. He looked at Della, concerned, and rang it again.

The door suddenly opened. A young man in a leather jacket peered at them from behind it. "What yer want?" he demanded.

Chris drew Della closer. "We're from America," he drawled. "Just got in from the airport and we're lost. Trying to find a cousin of ours, a...wait a sec." He drew a piece of paper from his pocket and read, "Billy Withers, 44 Truebridge Lane, London." He looked around. "This is Truebridge, but we can't find number 44."

The man looked irritated and impatient. "T'ain't no such number!"

Chris's face fell. "But we've come all this way! Are you sure you have no idea?"

There was a crashing sound in the back of the apartment. The young man scowled, turning toward the inside of the dark room. His hand went to his jacket.

Della never saw Chris move, but the next minute, the young man was on the floor and Chris was standing over him with an automatic weapon. He cocked it with confident ease and leveled it at the downed man.

"Seth!" he called loudly.

There was another scuffle, another crash, and a familiar face appeared in the hall.

"Damn!" Seth exclaimed when he saw the man on the floor. "That was a neat piece of work," he murmured, grinning as he bent to drag the young man up from the floor. "Come along, Tansy's in here."

"Is she all right?" Chris asked quickly, drawing Della's cold hand into his free one.

"She's a little rocky, but I gave her a pack of glucose. She's rallying."

Tansy was sitting on the edge of a ragged little

cot, sucking on a glucose packet, looking weary and almost defeated. She looked up and saw Chris and burst into tears.

Chris put the safety on the pistol and tossed it to one of Seth's men before he bent and gathered Tansy close.

"You idiot!" he muttered at her ear, holding her closer. "Dear God, you gave us a scare!"

"Which is nothing compared to what I got, my dear," Tansy sighed, clinging to her son. "My globe-trotting days are over. This is the absolute end." She lifted her head. "Did they find poor Cecil?"

"Yes, just after you vanished. Have you been here the whole time?" Chris asked.

She nodded. "They snatched me and held me until they got their money from Lady Harvey. I was a material witness and she told them to keep me here for collateral until she could get to her funds." She laughed hollowly. "I gather from what those goons said that she reneged and expected them to finish me off. They decided it might be better to hold on to me, because I could implicate her. She doesn't know that," she added. "But I was wearing a wire when she confessed that she and Tony Cartwright had planned Cecil's death."

Seth was suddenly all business. "What happened to the recording?"

"He had it." She pointed to the man on the floor.

Seth pulled out a nasty-looking knife. "Get them out of here," he told Chris.

Chris moved the women ahead of him and looked

back at the nervous man on the floor, presumably the vile Tony. "He usually only takes a finger. For his collection," he added with a cold smile. "In your case, it might be an organ. A vital organ. If I were you, I'd tell him what he wants to know. In any case, I'll remove the ladies before you start screaming."

They were in the next room with the door closed before Tansy turned to him. "You enjoyed that," she accused.

He smiled grimly. "Yes, I did. After what he put you through, I'd have enjoyed slugging him even more, but I think our friend Seth will do what's necessary."

"Lord Bainbridge, you mean," she corrected.

"We met Lord Bainbridge," Chris said carefully. "He's seventy."

"He's sixty-five," Tansy stated. She jerked her head toward the door. "That's his son—his only son—a colonel in the SAS until he retired year before last. Now he's what the secret agencies call a problem-solver. Thank God he came after me. I don't think I could have made it another day. I'm so weak, son."

"We'll get you to a hospital and have you checked over, just to be safe," Chris said.

Tansy was staring past him at the pretty little blonde. "Who's this?"

"Della Larson," he introduced. "She's eventually going to be your daughter-in-law when she makes up her mind that I'm serious about marrying her. But for the meantime, she's a reporter. I promised her an exclusive interview if she came with me to find you."

"She came right in here with you?" Tansy pursed her lips. She was impressed. "Brave girl."

Della grinned. "That makes several of us. I'm glad to meet you, Mrs. Deverell, and I'm very glad that we got here in time!"

Tansy shook the hand that was offered and smiled broadly. "So am I, dear." She lifted both eyebrows. "You're going to marry my son, are you?"

Della sighed. "I think so," she mused. "Of course, he may change his mind now that we're all out of danger."

"He won't," Chris drawled.

"He's my son," Tansy said. "I taught him always to do what he said he would." She seemed to slump. "I want a steak," she said. "And French fries and cherry cobbler and—"

"No cherry cobbler," Chris informed her.

She made a face at him. "Even the most rigid diet allows sweets occasionally."

"Not yours."

"Just wait…"

Chris put an arm around her and drew her close. "You can have mangoes and bananas and coconut."

She sighed. "My dear, you remembered!"

"How could I forget? The kitchen was always cluttered with mangoes," he told Della. "She likes desserts, but fruit was always her favorite." He glared at Tansy. "This time, you're going where you can be found. No more adventures."

"Spoilsport!"

"You could have died," he retorted.

"Eventually we all do." She shook her head. "Poor Cecil. He and I were friends years ago. He wrote to me and invited me to visit. I hadn't met his new wife, so I accepted. But after I'd been there for a few days, I realized that not only did his wife not love him, but she was obsessed with getting her hands on the estate. He vanished one night, just after that shady man in there—" her head jerked toward the closed door "—came to visit Lady Harvey. She woke me the next morning and said that Cecil was dead and I was the prime suspect, because his will named me as executrix and chief beneficiary. Lies, of course, but I was too stunned to question her. Tony Cartwright hustled me out the door and into his car, and said he'd hide me. But that wasn't what he did. He and his cronies brought me here and held chloroform to my nose and mouth. When I woke up, I was locked in that room." She smiled wearily. "I thought I'd never get out alive. I heard them discussing what to do to me after her ladyship went public and accused Tony of killing her husband. He'll be the prosecution's best witness at her trial, unless I miss my guess."

"Not without that tape recording he won't," Chris said solemnly. "Speaking of which…"

He turned toward the door just as Seth came out, all dressed in black, with cold eyes. He had something in his hand—a tiny tape recorder.

"The evidence!" Tansy exclaimed.

Seth nodded. "Irrefutable. Tony's decided to become the state's own witness. One of my men is telephoning the police even as we speak. I'm going to slip out with my men before they get here." He put a heavy hand on Chris's shoulder. "You're a hero. I'm proud of you."

"I didn't do anything except disarm one of the henchmen," Chris argued.

"Well, I sure as hell didn't do anything," Seth remarked haughtily. "I wouldn't soil my hands with such filth."

Tansy went to Seth, stood on tiptoe and kissed his lean cheek. "Thank you, dear."

He kissed her back and smiled warmly. "Come visiting again. But do it in a conventional way this time, hmm?"

"Behave yourself," Tansy directed.

"I'm the soul of discretion," Seth assured her. He grinned at Della, glanced at Chris, and suddenly caught Della around the waist, bent her back over his arm, and kissed her with exaggerated passion.

He let her up, breathless and flushed, and grinned wickedly. "You should have met me first," he repeated. He waved at the others, went to gather his men, and went stealthily out the back door.

"Damned bounder," Chris muttered, staring at Della.

"Don't you worry," Della assured him as she smoothed down her hair. "He's very good—but you're better."

Chris's expression lightened. "Am I?"

She grinned. "Much."

Tansy burst out laughing. "And that answers that question, doesn't it, my boy?" she asked her son.

"Yes," he agreed with a warm smile. "I suppose it does."

THEY GAVE THE tape recorder and the men over to the police when they arrived and gave statements as well. Tansy was taken to the hospital to be checked over. They kept her overnight and Della stayed in the room with her while Chris wound up the details of their trip, returned the rental car and got Tansy a seat on their flight back to Texas.

"It's been a very exciting trip," Della told the older woman, "although I'm sorry for what you went through."

"It was an adventure, and it will improve with every retelling," Tansy assured her with a wicked chuckle. "You and I are going to get along very well, my dear. I can tell that we're the same sort of people."

"Well, not exactly. But you should meet my grandfather," she told the older woman. "He was a war correspondent."

"War correspondent?" Tansy frowned. "Your last name is Larson? Is your grandfather Herbert Larson of UPI?"

Della blinked. "Well, yes."

"For heaven's sake!"

"You couldn't… You don't know him?" Della asked.

"Know him!" Tansy caught her breath and laid

back among the pillows. "I'm surprised that he's still alive, the chances he used to take!"

"You *do* know him!" Della exclaimed.

"About forty years ago," Tansy said, "he and I were pinned down by Latin American revolutionaries when I was in South America, just after my first husband's death. Your grandfather got me to the airport and onto a plane bound for home. I never met a man with such grit, such fire. He was…superb."

Della smiled. "He still is. He doesn't get around as well, and his sight isn't what it should be, but he's kicking." She hesitated. "He's diabetic but he won't give up sweets. That sounds familiar, too, doesn't it?" she added.

Tansy flushed. "Well, well."

"He and I live together," Della continued. She stopped dead and frowned. "Oh, dear."

"Oh, dear, what?"

"I can't leave him," she said plaintively, staring at Tansy with huge worried gray eyes. "He'll die if I'm not there to make him take his medicine and keep him away from the sugar bowl!"

Tansy reached over and patted her hand where it lay on the coverlet. "You marry Chris," she said firmly. "And let me worry about Herbert. I think I may have a solution to your problem."

Della didn't believe her. But when they arrived back in the States, and found Herbert Larson sitting in a seat next to the concourse entrance at the Houston airport, she began to understand what Tansy meant.

The old man, silver haired and dignified, rose as

the travelers came out of the airplane down to the concourse in the covered tunnel. He opened his arms and a happy Della ran into them to be hugged firmly and kissed. Tansy came out of the tunnel after her and stopped as the elderly man let go of Della and stood just looking at her. She was holding on to Chris's arm, but she let it go and moved slowly toward the elderly man.

They just looked at each other for a long moment. "You've got wrinkles," Herbert said abruptly.

"You've got flat feet," Tansy shot back.

"My granddaughter says she's going to marry your son."

"Too bad if you don't like it," Tansy said huffily.

He shrugged. "Looks like a nice boy," he mused, glancing at Chris with a faint smile. "I like it. Della needs looking after. She's too soft to be a reporter."

"She's not too soft to be a political featurist," Tansy said firmly. "It's what she likes to do best."

"She'll enjoy having kids and raising them more," Herbert Larson said. "She's a homebody, like my late wife was. No traipsing around the world getting into scrapes for Martha, no, sir!"

"Well, let's hear it for Saint Martha!" Tansy said through her teeth.

Herbert raised an eyebrow and studied her closely. "Still jealous after forty years, hmm?" he taunted.

"Della says you won't give up sugar," Tansy remarked, ignoring his question.

"She says the same thing about you. Trying to die?" he accused bluntly.

Tansy went scarlet. "I could ask you the same question!"

He shrugged thin shoulders. "I thought about it. Not anymore, though." His eyes narrowed. "I've just found a new lease on life. You like nightclubs?"

She nodded jerkily.

"Dancing?"

She nodded again.

He pursed his lips. "Maybe I'll give you a whirl, if you play your cards right. You never could do a tango."

"And you can?"

"I taught Valentino how," he bragged.

"You were in short pants when Valentino died," she accused.

"If I'd been old enough, I'd have taught him how," he said with a grin. He went forward and took her arm. "Come on, Grandma. I'll help you out to the car."

"You can drive?" she asked mockingly.

"No, but I hired a man who could. Nothing's too good for my granddaughter."

They walked ahead of the others, still arguing. Chris drew Della close to his side as they walked, pulling luggage on wheels behind them.

"I think some of our problems are about to be solved. Apparently, they know each other."

Della nodded. "And fairly well, from the look of things. Miracles never cease."

"I hope they won't kill each other before we get married."

She chuckled. "Oh, I don't think there's much danger of that." She slid her hand into his and looked up at him with her whole heart in her soft gray eyes. "I can't wait to marry you," she added in a breathless whisper.

He squeezed her hand, hard. His dark eyes were expressive on her face. "Neither can I." He hesitated. "You really don't mind the scars?"

She smiled and pressed close against his side. "Don't be silly."

His eyes closed briefly and his arm went around her, contracting almost painfully. It was like having every single dream of happiness he'd ever had come true. He could hardly contain the feeling it gave him to know she loved him.

"I love you, Della," he said tautly.

She looked up into eyes that adored her. "I love you, too." She smiled impishly. "How soon can we get married?"

He searched her soft features warmly. "As soon as I can get a license. You're not about to get away from me!"

THEY WERE MARRIED by a justice of the peace exactly three days later, with Tansy and Herbert for witnesses. The elderly couple were holding hands, apparently having decided that fighting was less fun than exploring each others' personalities. In a relatively short time, they'd rediscovered the feelings they had for each other years ago, and they were inseparable.

Chris and Della drove them back to Herbert's

apartment before they drove to the airport to catch their plane to Spain. They were going to Malaga, on the southern shores of Spain, along the Costa del Sol, for an extended honeymoon. Della, who'd traveled little in her life, was exuberant about the adventure of it. She couldn't wait to get there.

When they arrived and passed through customs, they took a cab to their hotel overlooking the blistering white beach and blue sea. The hotel was white stucco with gardens full of blossoming flowers. It was a dream of a place, with wrought-iron balconies and the smell of the sea air fresh and clean.

"The Rock of Gibraltar is very close by," Chris told her when they were installed in their suite, "and so is Morocco. We might take a day trip over there and explore the *souq*—the marketplace."

She turned from the window that led out to the balcony and stared at him hungrily, drinking in the sight of his long, lean body in white slacks and a red designer knit shirt. She was wearing a loose, comfortable crinkly cotton dress with tiny shoulder bows and little beneath it, because of the heat.

"Alone at last," she said with a soft smile. Her hands went to the shoulder bows and slowly undid them, letting the dress fall to the floor. Under it, she wore a white lace teddy that emphasized every sweet curve of her young body.

Chris caught his breath. He went to her, his hands slow and caressing on her shoulders. "You don't want supper first?" he asked quietly.

She shook her head. Her arms went up and around

his neck. "I want you first," she whispered, and drew his mouth down on hers.

The passion was explosive. She'd dreamed of being in his arms without fabric between them, and here it was happening, so naturally that she never thought to feel embarrassed. He eased her out of her clothing between soft, brief kisses that traveled the length of her body, each one more sensual and arousing than the one before.

She knew that he was experienced, but until now she had no knowledge of the reality of intimacy. He aroused her expertly, slowly, taking his time, soothing all her secret fears until she was dazed and shivering with the pleasure he gave her.

By the time he drew her carefully under him and eased down, she was eager and totally without fear or reserve. She lifted to meet the slow, sensuous downward thrust of his hips and laughed with pure pleasure when the tiny flash of pain was experienced and abruptly replaced by delicious sensations that rippled over her like waves.

His lean hands moved her, teased her, taught her, while his mouth devoured hers in the stillness of the cool room. There was a rhythm that she hadn't expected. It built the new sensations she was feeling into torrential spasms of pleasure that overwhelmed her unexpectedly and lifted her against him in a fever of submission.

She hid her face in his hot throat as the spasms broke against themselves, twisting her under his demanding body as she reached and reached and finally

found the exquisite source of the tiny sips of fulfill-
ment she'd only sampled.

He felt her go rigid, and at once, he drove for his
own satisfaction, his mouth hard against her breast
as he soared into the heights with her.

When he collapsed at her side, she was still shivering, and laughing through the little aftershocks of
ecstasy that left her moving restlessly on the bed.

"So it's like that," she whispered, awed.

"It's like that," he whispered back. He smiled and
rolled over, his face damp with sweat, his eyes blazing with love. "Was I worth waiting for? You certainly were!"

She chuckled and drew him down, so that she
could kiss him with lazy enthusiasm. "Yes, you were,"
she murmured. "I'm sleepy."

"So am I. We'll have a nice nap and then we'll go
and find the nearest seafood bar."

"I love seafood," she murmured drowsily.

"Me, too."

He drew her close at his side and pulled the sheet
over them, because the room was cooling. His last
thought as he slid into oblivion was that a lifetime of
Della wasn't going to be quite enough....

THEY CALLED TANSY and Herbert the next morning to
enthuse about the sights and sounds of Spain.

"I'm glad you two are having fun," Tansy said with
laughter in her voice. "When you come home, we'll
have another wedding."

"What?" Chris burst out.

"Herbert proposed," Tansy said. "And *this* time, I accepted."

He handed the phone to Della. "You aren't going to believe this," he told her.

"What?" she exclaimed when her grandfather told her the news.

"Haven't you people ever heard that you can marry more than once?" Herbert asked with disgust. "For heaven's sake, she's a dish. No way am I letting her get away from me now!"

"Well, congratulations, Grandad," Della said with love in her voice. "I couldn't be more pleased."

"Neither could I," Chris said loudly.

"You two enjoy yourselves. Tansy knows this little Japanese place downtown where they have that strange fish. Can't think what it's called. Anyway we're going there for a snack. You kids have fun. Talk to you soon. Bye!"

He hung up. Della glanced at her husband with a frown. "They're going to a Japanese place to have a strange fish."

Chris went pale. "Not fugu. Please. Tell me it's not fugu."

"What's a fugu?"

He grabbed up the receiver and placed a call to Tansy's apartment. Herbert answered.

"If you eat a fugu fish, I'll hire a man to do nothing but follow the two of you around, full-time, I swear it!" Chris said harshly.

"Fugu? Are you daft, son?" Herbert sighed. "Tansy, what's the name of that fish?"

"Sushimi," she called back.

Chris went red. "Oh," he said.

"Fugu, indeed. He thought we were going to eat fugu fish!" he called to Tansy.

"He's on his honeymoon, Herb, what do you expect? Now hang up and come help me get into this dress. We'll be late for our reservation!"

Chris laughed until Della was worried about him. When he told her what was going on at the apartment, she only grinned.

"They'll be happy together," she said.

"Each of them alone is a handful. Can you possibly imagine what it's going to be like to have *two* of them conspiring?"

Della grimaced. "I hadn't thought about that."

"Well, don't. Not now, anyway." He picked her up and kissed her gently. "We have six days of our honeymoon left, and we're not wasting a minute worrying about them."

"What are we going to do, then?" she whispered wickedly.

He chuckled as he turned toward the bed. "I'm glad you asked…"

So was she.

* * * * *

LUKE

CHAPTER ONE

LUKE CRAIG WAS a rancher, and he'd battled all sorts of problems over the years. He'd had to deal with falling beef prices, closed markets, crazy winters and bad fall harvests that required him to buy feed for his livestock over the winter. But the problem that had just cropped up was one he'd never seriously considered. A summer camp for underprivileged city kids had just opened right next door to his ranch, and he was having to come to terms with invaders who made the Mexican Army in 1836 look tame by comparison.

To top it all off, the owner of the camp was a feisty young woman who seemed to have cornered the market on bad temper and stubbornness. Her name was Belinda Jessup. He knew her brother, Ward, slightly, having met him at cattlemen's association meetings in the past. Ward was more interested in oil wells than cattle, as a rule, but he still kept his membership in various groups that dealt with livestock. Belinda didn't resemble her brother all that much, but they shared the same hot temper. She wasn't bad looking, with her dark blond hair and green eyes and outgoing personality. Strange how she rubbed Luke the wrong way.

His sister Elysia liked Belinda. Of course, Elysia had just married Tom Walker, the father of her young daughter Crissy, and right now, in the glow of nuptial bliss, she liked everyone. Luke, living alone for the first time in years, was heartily sick of his own cooking and his own company. Belinda's project made him even more irritable than he normally was.

It had come as a shock to discover that old man Peterson had sold the river property that adjoined Luke's to an outsider. It had been sudden, too. The land hadn't been advertised, not even with a sign on the roadside. One day, old man Peterson owned it. The next, it was being developed as a youth camp, complete with roofed pavilion, small cabins and a pier on the river. Luke's pasture adjoined the property. It was delineated by a sturdy electrified fence and a steel farm gate with a padlock. The very first morning Ms. Jessup's city kids came to stay, the padlock was skillfully removed and the gate opened. Neighbors had called the sheriff's office to complain that Luke's Hereford steers were roaming the neighborhood—and the highway.

Luke and his men had rounded up the cattle, put them back into the fenced pasture, and the padlock had been replaced by a chain half the size of one that held a ship's anchor, affixed with eight combination locks.

The next morning, the sheriff's deputy was back with the same complaint about loose cattle. Luke checked and all eight combination locks were lying on the grass, rusting.

It was inevitable that the rancher would go straight to the source of the problem.

Belinda was working out the next day's recreation schedule when she heard the sound of a horse's hooves outside the large cabin that served as her main office. She'd heard about the liberated cattle and she had a cold feeling that retribution was at hand.

She went out to meet trouble head-on. It was trouble, too; a lean, lithe man in denims and wearing an expensive wide-brimmed hat and hand-tooled boots with silver spurs that even her brother would have coveted.

As he came closer, she saw that he was incredibly handsome, with thick blond hair and eyes as blue as a china plate. He had a firm mouth and a square jaw, and an expression on his lean face that could have curdled milk. She didn't need telling that this was Luke Craig. She'd already heard about him in town, although most people said he was easygoing and friendly. He didn't seem that way to Belinda.

She held up both hands. "We're quite willing to pay damages," she said at once. "I know who the culprit is, and I've had words with him. Strong words."

He put both hands on his narrow hips and glared down at her. It was a long way down, too. She was a little woman. "If those had been my breeding bulls instead of steers, we wouldn't be having words, Miss Jessup," he said in a deep, cutting tone. "You'd be locked up in the county jail, alongside your larcenous cohort."

"My larcenous...!" Her mouth closed with a snap.

"You hold it right there, cowboy," she said shortly, losing patience and diplomacy in one breath. "These kids have never had much. They live in abject poverty with parents who don't want them. Some of them have been beaten, some have been addicted to alcohol and drugs, some have been in jail. The oldest is barely seventeen, and I'll leave you to imagine the sort of upbringing they've had. I opened this camp to give them a glimpse of life as it could be, as it should be! I brought them here to learn that there's more to the world than dirty houses and drunk parents and the sound of gunshots every night they live."

He studied her with open curiosity, his expression giving away nothing of his thoughts. "You're a one-woman salvation society, I gather."

"Actually, I'm a poorly paid public defender in Houston," she replied. "In the summer, I take a few kids camping. This year I decided to buy some land and make it a permanent camp."

He nodded. "Right next to my largest pasture."

"This is Texas," she reminded him. "You've got lots of room. I only want this little tiny bit of land, right here, that I bought and paid for."

"You didn't pay for the right to let my cattle loose."

She sighed heavily. "You're right, I didn't," she admitted. "And if I hadn't insisted on bringing Kells along with me, you wouldn't have been inconvenienced twice in one week. I'm sorry."

She'd piqued his curiosity. He'd known several do-gooders, but most of them were all talk and no action. "Kells?"

"The seventeen-year-old," she continued. "I defended him when he was arrested for shoplifting. Last month I convinced the judge to give him a second chance and asked for him to be remanded into my custody from juvenile hall." She grimaced. "He's not your ordinary slum kid. There hasn't been a lock built that he can't pick. If they put him in prison, he'll be a master safecracker by the time he gets out, complete with diploma."

"Having learned the trade from pros, in the slammer," he agreed.

"Exactly." She searched his blue eyes curiously. "Socially conscious, are you?"

"I watch the six o'clock news," he returned. "And I'm all for prison reform. I just don't want it next door to me."

"That's how everyone feels," she told him. "It's the same with any unpleasant thing. Yes, let's have a new sanitary landfill, but not on land adjoining mine. Yes, let's have an incinerator, a water treatment plant, a new factory—but not on land adjoining mine."

"You can't blame people for guarding their investments," he pointed out. "And I work as hard for my income as you work for yours, Miss Jessup."

She smiled. "I know a little about cattle. My brother's into oil exploration these days, but he still runs a thousand head of Santa Gertrudis on his ranch up in Ravine."

"He's from Oklahoma originally, isn't he?"

"No, but our mother was," she corrected. "We still have relatives there," she murmured, without adding that they never had any contact with those relatives, or their scandalous mother, who'd deserted them to run off with a married man.

"I know your brother," he added unexpectedly. "I go to a few cattlemen's conventions, when I can manage time. He got married a few years ago, didn't he?"

"Yes, to one of the few women in the world he actually likes," she murmured dryly. She looked past him at the big black-spotted white horse he was riding. "Nice mare."

"She's four," he said with a smile. "An Appaloosa. I breed a few of them."

"My boys would love to ride a horse," she murmured.

His face hardened. "Would they? There's a riding stable a mile down the road—Stan's Bar-K Ranch."

"I know. I've already approached him about riding lessons," she said with a smug grin at his chagrin. "Spiked your guns, huh, Mr. Craig?"

He looked around at the cabins. Curtains moved in one. He'd have bet money it was the boy she'd mentioned—Kells. He glared toward the spot and the curtain fell together and remained still.

"Nice glare," she murmured. "How long did it take you to perfect that?"

"All my life." He pulled the hat farther over his eyes and glared down at her. "No more opened gates. I'm putting a man out here on night duty. A city policeman. He'll be armed."

She drew her breath in sharply. "You'd have him shoot a child for trespassing?"

"I would not," he said coldly. "But I'm trying to make you see the seriousness of the situation. It wasn't so many years ago that leaving a gate open could get you hung in Texas."

"So could insulting a lady," she drawled.

He lifted a blond eyebrow and a corner of his mouth tugged up in a very sarcastic smile.

She actually blushed. Her hands clenched at her sides. "I'll be sure and tell Kells that your storm trooper is lying in wait for him."

"Some storm trooper," he murmured. "A family man with six kids and ten grandkids who can't make it on what they pay him to risk his life every shift he works."

She had the grace to feel ashamed. "Sorry."

"You've been standing on the wrong side of the law for a while, haven't you?" he asked coolly. "Perhaps you should spend a little time with the victims of the people you defend and broaden your view of the world around you."

Her indrawn breath was audible, even above the brisk wind in the trees around them. "That was uncalled for! You have no idea what I do—"

He cut her right off. "I have every idea! I sat in court and watched an ambitious public defender accuse my mother of asking to be beaten every night of her life by a drunken lunatic who caused her to miscarry two children." His blue eyes blazed in a face gone taut with horrible memories. His fists clenched at his sides. "To hear him tell it, my father was a victim of his family, not the reverse. Well, sadly for him, there were color photographs of my mother and my sister, very graphic ones, that the jury got to see." The hatred he felt for the whole legal system was written all over him as he spoke in curt, deep tones laced with bitterness. "They put him away for five years, despite all the legal chicanery and smooth talk, but not in time to save my mother. She'd suffered so much abuse that years were taken off her life. She died right after he was convicted."

Belinda was shocked that a total stranger would tell her such a thing about his family. She was more shocked that he made her feel dirty with his confession, and vaguely guilty, as well.

"I'm sorry," she said with genuine sympathy.

"Sorry." He looked her up and down coldly. His eyes went past her to the cabins. "Yes, you're sorry for the way the legal system works, Miss Jessup. So sorry in fact that you've brought a few future lawbreakers down here to the brush, to coddle and baby them so that they're even more convinced that society owes them a living for the horribly bad lives they've lived." He glared at her. "I could write you a book on dysfunctional families and physical abuse, but I've never picked a lock or stolen a car or shot another person in my life, except during Desert Storm when my army reserve unit was called up."

She moved back a step. "I'm not trying to defend criminals, Mr. Craig. I'm trying to turn some potential criminals around before they become the real thing."

"Pamper them, then," he mused. "And see how

long it takes one of them to slit your throat while you sleep." He leaned forward. "But don't take my word for it," he added sardonically. "It's been my experience that stubborn people have to learn the hard way."

"You have a very narrow view of life," she replied.

He looked down his nose at her. He knew he was being harsh, but something about her egged him on. "I'll bet you were loved and wanted and spoiled, weren't you?" he asked.

She was unnerved by that blue glitter. "My childhood is none of your business."

He laughed hollowly. "To hear you tell it, every criminal's childhood is my business. Poor little murderers and thieves and rapists. They just needed a little more love to be good citizens. And the people they victimized probably deserved it, didn't they?"

She was shocked. "I never said that!"

"You do-gooders think it. They said my mother asked to be beaten."

She winced. "Of course she didn't!"

"Really? The public defender was eloquent about that. He had dozens of reasons why she enjoyed having her face broken time and time again."

"He was doing his job," she said. "Even the worst criminal has the right to an attorney."

"Of course," he drawled. "And every public defender has the right to build a reputation for setting the guilty free."

"Was your father set free?" she asked pointedly.

"The public defender convinced the parole board to let him loose early," he told her. "He'd have come back with blood in his eye and taken his rage out on my sister and me. But he dropped dead in his cell of a heart attack. I suppose God still believes in justice, even if the legal system has forgotten the meaning of the word." He turned around. "I won't have the boy shot if he picks that lock again. I will have him arrested and prosecuted." He paused, glancing back at her. "I'm not a poor country kid at the mercy of the system now. I can afford the legal help of my choosing, and pay for it. If I lose any more cattle, you won't be taking one of your charges back to the city after summer camp. And that's the only warning you'll get."

He swung back into the saddle, turned the horse and rode back the way he'd come, his back as straight as a board.

Belinda watched him go with more conflicting emotions than she'd felt in her life. He was a bitter man, and they'd made an enemy of him because Kells couldn't keep his fingers to himself. If she wasn't careful, if she didn't keep a close watch on the boy, she'd land him in jail herself, when her whole purpose in coming here was to keep him and his mates out of trouble.

SHE WORRIED THE thought all through the evening meal of hot dogs and French fries, her green eyes on the lanky boy with his curly black hair and youthful brown skin. He sat idly at the table taking a pocket watch apart and putting it back together for amusement.

Kells was hard to reach. He was ultrasensitive

about his lack of grace and looks as well as his background. He had five brothers and sisters scattered around the country with various relatives. He'd moved here with his mother and her boyfriend, but the boyfriend didn't want him and his mother wouldn't fight for him. He'd stolen a CD player on purpose to get back at her when her boyfriend had beaten him. In his neighborhood, many people had criminal records. But Kells had magic in his fingers and something in his manner that set him apart from his peers. Belinda had recognized the potential in him. She believed in him. She was the only person who did. She'd had to fight his mother and the whole juvenile court system to get him here to summer camp. Now he was seventeen and he could go to jail if he was arrested. She might have taken him out of the frying pan only to land him in a fire.

He noticed her scrutiny and his black eyes came up, hostile and faintly defensive. "I can put it back together," he muttered when he saw her eyes on the watch.

"I know you can," she said, and smiled. "You're very clever with your hands, Kells. I don't think I've ever known anyone your age who had the facility you have with mechanical things."

He averted his eyes and shrugged, but she sensed that the compliment had pleased him. "That cowboy going to arrest me?"

"He's a rancher. It was his cattle you turned loose, twice."

"I never turned no cattle loose," he said with his head down.

"You picked his locks and opened the gate. The cattle turned themselves loose."

He made a jerky motion with his head. "Never seen cows before," he mumbled.

"Steers," she corrected.

His eyes came up and he seemed suddenly alert. "Steers? What's the difference?"

"Cows are mothers of calves. Heifers are unbred cows. Bulls are stud cattle. Steers are neutered cattle raised for beef. Those were steers. They're beef cattle."

His whole face seemed entranced. "Like at the supermarket, ground beef and all."

She smiled. "Yes, that's right."

He lost interest in the watch. "Why does he keep them apart from the others?"

"Bulls won't tolerate a steer, and mother cows will fight them to protect their calves," she explained. "Besides that, it's logistics. It's easier to have different categories of cattle in a bunch, easier to work them when it comes time to separate them."

He leaned forward. "Work them?"

She chuckled. "During roundup. You have roundup twice a year on the ranch, once in the spring when the calves come and once in the fall, when you're rounding them up for sale or culling nonproducers. Calves have to be dehorned, branded, given their vaccinations, castrated if they're to be beef cattle, and tagged."

He was really interested. His eyes were more alert than she'd ever seen them. "Do they have names or something?"

"They have numbers, usually on their ear tags, but sometimes they're tattooed or a computer chip with the individual animal's history is implanted under the hide to be read with a scanner."

"You're kidding!"

"I'm not. We still have rustlers in the cattle industry, even today."

"Did those steers have computer chips?"

"I don't know." She pursed her lips. "We could ask Mr. Craig."

He grimaced. "Oh, he won't talk to me," he said. "I know how people are around here."

She studied him quietly. "How are they?"

"Prejudiced," he muttered.

She smiled. "Did you know that a quarter of all the cowboys in the west during the last century were black?"

"They were?"

"African Americans and Hispanic Americans still make up a good portion of the numbers out here on ranches—they certainly do on my brother's. And I'm sure you've heard about the Ninth and Tenth Cavalry—the Buffalo Soldiers—and the Fifty-sixth and Fifty-seventh Infantry units. All African American."

"You mean, the Buffalo Soldiers were *all* black?"

She nodded. "They had the highest reenlistment rate and the lowest desertion rate of any group in the army."

He seemed to grow taller as she spoke. "They didn't say nothing about that in history class."

"It's changing," she said. "Slowly but surely American history is starting to include contributions by all races, not just the whites."

His lips tugged into a reluctant smile as his long-fingered hands toyed with the watch. "You're okay, Miss Jessup."

"So are you, Kells. Don't worry about Mr. Craig. Everything's going to be fine."

"I don't know," he said quietly. "It's not hard to see that he don't want us here."

"Sure he does," she countered. "He just doesn't know it yet!"

CHAPTER TWO

LUKE WAS FUMING when he got home. He hated the whole idea of his new neighbors. It wasn't bad enough that the largest part of his hay crop had been ruined by too much rain, or that cattle prices were falling after a bacteria scare. Some days it didn't pay to be a rancher. He wondered why he hadn't gone into some better-paying profession, like plumbing. It was sheer lunacy to hang on to a ranch, even if it had been in the family for three generations.

He tossed his hat onto the sofa and sat down in his big recliner to watch the news. There was a feature on about the rise of juvenile crime and the lack of proper punishment in the juvenile justice system. He laughed without mirth. The same old tired theme again, and now he had a better knowledge of juvenile crime than most people. He'd put the eight combination locks back on the farm gate between his pasture and the summer camp, and he'd talked to his friend in the police department about working two nights a week out there.

He allowed himself a moment to ponder the trespasser's future if he'd left a gate open on the other side of that summer camp, on land that belonged to

Cy Parks. Luke was fairly easygoing, even in a temper. Cy Parks was so bad-tempered that delivery boys had to have double pay just to take things out to his place. Luke had considered talking to him about the summer camp, because there was safety in numbers. But he decided against it. Cy was a newcomer to Jacobsville and he'd never made any attempt to get to know local people. Rumor had it that he'd been burned out on his Wyoming ranch and had barely escaped with his life. He'd bought old man Sanders's place on Verde Creek and was building a herd of pure-bred Santa Gertrudis cattle. If Kells had so much as sneezed on one of those expensive young bulls, there was no telling what Cy would do. Luke, of course, was a kindhearted man. That being the case, he had to resort to desperate measures to protect his cattle. So he planned to hire a watchman.

His property contained a little line cabin near the fence, which Luke had furnished with a stove and refrigerator, chairs, a table and a cot for the men when they were working out there during roundup. It was a good few miles from the ranch proper, and he didn't run a chuck wagon to roundup, so the cabin was largely self-sufficient. There was a kitchen, so the men could cook for themselves, and the small building even had a telephone. Luke would provide his security man with a pair of binoculars, special ones with infrared, so that they allowed night vision. He wasn't going to lose any more cattle through open fences. No matter what it took.

THE NEXT MORNING, on a day when he was going to install the security man in the line cabin, he rode out to the steer pasture to find the gate closed. But the steers weren't alone in the pasture. A tall, lanky kid was stalking one of the steers.

Luke spurred his mount, something he rarely ever did, and put on a burst of speed, insinuating the horse in front of the boy, who backed away with huge wide eyes and upraised hands.

"Get that thing away from me!" the boy yelled. "Don't let it kick me!"

The fear in the youth's face was a surprise. Luke reined in the horse and sat quietly, leaning slightly forward in the saddle to study the nervous youth on the ground.

"What the hell are you doing in my pasture?" Luke demanded in a cold tone.

"Looking…looking for them computer chips," Kells stammered.

It was the very last thing Luke had expected to hear. He sat hesitating, his mind working furiously.

He wasn't aware of Belinda's cry or her headlong rush over the locked gate, so frenzied that she almost ripped a hole in her elegant designer jeans and scarred her boots.

"It's all right!" Belinda cried, panting as she ran up to join Kells, moving just in front of him. "He wasn't doing anything to the cattle!"

"Steers," Kells corrected, feeling a little smug.

Luke looked at him with new interest. "You know something about cattle?" he asked unexpectedly.

"She was teaching me," he replied, jerking his head toward the small woman in front of him. "About the difference. You know, steers and heifers and such. And about the computer chips under the hides."

Luke's hostile expression had faded to curiosity. "She told you about that?"

He nodded. "I wanted to see the chips. I wasn't going to hurt nothing," he added with faint belligerence.

Luke actually chuckled. He abruptly rode off toward where the steers were congregating near the fence, lifting his lariat from the saddle horn. He spun a loop and lassoed one of the steers with easy grace, the result of years of long practice, and got down out of the saddle to catch the rope tight. He motioned to Kells.

"That was great!" Kells exclaimed. "That was just great! How you learn to do that, spin that loop and lasso that cow...that steer...so easy?"

Luke grinned. "A lot of practice and a few bruises," he murmured. He was petting the steer behind its ears, and the animal stood very still and looked content. "Come on, he's not dangerous. I only run polled cattle here."

"Polled?" Kells asked, curious.

"Dehorned," the older man qualified. He searched behind the steer's neck and felt for a small lump. He found it. "Here." He caught Kells's dark hand and smoothed it over the spot. "It's a computer chip. I resisted this technology for years, but it makes roundup so much easier that I finally gave in. We can keep an animal's entire herd history on one chip and get the information in seconds with a scanner when we sort the animals for sale."

"I didn't think ranchers used it on steers," Belinda interjected.

"Oh, we don't usually," he agreed. "But this lot is an experiment." He shifted a little self-consciously. "I've been reading about some new methods that our local cattlemen's association is using. Vasectomy, for one."

"What's that?" Kells asked.

"Ordinarily, you create a steer by removing what makes him able to reproduce. But by giving the steer a vasectomy," he explained, "the animal still produces testosterone, which we think is responsible for fast growth. But since the steer is effectively neutered, it tends to be easier to handle. You get a higher weight-gain ratio the same as with bulls, but you get the lean carcass of a steer."

"Isn't it expensive to do it that way?" Belinda asked.

He smiled. "Not really. It takes about the same amount of time, and we do it ourselves instead of calling out the veterinarian. But even if it did take more time, we think the benefits outweigh the cost. That's why we're experimenting with it. Since the animal gains weight without the use of growth hormones, we save some money there, too."

"My brother says a lot of consumers are getting scared of those additives, like growth hormones and antibiotics," Belinda agreed.

"There's definitely a market for organically grown beef, and at least one cattleman I know of is offering custom-grown lean beef to supermarket chains," he added. He noted Kells's light, fascinated touch on the animal's shoulder.

"Isn't it hard to kill them?" Kells asked unexpectedly.

"Yes," Luke replied unexpectedly. "I'm in the cattle business because I like animals, so I get attached to the damned things. They all have personalities. They're all different. I try not to get too close to the beef cattle, but I've got a ton-and-a-half bull who follows me around like a pet dog, and two Holstein milk cows who think they're cats."

Kells chuckled. "No fooling? What's a Holstein?"

"They're dairy cattle…. Look here, are you really that interested in cattle?"

Kells shrugged and lowered his gaze to the steer. "Never saw cattle before," he murmured. He glanced shyly at Luke and then away again. "I like them. I didn't mean to let them get loose. I wanted to see them up close, you know. And after she told me about the computer chips…" He grimaced. "I just wanted to see what it looked like."

Luke pursed his lips, aware of Belinda's stillness. "Want to come see the Holsteins?" he asked.

Kells caught his breath. "Really?"

Luke shook his head. "Nothing a cattleman likes better than to show off his operation." He almost laughed aloud at the expression on Belinda's face.

Kells was fascinated. "Reckon I could see that bull?"

Luke chuckled. "Sure. Why not."

"Aren't you scared of that thing?" Kells persisted, moving back from the big black-spotted white horse.

"She's gentle—a mare," Luke explained. He frowned. "Why are you afraid of horses?"

"I lived in New York City until this year," he muttered. "A cop on a horse tried to run me down. It reared up and if I hadn't moved, it would have pawed me."

Luke wisely didn't ask what Kells had done to provoke the man. Still, trying to ride a boy down, for any reason, was reprehensible. "You should have told someone in authority," he said curtly.

Kells shrugged. "Nobody ever wanted to do anything for me until my mom moved us to Houston a few months ago and I got in trouble for taking a CD player out of a shop. She—" he indicated Belinda "—went to bat for me and got the owner not to press charges. But I got sent to juvy anyway, 'cause I was sixteen then."

"Juvy?"

"Juvenile hall," Belinda told him. "Courts are harder on juveniles these days, because there's so much violence in the inner city."

"I see." He didn't. He studied Kells, who was watching the cattle with such fascination that he was drawn to the boy. All his prejudices about "coddling juvenile delinquents" were going up in smoke. It was easy to be intolerant when you didn't know the people you were intolerant toward. Kells was giving him an education in gray areas, where before he'd seen only black-and-white.

"When do you want me to bring the guys over?" Belinda asked him.

"No time like the present," he said. "Load 'em up and come on. Know how to find it?"

"Yes, I've seen it from the road," she replied. She smiled with genuine gratitude. "Thanks."

He shrugged. "Just being neighborly." He took the loop from the steer's neck and coiled the rope, with Kells watching every move. The young man had a quick mind and nimble fingers. Suddenly he had an idea that might bear consideration.

THERE WERE SIX kids from the same neighborhood in Houston in Belinda's group, ranging in age from nine to fourteen. Kells was the oldest. The youngest was Julio, a Mexican boy. Two were white and one of the others was black, like Kells. The middle boy, Juanito, was Native American, although he wouldn't say which tribe. He didn't talk about himself at all. In fact, he didn't talk much, period. He was living with an uncle and aunt who didn't seem to notice what he did, or care. It was the same story with most of the others. That's why they'd landed themselves in juvenile court and detention centers. They cared as little for themselves as the adults around them did. It was important to Belinda that someone cared about them, built their self-esteem, made them proud of their races and history. She didn't delude herself that she could change the whole world. But maybe she could change one person.

She drove the boys to Luke's ranch in the rickety old van she'd bought for the occasion. It was in good mechanical shape, even if it did look like the dark side of the moon. She thought of having it painted, but it seemed a waste of time and money.

As she reached the end of a long, winding graveled road that led off from a paved highway, she noticed Luke was waiting for them. The house was nice, big, white and friendly with a long porch. There was a stable and corral back away from the flower garden that Luke's sister had kept until her marriage, and there were fenced and cross-fenced pastures reaching all the way to the main road.

Belinda got out of the battered old van and opened the side door so the boys could get out with her. "Remember not to go through any fences, okay?" she cautioned them. "Bulls are dangerous and unpredictable. If you've ever watched rodeo, in person or on television, you'll know that already."

"Mr. Craig said his bull follows him around," Kells reminded her.

"So he does. But the bull knows Mr. Craig, doesn't he?" she replied.

Kells grinned. "I guess so."

Luke came down the steps to meet them, greeted the boys and led them toward the barn. "This ranch has been in my family for three generations," he began. "My grandfather started out with longhorn cattle and I ended up with Herefords. Most ranchers have a breed they prefer above others. Cy Parks, who lives across there—" he gestured back toward the space the summer camp occupied "—runs pure-bred Santa Gertrudis. One of his bulls cost a million dollars."

Kells eyes widened and then his face fell. "Gosh, I guess you got to be rich to have cattle, huh?"

Luke smiled at him. "Not really. You could start out with a young bull and a few heifers and build a ranch from there. It's not as expensive as you think."

The light came back into the youth's eyes. He looked past Luke to the big Hereford bull in the pasture adjoining the barn and his breath caught. "Oh, Lord, what an animal!"

Luke burst out laughing. "He sounds just like me at his age," he explained when everybody looked at him. "I thought there was nothing on earth as pretty as a bull."

"There isn't," Kells agreed. He got up on the bottom rung of the high wooden fence and wrapped his arms around the top rung. "Isn't he great?"

"His name's Shiloh," Luke told him. "I raised him from a baby and now he's mentioned in just about every major cattle journal as a top stud bull. I can't keep up with the demand for his progeny. There's even a waiting list."

"Got any buffalo?" one of the boys asked.

Luke shook his head. "I know of a ranch or two that runs some, but they're dangerous to keep. They'll charge at the least provocation and they can go right through a fence."

"They have buffalo up on the Yellowstone," Juanito said. "I saw a whole herd when my uncle drove us through the park."

"I never saw a buffalo," another boy murmured.

Belinda smiled at her charges. "The whole of the western states used to have herds of them, before white people came along and killed them off."

"Why'd they do that?" one of the others wanted to know.

"Greed," Luke said flatly. "Pure and simple, greed. They wanted the money that people back East and even overseas were willing to pay for buffalo hides. And, too, there was a lot of money to be had for guiding shooting parties out on the plains so that they could kill hundreds of buffalo for sport and leave them lying in the sun."

Belinda stared at him curiously and then she smiled. They were kindred spirits. She hated the loss of the buffalo, too.

He glanced down at her while the boys murmured to each other about the size of that big bull in the fenced pasture. She had a pretty face, he thought, and a big heart to go with it. He liked her already. He smiled slowly and was surprised and delighted to see her face flush.

She had to drag her eyes away from his. That look had gone right through her. Over the years she'd had plenty of boyfriends, but they were all just casual acquaintances. Or they had been until Russell, who gave her an engagement ring and swore he loved her, and then eloped with her best friend. That had been

four long years ago. She hadn't looked at another
man since.

"What's wrong?" Luke asked perceptibly.

She caught her breath. "Wrong? Why…noth-ing."

"You were thinking about something and it hurt.
What was it?"

She shifted. "I was engaged. He eloped with my
best friend."

"Well, well." He studied her carefully. "So that's
why you aren't married. No inclination to try again,
I gather."

"None at all."

"Join the club."

She shot a quick glance at his averted profile.
"You, too?" she asked softly.

He nodded, a jerk of his head. "Me, too. She promised to be true, but the minute I went off on business,
she was entertaining an old boyfriend at the local
motel." He laughed coldly. "You can't do that sort of
thing in a town this small and not be gossiped about.
Two people told me about it when I got off the plane."

"It's the world we live in," she said quietly. "Fidel-
ity doesn't seem to mean much, anymore."

He turned to face her. "It means the world to me,"
he said flatly. "I'm an old-fashioned man. When I
give my word, I keep it."

She grimaced. "So do I." She smoothed her fingers carefully over the hard wood of the fence. "He
said I was a dinosaur."

One eyebrow levered slowly up.

"I wouldn't go to bed with him because we weren't

married," she said simply. "So he found somebody who would." She shrugged. "I can't blame him, really. I mean, every woman does it."

"Not every woman," he said coldly. "Virtue is so rare as to be priceless these days."

"Show me one virtuous man," she dared.

"That would be difficult," he agreed, "although it's not impossible. I've known a man or two who felt the way you do about it. Still, men can't get pregnant, can they? Women are the childbearers, the civilizers. I believe that when children are going to be involved, there should be one man, and no others."

She stared up at him quietly. "You're a dinosaur, too."

"You got a dinosaur?" one of the boys, overhearing, asked.

"Don't be stupid," another boy answered him, "there's no such thing!"

"I read that dinosaurs turned into birds," another ventured.

Juanito grinned for the first time. "My grandad used to say he could turn into a bird when he liked. And my mom said no wonder he ate like one."

Everybody laughed, but kindly.

It broke the ice. Luke showed the boys around, and they warmed to his easy, friendly manner. He led them through the barn, where he had two calves being treated for scours and a heifer with a snakebite.

"They're all improving," he said, watching the boys stare at the animals. "They'll go out into the pasture in a day or two. There were three calves in here, but we lost one of them yesterday."

"What's scours?" Kells asked.

"It's a disease calves get that prevents them from keeping anything in their stomachs," he replied. "They die if they aren't treated. The vet has been giving them medicine for it. Usually it works. Sometimes, it doesn't, no matter how hard you try."

"I guess you have to use a horse to work cattle," Kells continued.

"I'm afraid so. Although," he added with a chuckle, "I used to know a man who used an all-terrain vehicle to do it."

"One of those four-wheeled things like a big lawnmower?"

"The very thing. He hit a stump unexpectedly and went headfirst, right into the lagoon. I hear he gave the vehicle to his nephew the next day and went back to using horses." He saw the question in Kells's eyes and before he could ask it he added, "A lagoon is where animal waste is collected."

Kells doubled over laughing. "No wonder he gave the thing away!" He sighed. "I guess I could learn to like horses."

"Sure you could," Luke assured him. "A horse that's trained right will do what you tell it to, although I've seen some bad horses. In fact, a neighbor of mine has a twenty-year-old horse that killed a man in an arena and was about to be destroyed. He saved it."

"Must be a nice man."

He shook his head. "Not a chance. He's like a rattlesnake, coiled up and waiting for somebody to come within striking distance." He grinned. "Most people walk wide around him."

"Can we go back out there and look at the bull?" Kells asked.

"Sure, go ahead."

They ran out almost in a unit, leaving Luke and Belinda together at the steel gate that contained the calves in their stall.

He glanced at Belinda. "That neighbor lives on the other side of your camp, by the way. You'd better make sure nobody trespasses in his direction. I'm a reasonable man. He's not."

"I'll remember," she promised.

He watched her openly, his blue eyes narrow and thorough on her soft oval face. "Do you like your job?"

"I like kids," she said. "Especially kids who need something society isn't giving them." She jerked her head toward the boys. "There's not one thing wrong with them that a little love and attention wouldn't have taken care of. They just want someone to care about them, and they find unorthodox ways to attract attention."

"Kells said he stole a CD player."

She nodded. "But not because he wanted it," she murmured. "His mother's boyfriend had beaten him up that morning. He was getting back at her, for exposing him to that sort of treatment." She shrugged. "The boyfriend is the reason they're out here. He sent for her, but he doesn't want Kells. Neither did his father."

"What a shame."

She nodded. "The boyfriend's idea of discipline is a fist to the jaw. I've had the D.A.'s office looking into it, but Kells's mother won't say a word in Kells's defense. In fact, she told the investigator that he asked for it, by being sassy."

"Nobody asks to be beaten up." He said it with such ferocity that she turned and looked up at him. His face was hard, set with lines of pain. She had the most terrible urge to reach up and touch it, to make the lines relax. She remembered very well what he'd told her about his father, about the beatings. It would have been worse, to watch his mother taking that sort of abuse and not being able to stop it. It was a sadly familiar story in her circles. She reflected on women she'd worked with who had been victimized by abusive husbands.

There seemed to be so many women who tolerated the abuse out of fear, a kind of fear that well-meaning outsiders could never understand. Belinda tried to explain that everything would change once the woman was out of the house. It rarely worked until a beating landed her in the hospital, or until the man injured, sometimes killed, one of her children.

"What are you brooding about?" Luke asked abruptly.

She smiled sadly. "About women who won't accept help, feeling they're better off where they are. I was thinking about why they won't leave men who hurt them."

"Because they're afraid," Luke replied curtly. "Everybody says, just get out, you'll be okay." He laughed bitterly. "Once, after the police left, my father held a butcher knife to my mother's throat for ten minutes and described to her, graphically, what he'd do to my sister, Elysia, with it if she ever called the police again."

"Dear Lord," she breathed.

"He meant it, too," he added. "He said he'd have nothing to lose if they were going to put him in jail anyway."

She put out a hand and touched the back of his, just lightly. "I'm sorry you had to go through that."

He turned his hand and caught her fingers in his, tightly. "Why did you become a public defender?"

She smiled ruefully. "My best friend was raped by her stepfather, and the public defender on her case had such a heavy workload that he plea-bargained the case to get it off his schedule. She was devastated when her stepfather didn't even have to serve time for what he'd done. She couldn't go back home, because by then her mother believed she'd invited it." She shook her head sadly. "I decided then and there that I wanted to make a difference in the world. I studied law and here I am, despite my brother's assurances that I was wasting my time."

He chuckled. "I remember your brother very well," he mused. "He was the most ruthless businessman I ever met."

"Yes, he was. His wife has changed him," she added. "He's given up being stone-hearted. Now, he's my biggest fan."

His blue eyes met hers and he smiled slowly. "Maybe, but he's not your only one." He leaned closer deliberately, pausing with his lips a breath away from hers. "I like you, too, Miss Public Defender." And then he kissed her.

CHAPTER THREE

HE'D MEANT IT to be a brief, teasing kiss. It didn't work out that way. The touch of that soft mouth under his was explosive. He caught his breath, lifting his head just enough to see the mutual shock and pleasure in Belinda's eyes before he bent again.

This time, it wasn't brief, or particularly gentle. He lifted her completely against the length of his tall, muscular body and kissed her until he had to come up for air. He looked into her stunned eyes with quiet curiosity, breathing raggedly.

"You should…put me down," she whispered.

"Are you sure?" he murmured while he searched her face.

"Yes. The boys…"

He eased her back onto her feet, shooting a glance toward the barn door. The youngsters weren't in view at all. "Nobody saw," he said. He traced her swollen lips with his forefinger. "I could get used to this," he added quietly. "How about you?"

She swallowed and then swallowed again. She had to move back from contact with him before her mind would work again. "I'm only here on my summer vacation," she managed in a voice that didn't sound like her own.

He smiled slowly. "Houston isn't that far away."

She didn't know what to say. She was overcome by feelings she'd suppressed, tucked away and forgotten. Her body felt like a rosebud subjected to rain and sun and wind, blooming and lifting its face to the elements. He was very attractive, and he had qualities that she loved. But it was too quick; too soon.

"I'm rushing you," he mused, seeing the confused uncertainty in her eyes. "Don't get uptight. I won't back you into a corner. But I'm interested. Aren't you?"

She took time to catch her breath. She lowered her eyes to his shirt. "Yes."

He grinned. His heart felt lighter than it had in years. He curled her fingers into his and led her toward the barn entrance. "Come on. I'll show you my horses."

Belinda went along silently. She couldn't believe he'd done that, right out in the open, in plain daylight. It had been a passionate kiss, deliciously arousing and hungry. The warm, hard contact left her confused and quiet.

He had several horses, all Appaloosas. He explained the markings and called their names. "I'm crazy about them," he remarked. "I belong to an Appaloosa club and we talk on the internet about our passion. This is one special breed."

"Everybody says that about whichever breed they

like best," she said with a laughing smile. "But I can see why you like Apps. They really are beautiful."

"Cy Parks has Arabians," he told her. "A small herd, with a glorious stallion herd sire. He's pure white, like beach sand on the Gulf of Mexico. I think he used to race them, before he moved here."

"Is he really such a rough customer?"

"Yes, he is," he said bluntly. "Keep your brood well shy of his ranch. He can't tolerate children at all," he added, without mentioning why.

She let out a soft whistle. "Thanks for the warning," she said. "I started this camp because I wanted to make a difference for these boys, if they could see another sort of life from the one they live in the inner city. Yet I never stopped to consider the potential pitfalls… Still, I'm encouraged by Kells's interest in ranching. He didn't seem the kind of teenager who'd fall in love with cattle so quickly, but he's genuine about it. This will give him something to work toward."

"I had an idea about that," Luke confided. "I thought I might ask him to stay at the ranch and learn the ropes while you take the others back to your camp. Then if he decided to come back here and work after graduation, I'd hire him."

She caught her breath. "You'd do that for him?"

"For myself, too," he said. "He's a quick study and he loves the business. A cowboy like that would be an asset anywhere. If I train him, I can hire him when he gets through school."

"He'd be over the moon."

"Don't tell him until we can get the details worked out," he cautioned. "I don't want to build him up to a big letdown."

"I won't say a word." She searched his face. "You're good with children."

"I learned on Elysia's little girl," he told her with a grin. "I took her to movies and the park and carnivals. Her dad does those things now. I've missed her since Elysia remarried."

She studied the Appaloosas. "You should get married and have kids of your own."

"You know, I've just realized that."

She didn't dare look at him. Her heart was leaping around madly in her chest.

He turned away from the horse pasture and tugged her along with him. "We'd better get back to the boys and make sure they aren't trying to climb aboard that old bull," he murmured dryly. "I still remember how I was as a kid."

"How did your father make a living?"

"My grandfather made the living for him," he replied. "He had this ranch. Dad worked for him, when he was sober enough, and my grandfather protected us as long as he was alive. When he died, everything changed."

"But you managed to hang on to the ranch."

"I had help," he said. "Neighbors, friends, relatives…everybody did what they could for us, despite my father. That's why I'm still here," he added seriously. "Jacobsville is the sort of place where you're not a resident, you're part of a family. Maybe people know your business, but they care about you, as well. I couldn't think of living anywhere else."

"I can understand why," she murmured. Her hand in his felt small and vulnerable. *She* felt small. He towered over her, and she liked him very much. Too much. It wasn't possible to feel so strongly for someone she'd only just met, but she seemed to fit into his life as if she'd been conditioned to it.

He glanced down at her with a warm smile. She was pretty and feisty and she really did care about these boys of hers. He could see her with children of her own. She'd be a veritable mama lion if her kids were threatened. He found himself wondering about having a child of his own. He loved Elysia's two, but he had to start thinking about the future, about kids of his own to inherit this place when he was gone. It didn't really surprise him that he was beginning to see Belinda in a new light. She came from a ranching background, and she had a soft heart. He'd had his fill of women who wanted a good time and no ties of any kind. He was old enough to start looking for a settle-down sort of woman.

THE BOYS LEFT the ranch late that afternoon with Belinda, after a long tour of the ranch on saddle horses that left them all sore but happy.

"They'll be uncomfortable tomorrow," Luke chuckled as he saw Belinda to the van. "They used muscles they didn't know they had on that trail ride. Kells took to it like a pro, did you notice? For a boy who was afraid of horses, he's come a long way in a short time."

"You were amazing with him," she said. "He was the one I couldn't reach, did you know? He was surly and uncommunicative until I started telling him about cattle. I found the door and you found the key. He's different."

"He's focused," he told her, glancing toward the van where the boys were conversing animatedly inside. "They're not bad kids," he said suddenly, as if the thought surprised him.

She smiled. "No, they're not," she replied. "The world is full of them. Young people get married and two years down the road, they realize they've made a mistake, but they've got a child. They get divorced and marry somebody else and the kids end up in a family where they're the outsiders. Sometimes they're not even wanted. It's worse in poor neighborhoods, of course." She nodded toward the van. "Kells could write a book on that. He said that most of the kids in his neighborhood in New York City were either wanted by the law or selling drugs. He thought he'd end up the same way." She sighed, her eyes seeing far away. "When people live in hopeless poverty, with a poor self-image and no way out, they give up. That's why they resort to alcohol and drugs, because it eases the pain, just for a little while. But pretty soon, they're hooked and they can't quit, and they'll do anything to get high again, so they can forget where they live and what they've become." She shook her head. "It occurs to me sometimes that a small percentage of people aren't constructed to live in a regimented, money-oriented, time-clock-mandated industrial society. These same people, placed on the land where they could work at their own pace, would be happy and useful."

"That's a new theory."

She shook her head. "It's not. I'm only quoting Toffler." He looked puzzled and she smiled. "Alvin Toffler... *Future Shock?* Mr. Toffler is a visionary and he sees right inside people. He said that some people will never fit into our fast-paced culture, and I think he's right."

"I'd like to hear more about that." He pursed his lips. "I don't suppose you could get away for supper one evening?"

"I've got no one to stay with the boys," she said regretfully.

"Then I'll just have to find an excuse to have them back over again, won't I?" he said, grinning down at her.

She chuckled. "You do that. I'd better get them back to camp. Thanks for letting me bring them over."

"I enjoyed it," he returned.

"So did I."

She went back to the van and climbed in with the boys. She couldn't help a glance into the rearview mirror as they went back the way they'd come, down the winding ranch road. Luke was standing in the yard with his hands in the pockets of his jeans, his wide-brimmed hat covering his head. He looked like part of the land itself, and something warm kindled inside her at just the sight of him.

FOR THE NEXT few days, Belinda found plenty of time to regret her lapse of control with Luke in the barn. She got cold feet and flatly refused the boys' request for another visit to the ranch.

She didn't realize that her refusal was about to have grave consequences. Kells, depressed with little to do and too much time on his hands, wanted another shot at roping cattle.

Late one sunny afternoon, he slipped away from the others. He'd found an old, limp rope in one of the old outbuildings near the camp and he'd spent hours every day practicing with it, as he'd seen Luke do. He was somewhat proficient, but he was bored with roping the old sawhorse that sat near the oak tree behind the building. He wondered if he could lasso a steer. Miss Jessup was occupied with the other boys, teaching them how to use her laptop computer. He preferred cattle to computers, so he coiled his rope and sneaked down the road toward a pasture full of red-coated cattle.

He didn't realize that Luke's cattle were only one side of the long, winding graveled road. He knew that most of Luke's steers were Herefords, which were white and red. These cattle were red, but they might be a variation on the same breed, he decided. They sure weren't steers, he knew that by looking at them, and they had horns. They'd be easy to rope!

He slipped through the barbed-wire fence stealthily, eased into the small line of trees that outlined the green pasture and started up a small rise where a red-coated young bull was grazing.

It was the perfect time to practice the lariat throw he'd been perfecting, as Luke had showed him how to do it. He missed the first time he tried, but the animal didn't run away. It stood chewing grass and staring at him curiously. He coiled the rope and patiently tried again. This time, he managed the throw perfectly, tossing the loop right over the short horns of the young bull. He chuckled and let out a whoop as he started reeling the bull in.

He was having the time of his life, leading the young bull around the pasture and down the hill toward the gate when he heard a loud yell, followed by a chilling report that sounded very much like a rifle being fired.

He stopped dead in his tracks, the rope in his hand, and turned to find a tall, threatening-looking man on a huge white horse sitting just a few hundred feet away on the ridge holding a rifle to his shoulder. His face wasn't visible under the wide-brimmed hat, but the threat in his posture was immediately recognizable to a teen who'd had several brushes with gangs.

Kells dropped the rope and threw up his hands while he had time. "I was just practicing with the rope, mister," he called. "No need to shoot me!"

The man didn't reply. He had a cell phone in his hand now and he was punching in numbers. A minute later he spoke into it and then closed it up.

"Sit down," a rough, deep voice called.

Kells wasn't thrilled with the idea of sitting down in a cow pasture where rattlesnakes might be crawling, but he didn't want to get shot. He sat down. This, he thought, was very obviously the landowner Luke had warned him about, but he hadn't listened. He knew with a miserable certainty that he was going to wish he had.

BELINDA WAS JUST beginning to clear the lunch dishes and wondering why Kells hadn't come in to eat when her cell phone rang. She picked it up and listened, and then sat down hard.

"They didn't have your number, so they called me," Luke told her grimly. "If you'll give me a minute to organize things here, I'll pick you up and we'll go to the police station together. I know these people better than you do."

"What are my chances of getting Mr. Parks to drop the charges?" she asked with resignation in her voice.

"Slim to none," he said flatly. "If Cy Parks had his way, they'd probably shoot him. I don't think we'll be able to talk Cy out of this, but we can try."

"How long will it take you to get over here?" she asked, not even protesting his offer to go with her.

"Twenty minutes."

ACTUALLY, HE MADE it in fifteen. He was dressed for work, in wide leather bat-wing chaps, old boots with caked spurs and a long-sleeved chambray shirt. He pulled his wide-brimmed hat farther over his eyes as he put Belinda into the huge double-wheeled pickup truck and drove her into town.

"Don't get the idea that our police department is gung-ho to arrest people for no good reason," he said as he drove. "Cy will have bulldozed them into it. By the letter of the law, Kells was trespassing, but nobody in his right mind would take a rustling charge seriously. What was he going to do with the damned bull, anyway?"

"He was practicing with the lariat, the way you taught him," she said miserably. "I suppose he got tired of lassoing the sawhorse and wanted something real to practice on."

"He heard me tell him to keep off Parks's place!"

"He wouldn't have known which side of the fence was Parks's," she returned. "He probably wasn't even paying attention to the color of the animals. At any rate, yours have red-and-white coats and Parks's have red coats, he might have thought some of yours were a solid color."

"It's a hell of a mess, I'll tell you that," he said angrily.

"Worse than you know. With his record, he may never get a chance to go home again. They'll want to send him right back to the detention center and keep him there."

"Damn!"

She felt furious at Cy Parks for this. Kells shouldn't have been on his property, but he was a kid, and he didn't think. Why did Parks have to abide by the very letter of the law?

It seemed forever before Luke pulled up in front of the neat brick building that contained the police and fire departments and the city jail.

"In here," he indicated, holding the door open for Belinda.

The building was air-conditioned and very neat. Luke opened the door that had Police written on it, and ushered her to the counter, behind which a clerk sat.

"We're here to see about bail for the Kells boy," Luke said.

"Ah, yes." The clerk took a slow breath and sorted through papers, shaking her head. "Mr. Parks was furious." She glanced at Luke. "He's still here, you know, giving the chief hell."

Luke's blue eyes turned to steel. "Is he, now? Which way?"

The clerk hesitated. "Now, Luke—"

"Tell me, Sally."

"He's in his office. I have to announce you."

"I'll announce myself," he said shortly and forged ahead, leaving a startled Belinda to follow him.

This was a side of Luke that she hadn't seen before. He barged right into Chief Blake's office with only a preemptory knock, and found the chief looking uncomfortable while a tall, whipcord-lean man with venomous light green eyes and jet-black hair raged at him.

Cy Parks turned as Luke entered the office, his lean face as unwelcoming as a brushfire. "I won't drop the charges," he said at once, narrow-eyed and threatening. "I don't want juvenile delinquents camped on my south pasture, and I'll have every damned boy on the place in jail if that's what it takes to keep them out of my cattle!"

"That sounds familiar," Belinda said under her breath.

Luke wasn't intimidated. He walked right up to Cy, almost on eye-level with the man, and pushed his hat back on his blond hair. "I taught Kells to use a rope," he said angrily. "He's crazy about roping. He's been practicing on my cattle, but they don't have horns."

Cy didn't speak. But he was listening.

"He's an inner-city kid who got arrested for swiping a CD player. He didn't want the appliance, he wanted to get back at his mother for letting his stepfather beat him up."

Cy's stiff stance relaxed just a little.

Encouraged, Luke plowed ahead. "He's not a juvenile now, so if you press charges, they'll lock him up for good. He'll never get out of the justice system. He'll become a career criminal in between terms in prison, and I'll lose the most promising young cowhand who's ever come my way."

Parks's eyes narrowed. "He likes cattle?"

"He's obsessed with cattle," Luke replied. "He's drained Belinda dry and now he's starting to pick my brain. He has a natural seat on a horse. He eats, sleeps and breathes cattle since he's learned how to tell one breed from another."

Parks's jaw clenched. "I don't like kids around me."

Luke didn't blink. He noticed that Cy always kept his left hand in his pocket, and he knew why. The man hated sympathy; it was probably why he was so mean. It kept most people at bay. "Hating kids isn't going to bring yours back," Luke said quietly.

The other man's face clenched. He stiffened and, for an instant, it looked as if he might throw a punch at Luke.

"Go ahead," Luke invited softly, evenly. "Punch me if you feel like it. I'll give you a free shot. But let the kid go. The last thing on earth he meant to do was damage any of your stock. He loves cattle."

Cy's fist balled by his side and then relaxed. He moved his shoulders, as if they felt stiff, and glared at the other man. "Don't mention my past again," he said in a tone that chilled. He glanced at the police chief. "If I drop the charges, do you let him go?"

"With a warning," Chief Blake agreed.

Cy hesitated. He turned toward Belinda Jessup, who was pale and quiet and obviously upset. "What was the idea behind this summer camp?" he asked curtly.

"I brought six inner-city kids to the country to see what life could be like," she replied calmly. "Most of them have never seen a cow or a pasture or a small town. They grew up in poverty, with parents who didn't really want them, and all they saw were people working themselves to death for minimum wage or men in luxury cars dealing drugs for big money. I thought, I hoped, that this might make a difference." She folded her hands behind her. "It was making a major difference in Kells, until now. I'm sorry. I should have been watching him more carefully. He's spent two days practicing with the rope. I suppose he thought he was in Luke's pasture when he roped the bull."

"Hell of a difference between a purebred Santa Gert and one of those damned mangy Herefords," Cy said curtly.

"Hey," Luke said testily, "don't insult my Herefords!"

They glared at each other again.

"What about Kells?" Belinda interjected before things escalated too far.

"Let him go," Cy said shortly.

Chief Blake smiled faintly. "I'm glad you decided that," he said, rising. "I never thought roping a bull should be a capital crime."

"You haven't seen my new Santa Gert sire," Cy returned.

Blake just chuckled and went to the back to bring out Kells.

Kells was chastised and miserable, and looked as if the world had ended. He grimaced when he saw Cy Parks standing there.

"I guess I'm going back to Houston, now, huh?" he asked Belinda with overly bright eyes.

"No, you're not," Luke said curtly, glaring at Cy. "You're coming over to the bunkhouse at my place for the rest of your camp leave."

Kells looked as if he'd been knocked sideways. "You're kidding, right?"

"I'm not," Luke assured him. "If you want to rope cattle, you have to be around them. Besides, we've got to talk about the future. Your future," he added. "Let's go."

Kells hesitated. He walked up to Cy Parks and bit his lip while he searched for the right words. "Look, I'm sorry about what I did, okay?" he asked hesitantly. "I knew them cattle didn't look exactly like Mr. Craig's, but I thought he might have had some more, and that was them. I never meant no harm. I just wanted something alive to practice on. Ain't no challenge in roping a few boards nailed together."

Cy looked uncomfortable. He made a strange gesture with his right hand. "All right. Don't do it again."

"I won't," Kells promised. "Them bulls sure are pretty, though," he added with a shy smile. "That breed started on the King Ranch in South Texas, didn't it?"

Cy's lower jaw fell a little. "Well, yes."

"Thought so," Kells said proudly. He smiled. "I'll know next time how to tell a Santa Gertrudis from a Hereford."

Cy exchanged a complicated glance with Luke. "I guess you could bring him over to see my new Santa Gertrudis bull," he said gruffly. "Call first."

Luke and the other occupants of the room gaped at him.

Cy glared back. "Are you all deaf?" he asked irritably. "I'm going home. I don't have time to stand around and gossip all day, like some I could name." He tipped his hat at Belinda in an oddly old-world gesture and stormed out the door.

Kells caught his breath as the rancher lifted his left hand out of the pocket to open the door, but Cy, fortunately, was out the door before it was audible.

"What happened to his hand?" he exclaimed.

"His Wyoming ranch burned up in a fire," Luke said quietly. "His wife and young son were in the house at the time. He couldn't get them out. Not for lack of trying, that's how he got burned."

"Oh, boy," Kells said heavily. "No wonder he hates kids. Reminds him of the one he lost, don't you think, Miss Jessup?"

She put an affectionate arm around Kells. "Yes, I do. Poor man. Well, let's get back. I left the others at lunch."

"Sorry about all the trouble," Kells said.

Luke grinned at him. "It was no trouble." He glanced at the chief of police and smiled. "Thanks, Chet."

Chet Blake shrugged. "All in a day's work. I was trying to get him to drop the charges when you walked in. But I didn't get far, I'm sad to say. I couldn't budge him."

"He's a hard-nosed fellow," Luke agreed. "But he did the right thing in the end."

"So he did. Maybe he's not frozen clean through just yet," Blake replied.

THEY DROVE BACK to Belinda's camp in a companionable silence.

"I'm taking Kells with me," he told her when he pulled up in front of the cabin, and the boys piled out onto the porch to greet Belinda. "I'll get him settled and you can come over in a couple of days and check on him."

"I thought you were kidding!" Kells exclaimed. "You meant it?"

"Of course I meant it," Luke told him. "You're a natural cowboy, Kells. I'm going to make you into a top hand. Then, when you get through school, and if you're still of the same mind, I'll take you on as a cowboy."

Kells could hardly speak. He stared down at his hands in his lap and averted his head. There were bright lights in those dark eyes until he blinked them away. His voice was still choked when he said, "Thanks, Mr. Craig."

"Luke," he corrected. "And you're welcome."

"Have fun," Belinda told Kells.

He got into the front seat beside Luke and closed the door, leaning out the open window to wave to his friends. "I'm going off to learn cowboying, you guys! See you!"

They waved back. Belinda joined them on the porch and waved the truck off with a grin.

"Is Kells going to jail?" Juanito asked.

"No, he isn't. Mr. Parks dropped the charges," she said with heartfelt relief. "In a day or so, we'll drop by the Craig ranch and see how Kells is doing. But for now," she added with a groan as she saw the disorder of the small kitchen and dining-room table, "we're going to have a dishwashing and housecleaning lesson."

The groans were audible even outside the cabin.

CHAPTER FOUR

BELINDA KEPT BUSY with the remaining boys in her small group for the next two days, taking them swimming and fishing. They were like prisoners set free, with plenty of time to enjoy the natural world around them, and no regulations and time schedules penning them in. It was more than a vacation for them; it was a glimpse into another world. With any luck at all, it would sustain them when they had to go home, give them goals to work toward, give them hope.

Two days after Kells's run-in with the law, they piled into the van and went over to Luke's ranch to see how the eldest of the group was making out.

They hardly recognized him. He was wearing new boots, jeans and chaps, a long-sleeved shirt and a raunchy-looking hat. He grinned at them from the corral fence, displaying blazing white teeth.

"Hey!" he called. He jumped down and went to meet them. "Miss Jessup, I rode a horse all morning and Mr. Craig even let me cut out a steer and lasso it! That's a quarter horse," he informed the other boys knowledgeably, nodding toward the horse in the corral. "His name's Bandy and he's a cutting horse. He's trained to cut cattle, so you don't have to do much work except sit in the saddle and let him do every-thing. He's one smart horse!"

"Well, he certainly thinks he is," Luke interrupted, joining the group. "What do you think of my new hand?" he asked Belinda, indicating Kells. "Looks the part, doesn't he?"

"Yes, he does," Belinda said, smiling. "We need a photo of him dressed like that," she added.

"I took one this morning," he replied smugly. "He'll have some interesting photos to show the folks back in Houston."

"I'm going to work hard, Miss Jessup," Kells said solemnly. "Harder than I ever did before. Now that I got something to look forward to, school won't be so bad."

"I'll tell you a secret, Kells," Luke told him. "School was hard for me, too. But I got through, and so will you."

"My real name's Ed," Kells said quietly. "Never told nobody else."

Luke smiled. "Is that what you want me to call you?"

Kells hesitated. "How about Eddie? I like Eddie Murphy, you know."

"I like Eddie Murphy myself," Luke replied with a grin. "I've never missed one of his movies yet."

"Son of a gun!" Kells was impressed.

"I actually saw him once," Belinda volunteered, "down in Cancun, Mexico, on holiday. He's just as nice in person as he seems to be on the screen."

"Did you talk to him?" Kells asked.

She shook her head. "I was too shy."

Luke pushed his hat back on his head and studied her with a keen, searching look. "Shy, hmm?"

She gave him a hard look. "Yes, shy! I do get shy from time to time!"

He looked pointedly at her mouth. "Do you, now?"

She flushed. "Do you think we could see those Holstein milk cows you mentioned the other day?"

"Sure we could!" Luke said at once. "Kells, suppose you take the boys along to the pasture and explain why we like to keep Holsteins for milk cows?"

The youth beamed. "I'd be tickled, Mr. Craig! Come on, guys. I know my way around here now!"

The group, impressed, followed Kells.

"Why can't I go, too?" Belinda asked.

"Because I have plans for you, Miss Jessup," he drawled. He caught her hand in his and led her toward the white frame house.

"What sort of plans?" she asked suspiciously.

He paused with a secretive grin. "What do you think?" He leaned closer, threatening her mouth with his, so that when he spoke she felt his clean, minty breath on her lips. "Well, I could be thinking about how big and soft the sofa in the living room is," he murmured. "And how well two people would fit on it."

She could barely breathe. Her heart was thumping madly against her rib cage.

"Or," he added, lifting his head, "I might have something purely innocent in mind. Why not come with me and find out?"

He tugged at her hand and she fell into step beside him, just when she'd told herself she wasn't about to do that.

He led her up the steps and into the house. It was cool and airy, with light colored furniture and sedate throw rugs. There were plain white priscilla curtains at the windows, and the kitchen was spacious and furnished in white and yellow.

"It's very nice," she said involuntarily, turning around to look at her surroundings.

"Can you cook?" he asked.

"A few things," she replied. "I'm not really good at sweets, but I can make rolls and biscuits from scratch."

"So can I, when I set my mind to it," he told her. He sat down at the kitchen table and crossed his legs across one of the other chairs. "Can you make coffee?"

"The best," she returned, smiling.

"Let's see."

He pointed her toward the cabinet where the coffee, filters and drip coffeemaker were located, and sat back to watch her work.

"There's a chocolate pound cake in the cake keeper, there," he indicated a huge rubbery container. "If you like it. My sister brought it over yesterday. She always bribes me when she wants something," he added on a chuckle.

"What did she want?"

"A babysitter," he replied. "I get to keep her son and daughter when she and Tom go to the opera at the Met in New York City. It's an overnight trip."

"You really must like kids," she observed.

"I like them more as I get older," he said. "I find I think more about having some of my own. After all, the ranch has to have somebody to inherit it after I'm gone."

"What if your children don't like ranching?"

He grimaced. "Horrid thought."

"Some people don't like animals. I've actually met a few."

"So have I. Not many."

"It could happen, though. Then what would become of your plans for a dynasty?"

"I suppose they'd go up in smoke." He dropped his hat on the floor beside his chair and stared at her until it became uncomfortable. The sound of the coffee dripping grew louder and louder in the tense silence. "Come here."

She just stood and stared at him, confused.

His blue eyes were glittery. There was a look on his face that made her knees weak. He was hypnotizing her.

"I said, come here," he repeated softly, his voice almost a sensual purr.

She walked to him, feeling every step all the way to her heart. This was stupid. She could get in over her head. She didn't really know him at all. She was letting herself be drawn in....

He reached up and pulled her down onto his lap. Before she could utter the confused thoughts rattling around in her mind, he had her head back against his shoulder and he was kissing her as if his life depended on it.

She gave in to the inevitable. He was strong and warm, and everything female in her responded to him. She hadn't realized how close two people could become in a relatively short period of time.

His arms contracted. Then, all at once, he let her go and stood up. His face was harder than she'd ever seen it. He held her tight by the upper arms, staring down into her green eyes with a curious expression.

"I think we should give the coffee time to finish," he said huskily. "Let's go find the boys."

"Okay."

She followed him back out the door, noticing the economy of his movements as he scooped up his hat and put it back on his head. He went a little ahead of her, keeping some distance between them. She felt uneasy, and she wondered if she'd been too acquiescent to suit him. Perhaps she should have hit him or protested or something. Obviously she'd done something wrong.

He opened the screen door and she started through it, only to be encased by his long arm as it shot out in front of her, blocking her way.

"I loved it," he said gruffly. "But we have to go slow. I don't do one-night stands any more than you do."

"Oh." She seemed to have developed a one-syllable vocabulary in the time she'd known him. She kept her eyes on his arm, instead of his face.

He tilted her face up to his. "If I wanted to give you the brush-off, I'd come right out and say so," he remarked. He bent and brushed his mouth gently over hers. "You don't gulp down an exotic dessert," he whispered. "You take your time and savor it, draw it out, make it last." He nibbled her lower lip gently before he lifted his head. "Suppose I come up to Houston after you get through with summer camp? We could go to the theater and the ballet, even a rodeo if you like. I'm pretty flexible in my entertainment, I like everything."

"So do I," she said, sounding breathless. "I love opera."

"Another plus," he mused, grinning. "We'll fly up to New York with Tom and Elysia one day and go to the Met."

"I've only been there once," she told him. "I loved it."

"It's unforgettable," he agreed. "The settings and special effects are every bit as enjoyable as the opera itself."

She shyly traced a pattern on his shirt. "I'd like to go out with you."

"Then it's a date." He glanced past her at the boys in the distance, standing in a group as if they were being lectured. Probably they were, he thought, because Kells was a quick study and he'd learned a lot in the past few days. "It wouldn't be very easy to go out even to a movie with that bunch in tow," he added with a chuckle. "They'd hog the popcorn."

"I suppose they would." She touched his arm where the muscle was thickest and enjoyed its strength. She liked the way it felt to be close to him. "You've been good to them, especially to Kells."

"He's had a raw deal. I guess they all have, but it shows more on him. Do you know, the guys in the bunkhouse took to him right away. One of them told me that it was flattering to have a teenager ask for information instead of trying to give it. He made them feel important by asking them things." He pursed his lips. "I wonder if he realizes what a gift he has for making people like him? Even Cy Parks, who hates just about everybody."

"He's learning that he has traits he can exploit, I think. But I don't know that he would have arrived at this point so soon if you hadn't intervened. Thank you."

He shrugged off her gratitude. "Like I said, I'll benefit from all his enthusiasm. He really loves cattle."

She searched his lean face. "So do you, I think."

He grinned. "There was never anything I wanted to be more than a cowboy when I was a kid. One of our wranglers had been a rodeo star. I used to sit and listen to him by the hour."

"We had one of those, too, on my brother's ranch," she replied. "Ward and I liked him a lot, until he had an affair with our mother."

He frowned. "What?"

She sighed. "You might as well know. Our mother was very promiscuous. Anything in pants would do. She finally ran off with one of her conquests and we had to stay and live down her reputation. Ravine is about the size of Jacobsville, so you can imagine the gossip. It was harder on Ward than on me."

"There are a lot of miserable kids in the world," he remarked.

"I noticed."

"Is that why you don't spend much time at your brother's ranch?"

She chuckled. "No. It's because of his house-keeper—excuse me, now his aunt-in-law. Lillian is a matchmaker. She brought her niece Marianne out to Texas from Georgia on some gosh-awful pretext and Ward fell in love with her. He didn't want to, so things got bad before he admitted he couldn't live without her. She's changed him. He isn't the same hard-hearted, ruthless man he used to be since he married Marianne. So Lillian had that great success and now she's got her eye on me." She smiled. "I don't like her choice of suitors, so I keep well clear of the ranch."

"What sort does she toss your way?"

"Big, husky mechanics and any delivery boy who comes within half a mile of the house."

His eyebrows arched. "You're not that desperate."

"Thank you," she replied. "How about writing and telling her so?"

He grinned. "Give me time. I'll take care of that problem for you, in the most natural sort of way."

She wondered what he meant, but she wasn't con-fident enough to ask. She smiled and went past him out the door.

IN THE DAYS that followed, Luke was almost a con-stant visitor to the camp. Sometimes he brought Kells, sometimes he came alone. He taught the boys how to make a fire from scratch, how to trap game, how to live off the land.

"They say these are outdated skills," he told the group after he'd started a small fire. "But what if the oil suddenly gives out and everything electronic or electrical goes dead one day? Frozen food would spoil. Computers wouldn't work. Since most telephone exchanges are computerized, communications would be out. Cars wouldn't go far, houses wouldn't have heat, air-conditioning wouldn't work. If all the old skills of survival are lost, one day the only humans who live may be the ones who can live off the land—assuming there's any land left after the developers get through."

The Native American boy, Juanito, touched a tiny bunch of twigs that Luke had bunched to use on the tiny fire. "My great-uncle says the same thing," he volunteered. "But he can trap game and find water in places where it usually isn't. He knows which cactus plants can give water or be eaten, and he knows how to make smokeless fires. His grandfather rode with Geronimo."

The other boys were impressed. "But even if you can do those things, what good are they in the city?" one of the other boys asked. "What are you going to trap in Houston?"

"Girls," one of the older boys said with a wicked grin.

"He's got a point," Luke said, nodding toward the boy who'd asked about country skills in the city. "People who live in cities are going to be the hardest hit if we ever have a major energy crisis. Look what happened during the last big power outage in the west."

"They had a movie about that. It was scary," another boy said.

"Well, we've got lots of dead dinosaurs lying around yet to be discovered, so I don't think it's going to be an immediate problem," Belinda mused.

That led to the obvious question of what did dead dinosaurs have to do with energy, and for several minutes she traced the evolution of petroleum products for the boys while Luke watched and listened attentively.

Later, when the boys were in for the night and he was ready to go back to his ranch, he paused with her in the shadows, beside the pickup truck.

"You make a good lecturer," he commented.

"Thanks," she said, surprised. "Some would say I have a big mouth and can't keep it shut."

He took her hand and drew it to his chest. "I like the way you treat the boys," he said quietly. "You never talk down to them or make them feel stupid when they ask questions."

"I try not to," she agreed. "I've had it done to me in school, and I didn't like it."

"Neither did I." He smoothed his thumb over her short, neat fingernails. "You have nice hands."

"So do you." She liked the strength of them, the way her heart jumped when they touched her own hands. She looked up at him through the darkness, trying to see his face in the dim light from the cabin behind her.

He chuckled. "I was just thinking how strange life is," he told her. "I was hopping mad when I found out some lunatic was going to open a summer camp for delinquent boys right on my boundary line."

"I remember," she chuckled.

"It was a surprising day all around, especially that Kells." He shook his head. "What a treasure he turned out to be. And your guy Juanito, whose grandfather rode with Geronimo. These boys are interesting, and they aren't at all what I pictured them as."

"These are unique," she said. "But for every success, I've had three failures," she added sadly. "When I started working in the public defender's office, I had the idea that all these boys were in trouble because of their home lives. It was a mistake. Any number of them had loving parents and an extended family that really cared about them, but they could never see anything criminal about stealing and lying and hurting people. One of my charges actually wrestled me down in my office and tried to rape me."

She felt him stiffen. "What did you do?"

"Oh, I'm an old hand at self-defense," she said, making light of the terror she'd felt. "I got an opening and almost made a eunuch of him. It taught me a lesson. Some of the juveniles can't be turned around, no matter how dedicated you are to saving them. There's always going to be a percentage who feel comfortable with making a living outside the law."

"I don't like the idea that you might be attacked," he said.

She smiled. "I'm glad. But I'm not as naïve as

I was. I never have closed-door sessions with any of my clients anymore. I have a good secretary and she's always there when I need her." She sighed. "But there are times when I feel so useless. Like with Kells in the chief of police's office. I really don't know what I would have done if you hadn't been able to get through to Mr. Parks."

"Cy's not so bad," he said. "You just have to stand up to him. He's the sort of man who'll be hell on anybody who's afraid of him."

"You weren't."

He shrugged. "I grew up swinging," he mused. "I learned early that fear is the worst enemy. Once I got past that, I wasn't afraid of much."

"I noticed." She leaned close and laid her cheek against his chest, feeling his arms come around her with a sense of wonder. She closed her eyes and let him hold her, drinking in the sounds of the night and the warm, safe strength of his body. "I only have a week left here."

She felt him stiffen. His hands stilled on her back. "A week?"

"Yes. I have cases waiting and my vacation's almost over."

"I didn't realize it was that close."

Her eyes opened and she saw the faint light of the horizon far away. Crickets were chirping madly in the night. "I've been enjoying this so much that I didn't want to spoil it," she confessed.

His arms tightened around her. "So have I. But I've already told you that Houston isn't that far away."

"Of course it isn't."

They both knew it wasn't quite true. It was a great distance, and Luke couldn't leave his ranch to run itself. A long-distance romance was going to be difficult, even though they both knew it was what they were leading up to.

"I don't suppose you might like to come and work in Jacobsville?" he asked.

She hesitated. "That would be nice," she said. She wondered why the thought made her so uncomfortable. He was asking for more than a move on her part, and it frightened her. He was thinking about a future that included both of them, but all she could think about was the disaster of her parents' marriage. Ward had made it work with his Marianne, but Belinda had been on her own for a long time. She wasn't ready to think about spending her life with anyone.

"We have a juvenile court system here," he continued. "It's on a circuit, and we may not have the caseload you do in Houston, but you'd stay busy. We've got local kids who could use a good attorney."

"There are kids everywhere like that," she said tightly. "But Houston is home to me now. It's where my job is. I wouldn't feel comfortable starting all over again in a new town, especially a small town."

He was still for a moment and then he eased her away and stepped back. "The job is that important to you, is it?"

She felt a coolness in him that hadn't been there before. But she wasn't backing down now. She was fighting for her independence. "Well…yes, it is. I feel that I'm beginning to do some good."

"Is your job more important than marriage would be?"

She wouldn't think that far ahead. "I haven't thought much about marriage. Or if I have, it's a long way in the future. I don't want to be tied down just yet."

He studied her with pursed lips and a calculating stare. "Then you might be in the market for an affair."

It was like a stone between the eyes. She couldn't even find the words to express what she was feeling.

"No, I… I don't want an affair," she stammered. "I don't have time for that sort of thing. I have a caseload that's more than enough for three people, but there's only me to do it."

He let go of her completely and stood away, leaning against the hood of the truck to study her. "One thing I learned early is that jobs don't matter as much as people," he said coolly. "I've never put work before my family."

"Ward always did," she replied.

"You're not your brother. And you said he'd changed since his marriage."

"Yes, but I grew up learning that you gave everything in you to whatever job you were doing. My father hammered the work ethic into both of us from childhood."

"You don't think you could change?"

She frowned. The conversation was going far out of bounds. She wasn't sure what she believed anymore. She was drawn to Luke, but he was talking as if he wanted her to give up her job and just stay at home all the time. She knew she could never do that. Her work was fulfilling, important, almost sacred. She had a mission in life that she couldn't sacrifice for dirty dishes and housework.

"I'm not cut out to be a happy homemaker," she said on a hollow laugh.

"No pots and pans and dirty diapers for you, right?"

She wasn't sure about that, but he was being sarcastic. "Maybe so," she said after a minute. "I'm doing an important job, and it isn't one that everybody can do. I enjoy my work. I have to feel that I'm contributing something to the world."

He turned his head and stared toward the horizon without speaking. He hadn't counted on this. He was falling in love, and he'd thought she was, too. But she obviously wasn't the marrying sort of woman, and she didn't want an affair. That left nothing but friendship, and that wouldn't be enough for him.

"I've never been much on glorious causes," he said finally. "I raise cattle. It's what I enjoy, and it makes a good living for me. But I always thought that it would come naturally to me to be a family man. I want kids. I'd be good to them, and they'd have all the things I didn't have when I was growing up, like loving parents and security." He shrugged. "I suppose it's an old-fashioned ideal in this modern world, but it's still what I want most." He stared off into space, his chin lifted, the air cooling his face. He sighed and turned and looked down at her. "Well, I've enjoyed having you and the boys around, despite our bad beginning," he said and actually smiled. "And if you come back next summer, you can bring your brood over again and I'll show them what ranching is all about."

He was pleasant and friendly and all at once she felt a door closing. He was going to be her friend, her good neighbor in the summer, and not one thing more. She knew without a word being spoken that there would be no trip to the opera, no weekend visits to Houston. She knew it as certainly as if he'd spoken aloud.

"I'll remember," she replied in a subdued tone. "Thank you."

He shrugged. "What are friends for?" he mused. "Well, I'd better be going. Keep an eye on Kells for me when you get home, will you? He's a fine young man. I'd hate for him to backslide."

"I'll make sure he doesn't," she promised.

He nodded. "So long, then."

"So long."

She watched him climb into the cab of the truck, crank it and drive off with a careless wave. It was more than a door closing. It was the end of something that would have been sweet and fulfilling, and she'd smashed it with a few cold words.

She folded her arms around her chest and wondered why she'd felt compelled to say things that she didn't really even believe. She was afraid, she decided. Afraid to take a chance so risky, to get married and end up as her poor father and mother had. She wasn't the sort to be unfaithful and she didn't think

Luke was, either, but she'd seen a bad marriage first-hand and she was frightened.

Her job was safe, comfortable, secure. She knew where it would take her, she knew the path well. Marriage was a trek through a maze, with false turns and sudden stops and danger all around. She barely knew Luke. What if the man she saw on the surface wasn't the real man at all?

She turned around and went back inside. It was useless to speculate. She felt empty and alone, but she knew it was for the best. She was too uncertain to take that final step with Luke. He deserved someone who knew what they wanted.

CHAPTER FIVE

BELINDA STUCK TO her guns about being independent, but if she expected Luke to try to change her mind, she was disappointed. He came by frequently to talk to the boys, and he was making inroads into teaching Kells cowboying. He brought the youth over to see Belinda, and he was as open and friendly as he had been at the beginning. But he wasn't approachable.

"I guess you're packing already," he remarked a few days before her vacation ended as he stood leaning back against one of the support posts on the cabin's front porch. "Eager to get going?"

"Not terribly," she said carefully. "It's been educational and a lot of fun. But I've got work to catch up. Vacations can't last forever."

"They wouldn't be much fun if they did," he remarked. His blue eyes slid over her slender body in jeans and a knit shirt. "How old are you?" he asked abruptly.

She blinked, surprised. "I'm twenty-seven," she said.

His eyes narrowed. "The older you get, the harder it's going to be to give up your independence. You'll draw into a shell and never come back out."

She glared at him. "It's my shell."

"Pity to waste your youth on a job, no matter how important it is," he commented. "Plenty of women juggle marriage and a career and even children. It isn't impossible, especially with a partner who's willing to compromise."

"I don't want to compromise," she said stubbornly. Her green eyes flashed. "I told you, I'm happy as I am."

"Got a cat?"

She frowned. "What do I need with a cat?"

"For companionship," he emphasized. "You can't go on living completely alone. You'll get lonesome."

"I hate cats!"

"Liar."

She sighed angrily. "Okay, I don't hate cats, but I haven't got time to take care of a pet."

"You could get one of those Japanese electronic things that you have to feed and clean up after," he suggested.

"I don't want an electronic pet."

"I've got one on my computer," he drawled playfully. "It barks and growls and romps across the screen. Some of them even evolve."

"Wonderful. Just what I need. A dog to guard my computer."

"They're cute."

She hated the way her eyes kept going to his long legs and slim hips and broad chest. He was sexy and she was going overboard about him. She couldn't backslide now, when she was so close to getting away from him in time!

"Next thing you know, they'll have a life-size electronic pet that you have to feed and water and clean up after. What's wrong with the real thing?"

"Beats me, darlin'," he murmured softly, and chuckled when she flushed at the endearment. "You're the one who doesn't want to get married."

"Why should I need an electronic pet just because I don't want to get married?"

He smiled slowly. "You'd have something to lavish affection on. Something to keep you company. Something to cuddle."

"I'd like to see you cuddle an electronic blob!"

He shifted suddenly away from the post and stopped just a few inches away from her, his hands on his slim hips as he searched her flushed face. "I'd like to cuddle you, Belinda," he said softly. "We could sit on the sofa and watch TV together in the evenings when we were through with work. We could lie in my hammock on lazy summer evenings and kiss each other to a cricket and hound dog serenade. We could share coffee and cake at two in the morning when we couldn't get to sleep. Can you do that with a virtual pet or a legal pad?"

She hated what her heart was doing inside her chest. Her wide, worried eyes met his. "I'm scared!" she burst out.

"I know you are, and I know why." He touched her cheek with his fingertips, tracing a pattern on its flushed softness. "I'm uneasy, too. It's a big step from friendship to intimacy. But we've got a lot in common, and I don't mean just cattle." His fingers fell to her soft mouth. "Don't throw it away on a job."

She drew back as if his fingers scalded her. Her eyes were wide, her face drawn with misgivings and confusion. "I don't want to... belong...to anyone," she bit off. "If I stay by myself, depend on myself, I won't ever get hurt."

"Maybe not," he agreed. "But you'll never know what it is to really share love, either. You've got a big heart. You've given your time, your hard work, your heart to these boys in your camp. Why is it so hard to do the same thing with a man?"

She grimaced. "Love doesn't last," she groaned.

"It does," he disagreed. "If you can compromise, it does. Nothing comes with a money-back guarantee in this life, but people with kind hearts and things in common don't usually end up in divorce court. Try looking around you at elderly couples, people who've been together for fifty years or more. I believe love can last, if you give it a chance."

She sighed wearily. "I don't believe it," she said. "I'm sorry. For me, that's a fairy tale. There aren't any happy endings."

"You cynic," he chided. "Take a chance. Dare everything. Risk it all."

"I'm not a gambler," she replied. "I'm a conventional, conservative woman with no real sense of adventure. I don't take chances, ever."

He shook his head sadly. "Well, it's a waste," he

told her. "You've got so much to give, Belinda. But you're wrapped up in your own fears."

"I'm not afraid of anything!" she flashed.

"Except love."

She started to argue, but she couldn't find the right words.

He tapped her nose with his forefinger and smiled. "You may be a quitter. I'm not. Just keep running, darlin'. When you've worn yourself out, I'll still be here."

"Why?" she asked, almost in anguish.

His face sobered, and his eyes began to glitter in his lean face. "You're worth fighting for, didn't you know? And I'm a stubborn man when I want something that badly."

"It's just physical attraction!" she muttered.

"Nope."

"I'm something different, something out of the ordinary."

"You're that," he agreed. He tilted her chin and dropped a brief, hard kiss on her soft mouth. "Okay, no hard sell. But don't make the mistake of thinking I'll go away. I'm like a rubber ball. I keep bouncing back."

"I won't change my mind," she said through her teeth.

He only laughed, got back into his truck and drove off.

"I won't!" she yelled after him.

It wasn't until she realized the boys were all staring at her that she turned around and went back into the cabin.

THE NEXT COUPLE of days passed all too quickly, not only for Belinda but for Kells. He was almost in tears when he climbed into the van for the long drive back to Houston. The boys from the bunkhouse had come out en masse to shake hands and wish him well.

"See you back here next summer, young feller," one of the older men said jauntily. "Mind you keep well shy of trouble, too!"

"Yes, sir, I sure will," Kells promised with a sad smile. "Sure am gonna miss you guys."

"We'll miss you, too, son," another wrangler agreed. "Study hard, now. Cowboying is more complicated than it used to be. You need a good education even to keep tally books!"

"I'll remember," Kells promised.

Luke was standing beside the driver's side, where Belinda was trying to be cheerful and failing miserably. She looked up into eyes that were as blue as a robin's egg and felt her heart contract painfully. He was friendly and cheerful, but suddenly remote, as if he felt nothing passionate for her at all.

His attitude confused and even wounded her, but she tried to behave nonchalantly. She held out her hand. "Thanks for all the help," she said with a forced smile. "I'd never have gotten through this without you."

He glanced at the boys and smiled and waved to them as they climbed aboard. "You had a good group. Like I said, if you come again next summer…"

"I…don't think I will," she said, having made that painful decision the night before. She didn't want to see Luke again, ever. "I'm going to put the land on the market. If you're quick, you can get it before Mr. Parks does."

He was staring at her. "I thought you'd decided that the camp was a good idea."

She shook her head. "Too many unexpected pitfalls," she replied. "If you hadn't been around, Kells would have gone to jail. I had no idea what I was getting into, although it turned out better than I expected." She stared at his top shirt button instead of his face. "I've decided to leave the special camps to people who know what they're doing. I came close to causing a disaster, with the best intentions in the world."

"Funny. I thought you did a grand job," he said.

She smiled halfheartedly. "We'll have to wait and see about that."

He pursed his lips. "I guess you're glad to be leaving," he said carelessly.

She hesitated. She almost said that she felt empty and alone, more so than ever before in her life, and that she wasn't glad at all. But the moment passed. "Yes," she said with a faint smile. "I'll be glad to get back to work." She held out her hand. "Thanks again."

He took her hand and curled his fingers into hers, watching her breath catch at the contact. She felt something for him, something powerful, he knew she did. But she was frightened and ready to bolt. He could tell by the coolness of her fingers, the uncertain flicker of her eyelids as she tried and failed to meet his eyes.

"There are no great rewards without great risks," he said under his breath.

She lifted her eyes and had them trapped by soft blue ones. "My parents…"

"You're not your parents," he replied simply. "And I'm not mine. Life is a risk. Everything's a risk. If you never take a chance, if you always try to play it safe, what's life worth? You get nothing except monotony."

"I don't like taking chances," she said curtly.

"You could learn to like it," he mused. "But you'll have to find that out the hard way, I expect."

"It's my choice," she said doggedly. "You can't tell me how to live my life."

"I can't, hmm?"

"That's right, you can't," she said firmly. "I'm leaving now. I'm going back to my own life, to my job."

"And that's all you need to be happy, right?"

"Right!" She straightened. "I'm glad you finally understand that."

He smiled in a strange, calculating way. "I understand more than you think. Well, since you're determined to leave, here's something to take with you back to Houston and your perfect job."

He moved forward and swept her up against him, bent her back over his arm in the best Hollywood tradition, and with a wicked laugh, kissed the breath and the fight right out of her. She felt as if she was melting right down the front of him, her lips hungry and aching as he kissed them, her body throbbing at the long, hard contact with his strength. By the time he was through with her, she was clinging and moaning helplessly. He had to lift her arms away and steady her before she could stand alone.

Several hectic seconds later, she wobbled to the van and climbed in, fumbling the key into the ignition to the amused catcalls of her passengers.

"I bet he watches them old movies on TV," Kells said gleefully.

"Could you be quiet?" Belinda asked. "We've got to get on the road. Goodbye, Mr. Craig!" she said gruffly.

He swept off his hat and bowed mockingly. "Au revoir, Miss Jessup!" he called after her.

She stomped too hard on the accelerator and almost flooded the engine. As the van jerked its way out of the yard toward the gates, Luke was laughing wickedly. He was a keen fisherman, and this was the championship tournament of his life. He was going to land that feisty little fish. It would take patience and fortitude, but he'd never been lacking in those qualities.

He put his hat back on and went toward the barn, whistling all the way.

THE FIRST TWO weeks Belinda was back at work in Houston, she felt a new emptiness in her life. She hadn't considered how lonely it was going to be without the boys. Over the weeks, she'd gotten used to them. Now, she felt as if she'd left her family behind. And she missed Luke ridiculously.

She was just leaving the courthouse after a particularly rough morning when she almost ran into Kells at the bottom of the steps.

He grinned. "I got something to show you," he said, producing a handful of papers.

She took them, looked at them, and gasped. "Why, Kells, this is extraordinary!"

It was, too. He had straight A's on English, math and science papers.

He was still grinning. "They think I'm going crazy at home, cause all I do is study. I just ignore them when they start drinking. I stay in my room and crack those books. It's not so hard, after all, Miss Jessup. You just got to get motivated."

"That's exactly right. Oh, I'm so proud of you!" she exclaimed.

He looked sheepish. "Thanks. Reckon you might tell Mr. Craig?"

She closed up. "I haven't heard from him."

"You could write him, though, couldn't you?" he persisted.

She had to agree that she could, although she didn't really want to. She sighed. "I suppose I could, considering what a happy surprise those grades are going to be for him. I'll do it."

"Thanks, Miss Jessup. And not only for that, but for believing in me," he added solemnly. "Nobody else ever thought I was worth their time."

"You're worth my time," she said with a smile. "Mr. Craig believes in you, too."

"That's what keeps me going," he told her. "That job next summer. I'm going to work so hard, Miss

Jessup. I'm going to learn all I can before I go back. I'll make Mr. Craig proud of me."

"Indeed you will," she said.

"Gotta go. I'm taking a night course in Spanish," he added, surprising her. "They speak it on the ranch, you know, and there's a couple of Mexican hands. See you, Miss Jessup!"

She waved and then caught her breath at his ambition. To think that only a few short months ago, he might have ended up in juvenile hall for good, and then in jail. How many children like Kells never made it because they had no one to encourage and believe in them? She felt good inside. If she only pulled one child out of the hopelessness of poverty, her job was worthwhile. Why couldn't that hard-nosed cowboy in Jacobsville understand that, she thought furiously.

Then she remembered that he'd asked how she'd feel about working in Jacobsville, and what she'd told him. She'd said that she couldn't do such a job anywhere except Houston, and that was baloney. Of course she could. But she was frightened. She didn't want to fall in love and get married. She wanted to depend on one person, herself. She couldn't imagine risking her heart.

She went on down the street to her car, feeling despondent and miserable. If only she'd never met Luke Craig!

IT WASN'T EASY to ignore Kells's request about that letter to Luke. In the end, Belinda was all but forced by her conscience to send him a note. It was friendly, not too intimate, and factual. It took her twenty tries before she had the right words. She mailed it and waited.

But the reply didn't come in the way she expected. After a particularly long session in court with a client, she dragged herself up the steps to her apartment and found a familiar face leaning against the wall near her door. He was wearing a navy suit with a tie, and he looked more sophisticated than any rancher she'd ever known.

"Luke!" she exclaimed.

He chuckled and scooped her up in his arms, kissing her hungrily right there in the hall. Her raincoat, her valise, her pocketbook were scattered like grains of corn while she kissed him back. It was only then that she realized how much she'd missed him.

"No need to ask if you missed me," he murmured before he kissed her again. "How about supper?"

"I'm famished," she said breathlessly. "But I don't have anything to cook…."

"There's a nice restaurant down the street. I've made reservations," he said. "Put your gear inside and freshen up."

She was reluctant to take her arms from around his neck, and she laughed at her own feelings. "It's good to see you," she said, trying to act normally as she paused to scoop her stuff from the floor.

"It's good to see you, too," he replied with a smile. "You look worn."

"It's been a long week." She searched his eyes before she put her key in the lock and opened the door. "It's been a long several weeks," she added honestly.

"I know."

She put her things in a chair and turned to him. He looked tired, too. He was devastating to a heart that had gone hungry for the sight of him. For several seconds, she just stood there and looked at him.

He did the same. In her beige dress and high heels, with her dark blond hair in soft waves down to her collar, she looked lovely.

"If you want supper at all," he said huskily, "you've got ten seconds to stop looking at me like that before I do something about it."

She wanted him to. She really did. But there were things to settle first, so she dropped her gaze with a shy smile. "Okay," she said. "I'll freshen up."

While she fixed her makeup and added a touch of perfume, he stared down at the computer on her desk. A piece of new software was lying near it, with a scruffy-looking dog on the cover of the box. He grinned.

"Bought a dog, I see," he drawled as she came back into the living room.

She saw where he was looking and laughed self-consciously. "It sounded cute. And it is."

"Told you so. Ready to go?"

She nodded, grabbing her purse.

He stopped her just at the door before he opened it. "Does that lipstick come off easily?" he asked in a deep, lazy tone.

She was barely breathing. "It isn't supposed to."

"Let's see."

He drew her to him, stared into her eyes until

she felt her whole body vibrate with delicious sensations, and only then bent to take her mouth completely under his.

Absence had certainly made the heart grow fonder, she thought while she could. The purse dropped to the floor for the second time that afternoon, and her arms stretched up to hold him while the warm, hard kiss went on and on.

She was standing on her tiptoes when he stopped. His blue eyes, more vivid than she remembered them, stared straight into her green ones with all the evasions and teasing gone.

He was so somber that the expression on his face made her nervous.

"Tell me the job means more to you than I do," he said roughly. "And I'll leave right now before this goes any further."

Her eyelids flinched at the very thought. She drew in an unsteady breath. "It's been weeks," she managed to say in a tight tone.

"Hell, it's been years," he muttered, and his mouth came down on hers again. But this time it was rough, hard, insistent. This time it burrowed into hers with passion and purpose, and she was shaking when he lifted his head.

She held on for dear life. "If you go, I'm going with you," she said involuntarily, her face flushed, her eyes sparkling with feeling.

"That's what I came all this way to hear," he said in a harsh undertone. "It took you long enough!"

She burrowed against him and his arms came

around to enfold her. "I'm still afraid, Luke," she whispered.

"Everyone's afraid. Not only of falling in love, but of getting married, having children. These are big steps, important steps. People who aren't afraid to take them are the ones who end up divorced and miserable. You have to be sure, but even then, it's a risk."

"I'm willing to take it, if you are," she said after a minute.

His arms contracted again as he bent over her head and rocked her against him. "I've been willing to take it since the first time I saw you," he breathed. "I've spent my life waiting for a woman I could live with. And you didn't even like me!"

She laughed with delight. "Only at first," she protested.

"Ha!" he murmured. "You fought me every step of the way." He lifted his head to look down at her. "Jacobsville can always use a good public defender," he said firmly. "There are kids in trouble everywhere."

She smiled ruefully. "I was hedging," she confessed. "I couldn't bear the thought of being near you all the time if...well, if I was the only one who felt this way."

"Which way?" he asked in a soft, sensuous tone.

She stared at his tie. It was blue and had a paisley pattern—very nice. His thumbs jabbed her gently in the ribs.

"Which way?" he persisted.

She leaned her forehead against him. "I love you." There was a long, ominous silence. She lifted her head apprehensively and saw his eyes. They were such a vivid blue that they almost glowed. She got barely a glimpse of them before they closed as he lifted her against him and kissed her again. Under his breath, she heard him repeat the words back to her. And then, she stopped trying to hear anything except the beat of her own heart.

LONG, TEMPESTUOUS MINUTES LATER, he looked down at her, where she lay in the crook of his arm on the sofa, her body soft and fluid against his, her dress unfastened, her hair disheveled. His shirt was open, too, the tie long gone, and her fingers played lazily through the wedge of blond hair on his chest.

"We were going out to eat," she reminded him.

"To hell with food. I'm not hungry."

"Well, I am," she said, laughing. "Especially now."

He traced a slow pattern on the lace of her bra. "Spoilsport," he murmured. "Just when I'm getting to know all about you."

She laughed again, moving his hand aside so that she could button up her dress again. "You stop that," she teased.

"Stop? I haven't even gotten started!" he protested.

"There's plenty of time for all that," she reminded him. She searched his blue eyes. "I want a white wedding. Do you mind?"

"I want a white wedding, too," he agreed, smiling at her. "We'll have the works, a best man, a best woman, a flower girl—my niece, of course," he added with a chuckle.

"I'll have my sister-in-law for matron of honor. Best woman," she scoffed, and broke up laughing at the thought of pretty Marianne in a suit and bow tie.

"It will be an occasion," he said. "And then we'll raise cattle and look after kids and grow old together."

She snuggled close to him, so happy that she could barely contain it all. "I love the way that sounds."

"So do I. But we'll grow old slowly, if you don't mind. I've got a lot of ginger left in me, yet."

"I noticed," she said demurely.

He loomed over her with intent. "Did you, now?" he murmured, his eyes drawing over her sensually.

"I love you," she whispered.

He smiled slowly. "I love you, too."

It was the last thing they said for a long time.

THE WEDDING WAS truly a Jacobsville occasion. Everybody came, even glowering Cy Parks, who wore a suit and brought a wedding present. Ward Jessup and a very pregnant Marianne were present, along with Marianne's Aunt Lillian. Elysia Craig Walker and her husband, Tom, welcomed Belinda into the family, and their daughter Crissy acted as flower girl. Belinda was exquisite in a white lace gown with a train and a delicate lace veil. She carried a bouquet of white rosebuds and she wept when her devastatingly handsome new husband lifted the veil and saw her for the first time as his wife.

Outside the church, the Craig ranch's cowboys made a double line and threw confetti as the happy couple erupted from the front entrance. One of the cowboys had just graduated from high school and was the newest employee on the place. He wore a ten-gallon hat, a red bandanna, boots, jeans, a chambray shirt and a huge toothy smile—and his name was Edward Kells.

The happy couple waved at him as they rushed past to the limousine that would take them to the ranch to change clothes before they went on to the reception Matt Caldwell was hosting for them at his elegant mansion on the outskirts of Jacobsville.

They piled into the car and the driver pulled away from the curb.

Luke looked at Belinda with his whole heart in his eyes. "The best day of my life," he murmured, "Mrs. Craig."

"And the best day of mine, Mr. Craig," she echoed.

The words exemplified their vow of love. He drew her close and kissed her. Behind them, the crowd drew in on itself to rehash the details of the elegant society wedding. But inside the limousine, two pairs of sparkling eyes were already looking ahead to a bright and beautiful future.

* * * * *

GUY

CHAPTER ONE

IT WAS A cool autumn day, and the feedlot was full. A good many of these steers were already under contract to restaurants and fast-food establishments, but in these last weeks before they were shipped north, the cowboys who worked for the Ballenger Brothers in Jacobsville, Texas, were pushed to the limit. Guy Fenton hated his job when things were this hectic. He almost hated it enough to go back to flying; but not quite.

He pushed his hat back from his sweaty dark hair and cursed the cattle, the feedlot, people who ate beef and people who bought it in eloquent succession. He wasn't a handsome man, but he still had a way with women. He was lean and lanky, thirty years old, with gray eyes and a tragic past that an occasional date numbed just a little. Lately, though, women had been right off his list of pastimes. There had been too much work here at the feedlot, and he was responsible for mixing the various grains and nutrients to put just enough, but not too much, weight on these beef cattle. He enjoyed the job from time to time, but just lately everything was rubbing him the wrong way. A chance meeting with an old acquaintance several months ago from the days of his engagement had brought back all the bad memories and set him on a weekend binge. That was followed by another, when the man settled nearby and came to visit him occasionally, not realizing the damage he was doing to Guy's peace of mind.

"For two bits," he said out loud, "I'd chuck it all and become a beachcomber!"

"Keep your mind on that conveyor belt and thank God you don't have to climb down in there to inoculate those horned devils," came a drawling voice from behind him.

He glanced over his shoulder at Justin Ballenger and grinned. "You don't mean things could get worse around here?"

Justin stuck his hands into his pockets and chuckled. "It seems that way, from time to time, when we get this much extra business. Come over here. I want to talk to you."

The big boss rarely came out to talk to the hands, so it was an occasion for curiosity. Guy finished the settings on the conveyer belt that delivered feed to the dozens of stalls before he jumped down lithely to stand before one of the two owners of the feedlot.

"What can I do for you, boss?" he asked pleasantly.

"You can stop getting drunk every weekend and treeing Thompson's place," he replied solemnly, his dark eyes glittering.

Guy's high cheekbones went a little ruddy. He averted his gaze to the milling, mooing cattle. "I didn't realize the gossip got this far."

"You can't trim your toenails in Jacobsville without somebody knowing about it," Justin returned. "You've been going downhill for a while, but just lately you're on a bad path, son," he added, his deep voice quiet and concerned. "I hate to see you go down it any farther."

Guy didn't look at the older man. His jaw tautened. "It's my road. I have to walk it."

"No, you don't," Justin said curtly. "It's been three years since you signed on here. I never asked any questions about your past, and I'm not doing it now. But I hate to see a good man go right down the drain. You have to let go of the past."

Guy's eyes met the other man's almost on a level. Both were tall, but Justin was older and pretty tough, too. He wasn't a man Guy would ever like to have to fight. "I can't let go," he replied shortly. "You don't understand."

"No, I don't, not in the way you mean," Justin conceded, his dark eyes narrowing. "But all this carousing and grieving isn't going to change whatever happened to you."

Guy drew in a short breath and stared at the flat horizon. He didn't speak, because if he let the anger out, Justin would fire him. He might hate his job, but he couldn't afford to lose it, either. "Rob Hartford settled up in Victoria and he comes down to see me. He does it too often," he said finally. "He was there—when it happened. He doesn't know it, but he brought all the memories back."

"Tell him. People can't read minds."

He sighed. His gray eyes met Justin's dark ones. "He'd take it hard."

"He'll take it harder if you end up in jail. The one good thing about it is that you've got sense enough not to drive when you're in that condition."

"The only good thing," Guy said wearily. "Okay, boss, I'll do what I can."

Justin followed his gaze. "Winter's coming fast," he murmured. "We'll just get this batch of steers out before we have to buy more feed. It'll be close, at that."

"Only crazy people get into feeding out cattle," Guy pointed out, lightening the atmosphere.

Justin smiled faintly. "So they say."

He shrugged. "I'll try to stay away from Thompson's."

"It doesn't make a hell of a lot of sense to drink up your salary every weekend," the older man said flatly. "Regardless of the reason. But that isn't what I came out here to talk to you about."

Guy frowned. "Then why did you?"

"We've got a beef industry publicist coming tomorrow from Denver. She wants to visit a few area ranches, as well as our feedlot here, to get some idea of what sort of methods we're using."

"Why?" Guy asked curtly.

"The local cattlemen's association—of which Evan Tremayne was just elected president—wants to help punch up the image of the industry locally. The industry as a whole has had some bad press lately over bacterial contamination. There's been even more bad press about some renegade cattlemen and their practices. We don't follow their lead around here, and we're anxious to get the fact across to the beef-eating public. Evan also has an idea about customizing lean beef for a specialized market of buyers."

"I thought Evan was too busy with his wife to worry about business," Guy murmured dryly.

"Oh, Anna's doing his paperwork for him," he mused. "They're inseparable, business or not. Anyway, this publicist is expected in the morning. The Tremaynes are out of town, Ted Regan and his wife are at a convention in Utah and Calhoun is going to be tied up with a buyer tomorrow. You're the only cowboy we've got who knows as much about the industry as we do, especially where feedlots are concerned. We've elected you to be her guide."

"Me?" Guy cursed under his breath and glared at the older man. "What about the Hart boys? There are four of them over at the Hart ranch."

"Two," Justin corrected. "Cag's off on his honeymoon, and Corrigan went with his wife, Dorie, to visit Simon and Tira in San Antonio. They've just had their first child." He chuckled. "Anyway, I wouldn't wish the two bachelor Hart boys on her. We don't know if she can make biscuits, but Leo and Rey may be too desperate to care."

Guy only nodded. The Hart boys were a local legend because of their biscuit mania. Pity none of them could cook.

"So you're elected."

"I know more about rodeo than I know about ranching," Guy pointed out.

"Yes, I know." He searched the younger man's closed face. "I heard someone say you used to fly yourself to the competitions."

Guy's eyes glittered and he straightened. "I don't talk about flying. Ever."

"Yes, I heard that, too," Justin said. He threw up his hands. "All right, clam up and fester. I just wanted you to know that you'll be away from here tomorrow, so delegate whatever chores you need to before the morning."

"Okay." Guy sighed. "I guess you couldn't do it?"

Justin glanced over his shoulder. "Sorry. Shelby and I have to go to the elementary school in the morning. Our oldest son's in a Thanksgiving play." He grinned. "He's an ear of corn."

Guy didn't say a word. But his eyes danced and his lower lip did a tango.

"Good thing you kept your mouth shut, Fenton," he added with a wicked grin. "I hear they're shy a turkey. It would be a pity to volunteer you for *that* instead of the ranch tour."

He walked off and Guy gave in to the chuckle he'd choked back. Sometimes he didn't mind this job at all.

He went back to the bunkhouse after work, noting that it was empty except for one young college student from Billings, who was sprawled on a bunk reading Shakespeare through small rimmed glasses. He looked up when Guy entered the building.

"Cook's off sick, so they're shuttling supper out

from the main house," the college student, Richard, remarked. "Just you and me tonight. The other bachelors went off to some sort of party in town."

"Lucky stiffs," Guy murmured. He took off his hat and sprawled on his own bunk with a weary sigh. "I hate cattle."

Richard, who liked to be called "Slim" by the other cowhands, chuckled. He was much more relaxed when he and Guy were the only two men sharing the bunkhouse. Some of the older hands, many uneducated, gave him a hard time in the evenings about his continuing studies.

"They may smell lousy, but they sure do pay my tuition," Slim remarked.

"How many years do you have to go?" Guy asked curiously.

The younger man shrugged. "Two, the normal way. But I have to work a semester and go to school a semester, because it's the only way I can afford tuition. I guess it'll take me four more years to graduate."

"Can't you get a scholarship?"

Slim shook his head. "My grades aren't quite good enough for the big ones, and my folks make too much money for me to qualify for financial aid."

Guy's eyes narrowed. "There should be a way. Have you talked to the finance office at your school?"

"I thought about it, but one of the other kids said I might as well save my time."

"What's your field?"

Slim grinned. "Medicine," he said. "So I've got a long road ahead of me, even after I get my B.S."

Guy didn't smile. "I've got a couple of ideas. Let me think them over."

"You've got problems of your own, Mr. Fenton," Slim told him. "No need to worry about me, as well."

"What makes you think I've got problems?"

Slim closed the literature book he was holding. "You get drunk like clockwork every weekend. Nobody drinks that much for recreation, especially not a guy who's as serious the rest of the week as you are. You never shirk duties or delegate chores, and you're always stone sober on the job." He smiled sheepishly. "I guess it was something pretty bad."

Guy's pale gray eyes had a faraway, haunted look. "Yes. Pretty bad." He rolled over onto his back and pulled his hat over his eyes. "I wish you outranked me, Slim."

"Why?"

"Then you'd get stuck with the publicist tomorrow, instead of me."

"I heard Mr. Ballenger talking about her. He says she's pretty."

"He didn't tell me that."

"Maybe he was saving it for a surprise."

Guy laughed hollowly. "Some surprise. She'll probably faint when she gets a good whiff of the feedlot."

"Well, you never know." Pages in the book rustled as he turned them. "Man, I hate Shakespeare."

"Peasant," Guy murmured.

"You'd hate him, too, if you had to do a course in Elizabethan literature."

"I did two, thanks. Made straight A's."

Slim didn't speak for a little while. "You went to college?"

"Yup."

"Get your degree?"

"Yup."

"Well, what in?"

"In what," Guy corrected.

"Okay, in what?"

"You might say, in physics," he said, without mentioning that his degree was in aeronautics, his minor in chemistry.

Slim whistled. "And you're working on a cattle ranch?"

"Seemed like a good idea at the time. And it's sure physic-al," he added with a deliberate play on words.

Laughter came from across the room. "You're pulling my leg about that physics degree, aren't you?"

Guy smiled from under his hat. "Probably. Get back to work, boy. I need some rest."

"Yes, sir."

GUY LAY AWAKE long into the night, thinking about college. He'd been a lot like Slim, young and enthusiastic and full of dreams. Aviation had been the love of his life until Anita came along. Even then, she was part of the dream, because she loved airplanes, too. She encouraged him, raved over his designs, soothed him when plans didn't work out, prodded him to try again. Even when things were darkest, she wouldn't let him give up on the dream. And when it was in his grasp, she never complained about the long hours he was away from her. She was always there, waiting, like a dark-haired angel.

He'd given her the ring just before they went up together, that last time. He was always so careful, so thorough, about the plane. But that once, he was exhausted from a late-night party the night before, and his mind had been on Anita instead of the engine. The tiny malfunction, caught in time, might have been rectified. But it wasn't. The plane went down into the trees and hung, precariously, in the limbs. They could have climbed down, only bruised, but Anita had fallen heavily against the passenger door and, weakened by the crash, it had come open. He saw her in his nightmares, falling, falling, forty feet straight down to the forest floor, with nothing to break the fall except hard ground, her eyes wide with horror as she cried his name…

He sat straight up on the bunk, sweating, barely able to get his breath as the nightmare brought him awake. Slim was sleeping peacefully. He wished he could. He put his head in his hands and moaned softly. Three years was long enough to grieve, Justin said. But Justin didn't know. Nobody knew, except Guy.

HE WAS HALF-ASLEEP the next morning when he went down to the feedlot in clean blue jeans and a blue-and-white checked flannel shirt under his sheepskin jacket. He wore his oldest Stetson, a beige wreck of a hat, wide-brimmed and stained from years of work. His boots didn't look much better. He was almost thirty-one years old and he felt sixty. He wondered if it showed.

Voices came from Justin's office when he walked into the waiting room at the feedlot. Fay, J. D. Langley's pretty little wife, smiled at him and motioned him in. She was technically Calhoun Ballenger's secretary, but today she was covering both jobs in the absence of the other secretary.

Guy smiled back, tipped his hat and walked on in. Justin stood up. So did the pretty little brunette with him. She had the largest, most vulnerable brown eyes he'd ever seen in a human being. They seemed to see right through to his heart.

"This is Candace Marshall, Guy," Justin said. "She's a freelance publicist who works primarily for the cattle industry. Candy, this is Guy Fenton. He manages the feedlot for us."

Guy tipped his hat at her, but he didn't remove it. He didn't smile, either. Those eyes hurt him. Anita had brown eyes like that, soft and warm and loving. He could see them in his nightmares as she cried out for him to help her....

"I'm pleased to meet you, Mr. Fenton," Candy said solemnly and held out a hand toward him.

He shook it limply and without enthusiasm, immediately imprisoning both his hands in the pockets of his jeans.

"Guy is going to show you the ranches in the area, before he familiarizes you with the feedlot itself," Justin continued. He produced two typed sheets and handed one to Guy and one to Candy. "I had Fay type these for you. There's a map on the back, in case you don't recognize where the ranches are located. The local ranches contract with us to custom-feed their yearling bulls and replacement heifers," he explained to Candy. "We do some out-of-state business, too, with consortiums like Mesa Blanco, which Fay's husband, J. D. Langley, operates. Any details you need about daily routine and operation and costs, Guy can give you. He's been with us for three years now, and he's very good at his job. He's in charge of the feeding schedules, which are scientific in the extreme."

Candy studied Guy with new interest. "Scientific?"

"He minored in chemistry," Justin added. "Just what we need here to work out feed concentrates and nutritive combinations, all to do with weight-gain ratios, the bottom line of which is profit."

She smiled softly at Justin, pushing back a long strand of dark hair that had escaped from the French twist at her nape. "My dad was a cattleman, so I know a bit about the business. My mom runs one of the biggest ranches in Montana, in fact."

"Does she, really?" Justin asked, impressed.

"She and J. D. Langley and the Tremayne boys gang up on the others at cattlemen's conventions," she continued. "They're radicals."

"Don't tell me," Justin groaned. "No additives, no hormones, no antibiotics, no pesticides, no herbicides, no cattle prods—"

"You *do* know J.D.!" Candy chuckled.

Guy was trying not to notice her resemblance to Anita. She was very pretty when she smiled.

"Everybody around here knows J.D.," Justin said with an exaggerated sigh. He glanced at the Rolex watch on his left wrist. "Well, I've got a play to catch, so I'll let you two get down to business."

Candy was glancing hurriedly at the list. She grimaced. "Mr. Ballenger, we can't possibly see all these ranches in one day!"

"I know. We figure it will take a week or so. We've booked you into our best motel. The cattlemen's association will pick up the tab, including meals, so don't skimp on food." He frowned, noting her extreme thinness and pallor. "Are you all right?"

She straightened and smiled with something like deliberation. "I'm just getting over a bad case of flu," she said slowly. "It's hard to pick up again."

"So it is. Early for the flu."

She nodded. "Yes, it is, isn't it?"

Justin hesitated, then shrugged. "Take it easy, just the same. Guy, if you don't mind, check in with Harry every morning and give him his instructions. I know they're pretty much cut-and-dried for the next week, but do it just the same."

"Sure thing, boss," Guy said lazily. "Well, Miss Marshall, shall we go?"

"Of course." She started slowly toward her compact rental car when she noticed that Guy was going in the opposite direction.

"Mr....Fenton?" she called, having had to stop and remember his name.

He turned, his hands still deep in his pockets. "This way," he said. "We'll go in one of the ranch trucks. You'll never get that thing down Bill Gately's pasture without a broken axle."

"Oh." She stared at the car and then at the big black double-cab pickup truck with the Ballenger logo in red on the door. "I see what you mean." She went toward the truck in that same, slow gait, a little winded by the time she reached it. She stepped on the running board, displaying a slender, pretty, long leg as her skirt rode up. Catching hold of the handhold just above the door, she pulled herself up and into the seat with a gasp.

"You're out of condition," he murmured. "Bronchitis?"

She hesitated just a second too long before answering. "Yes. From the flu."

"I'll try to keep you out of feed dust on the tour," he said, closing the door tight behind her.

She had to sit and catch her breath before she could struggle into the seat belt. All the while, Guy Fenton sat holding the steering wheel in one gloved hand while he observed her pale complexion and flushed cheeks. She looked unwell.

"I got out of bed too soon," she said finally, pushing back a loose strand of dark hair. "I'm fine. Really." She forced a smile and her big brown eyes softened as she looked at him.

He almost groaned. Memories hit his heart and made his breath catch. He flicked the key in the ignition and put the truck in gear. "Hang on," he said tautly. "We've had a lot of rain and the roads are a mess."

"Muddy, huh?" she asked.

"Muddy. Some are washed out."

"Winter floods," she mused.

"El Niño," he informed her. "It's played havoc with the West Coast, the East Coast and all points in between. I don't think I've seen this much rain in Texas in my lifetime."

"Were you born here?"

"I moved here three years ago," he said tersely.

"Not a native Texan, then." She nodded.

He glanced at her. "I didn't say I wasn't born in Texas. Just that I wasn't born in Jacobsville."

"Sorry."

He looked back at the road, his jaw taut. "No need to apologize."

She was pulling hard at air, as if she couldn't get enough in her lungs. She leaned her head back against the seat and closed her eyes for a minute. Her eyebrows drew together, as if she were in pain.

He put on the brakes and slowed the truck. Her eyes opened, startled.

"You're ill," he said shortly.

"I'm not," she protested. "I told you, I'm still weak from the flu. I can handle my job, Mr. Fenton. Please don't…don't concern yourself," she added stiffly. She turned her head and stared out the window at the bleak winter landscape.

He frowned as he pulled ahead down the rough track that led to the main road. She was prickly when he referred to her health and he'd have bet she was hiding something. He wished he knew what it was.

THE FIRST RANCH on the agenda was owned by old Bill Gately, on the Victoria road. It wasn't the showplace of most ranches around Jacobsville, a fact which Guy pointed out to her when they arrived.

"Bill hasn't moved with the times," he told her, his eyes on the road ahead. "He grew up in the thirties, when ranching was still done the old-fashioned way. He doesn't like the idea of feeding cattle anything supplemental, but when we were able to prove to him the weight-gain ratios we could get, he caved in." He glanced at her with a wry smile. "Not that he's completely sold. And he's going to have trouble with you, I'm afraid."

She chuckled. "Women don't belong in the cattle industry, I gather, and how could the cattlemen's association be blind enough to let them do publicity—and why do we need publicity, anyway, when everybody loves steak?"

"Pretty good," he said. "He'll trot out all those arguments and a few more besides. He's seventy-five and he can run circles around some of our cowboys." He glanced at her. "We have it on good authority that he knew Tom Mix personally and once, briefly, had charge of grooming Tony."

"I'm impressed," she said.

"You know who Tom Mix is?"

She laughed. "Doesn't everybody? He was as much a showman as a movie star. I have several of his silent films, and even a talkie." She shrugged. "I don't care a lot for most modern films, with the exceptions of anything John Wayne starred in."

He navigated a tricky turn and changed gears as they went down what looked like a wet ravine. "See what I meant about this place?" he asked as she held on for dear life while the truck manfully righted itself at the bottom of the sheer drop.

"I sure do," she agreed, catching her breath. "What does Mr. Gately drive?"

"He doesn't," he informed her. "He goes where he has to go on horseback, and if he needs supplies, he has them brought in." He grinned. "The grocer in town has a four-wheel drive, or I guess old Bill would starve."

"I should think so!"

He shifted back into high gear. "How did your mother become a rancher?"

"My dad was one," she said simply. "When he died, she kept the place going. It was difficult at first. We had ranch hands like your Mr. Gately, who were still living in the last century. But my mother is a law unto herself, and she gathers people in without even trying. People just love her, and they'll do whatever she asks. She's not bossy or sharp, but she's stubborn when she wants her own way."

"That's surprising," he said. "Most women in positions of authority are more like overbearing generals than women."

"Have you known a lot?" she returned.

He pursed his lips and thought. "I've seen plenty in movies."

She shook her head. "Most of which are written by *men,*" she pointed out. "What you get in cinema and even in television is some man's idea of a woman authority figure. I've noticed that not many of them are true to life. Certainly they aren't like my mother. She can shoot a Winchester, round up cattle and build a fence—but you should see her in a Valentino gown and diamonds."

"I get the point."

"It's been a long road for her," she said. "I'm sorry Dad died when he did, because she's known nothing but work and business for most of her life. It's made her hard." And as cold as ice, she could have added, but didn't.

"Any brothers or sisters?"

She shook her head. "Just me." She turned her head toward him. "How about you?"

"I have a brother. He's married and lives in California. And a married sister up in Washington State."

"You've never married?"

His face became hard as stone. He shifted the gears again as they approached the rickety old ranch house. "Never. There's Bill."

CHAPTER TWO

BILL GATELY WAS white-headed and walked with a limp, but he was slim and as spry as most men half his age. He shook hands politely with Candy and lifted a bushy eyebrow but made no comment when he was told what her job was.

"Justin Ballenger said that you wouldn't mind letting us look over your place," Candy said. She smiled. "I understand that you've made some amazing progress here in the area of old forage grasses."

His blue eyes lit up as if plugged into an electrical socket. "Why, so I have, young lady," he said enthusiastically. He took her by one arm and led her around to the back of the house, explaining the difficulty of planting and cultivating such grasses. "It wouldn't be feasible on a large scale because it's too expensive, but I've had great success with it and I'm finding ways to bring down the cost with the use of mixing common grasses with cultivated ones. The calves forage on these grasses, on a rest-rotation grazing system, until they're yearlings, and then I send them over to Justin and Calhoun to have them fed out for market." He smiled sheepishly. "I've shown some pretty impressive weight gains, too. I should probably let the Ballengers do my marketing as well, but I like to do my own selling, keep my hand in. I only have about a hundred head at a time, anyway, and that's a small lot for the brothers to want to bother with."

"Where do you usually sell your stock?" she asked curiously.

"To a hamburger chain," he said and named it. It was a local chain that had started on a shoestring and was now branching out to larger cities.

Her eyebrows lifted. "I'm really impressed," she said. "Most hamburger joints were buying all their beef from South America until the news about the dwindling rain forest got out. After that, a number of chain restaurants lost customers because people were upset about South American ranchers cutting down rain forest to make way for pasture for their beef cattle."

He grinned. "That's the very argument I used on them!" he told her with a sweeping gesture. "It worked, too. They're even starting to advertise their hamburgers as the ones that don't come from the rain forest, and if they wanted to, they could advertise it as 'organically grown,' because I don't use anything artificial in their diets."

She sighed. "Oh, Mr. Gately, if only we could package and sell *you!* What a marvelous approach to cattle raising."

He blushed like a young girl. Later, he got Guy to one side and told him that he'd never met anyone as capable as Candy at publicizing the cattle industry.

Guy related the story to his companion as they

wound down the road toward Jacobsville. The Gately ranch had taken up most of the afternoon, because Candy checked Bill's research journal for his progress with several other strains of old grasses, like the old buffalo grass, which had largely been destroyed on the Western plains by farmers in the early days of settlement. It had been a productive session.

"You're very thorough," Guy commented.

She was reading her notes but she looked up at his tone. "Did you expect someone slipshod to do such important work?" she asked.

He held up a lean, strong hand. "I wasn't throwing out a challenge," he told her. "I only meant that you seem pretty good at what you do."

She leaned back against the seat with a little sigh. "I take pride in my work," she confessed. "And it hasn't been an easy job from the beginning. There are plenty of cattlemen like Mr. Gately, only less easily convinced, who enjoy making me as uncomfortable as possible."

"How?"

"Oh, they make sure I'm escorted past the breeding pastures when the bulls are at work," she mused, tongue-in-cheek, "and into the barn when the cows are being artificially inseminated. I once had a rancher discuss his cattle weight-gain ratios in front of a stable where a mare was being bred. He had to shout to make himself heard."

He whistled. "I'm surprised. I thought most men in this business had a little respect for the opposite sex."

"They do, as long as she's in a kitchen making biscuits."

"Don't say biscuits around the Hart boys, whatever you do!" he exclaimed. "Rey and Leo are still single, and I could tell you some incredible tales about the lengths they've gone to for a biscuit feast since Corrigan and Simon and Cag got married and moved out of the main house!"

She chuckled. "I've heard those all the way back at our main office in Denver," she confided. "At any cattle convention, somebody's got a story to tell about the Hart boys. They get more outrageous by the day."

"And more exaggerated."

"You mean it wasn't really true that Leo carried a cook bodily out of the Jacobsville café one morning and wouldn't let her go until she made them a pan of biscuits?"

"Well, that one was…"

"And that Rey didn't hire one of the cooks in Houston to make him four whole trays of uncooked biscuits, which he hired a refrigerated truck to take down to the ranch for them?"

"Well, yes, he did…"

"And that when Mrs. Barkley retired from the Jones House restaurant in Victoria, Rey and Leo sent her red roses and truckloads of expensive chocolates for two weeks until she agreed to give up retirement and go work for them last month?"

"She's allergic to roses, as it happens," he murmured dryly, "and she was gaining a lot of weight on those chocolates."

"She's probably allergic to those Hart boys by now, poor soul," she said with a tiny laugh. "Honestly, I've never been around any such people!"

"You must have characters back home in Montana."

She dusted off her skirt. "Sure we do, but only like old Ben who used to hang out with Kid Curry and Butch Cassidy, and served time for being a train robber," she replied.

He grinned at her. "Beats stealing a cook."

"I don't know. I understand one of the Hart boys keeps a giant snake. His poor wife!"

"He had an albino python, but when he married Tess, he gave it to a breeder. He visits Herman occasionally, but he wouldn't ask Tess to live with it."

"That's nice."

"Cag is a lot of things. Nice isn't one of them." He thought for a minute. "Well, maybe his wife likes him."

"No wonder his best friend was a reptile."

"You're sounding a little winded," he remarked. "That wheat straw in the corral wasn't too much for you, was it? The wind was blowing pretty hard."

She stared at him blankly. "Am I supposed to notice a connection between that and my being breathless?"

He lifted a shoulder. "Why don't you use your medicine?"

She stilled. "What medicine?"

"Surely you know you're asthmatic?"

She kept right on staring at him, her eyes turbulent, although he couldn't see them. "I don't—have asthma," she said after a minute.

"No? You could have fooled me. You can't walk ten steps without resting. At your age, that's pretty unusual."

Her jaw clenched and her pretty hands had a stranglehold on her purse as she stared out the window.

"No comment?" he persisted.

"Nothing to say," she returned.

He would have pursued it, but they were already going down the main street in Jacobsville, barely a block from her hotel.

"My rental car," she began.

"I'll pick up Slim. He can drive it over here and ride back with me. Got the keys?"

She handed them to him warily. "I'm perfectly capable of driving. There's nothing wrong with me!"

"I'd do it for anyone," he said, acting puzzled. "You've had a long day. I thought you might be tired."

"Oh." She flushed a little as they reached the hotel and he pulled up in front of it. "I see. Well, thank you, then."

He parked the truck, got out and went around to help her down from the high cab. She seemed to resent that, too.

He frowned down at her. "What put that chip on your shoulder?" he asked. "You're overly sensitive about any sort of help."

"I can get out of a truck by myself," she said shortly.

He shrugged. "I do it for a great-uncle of mine,"

he informed her. "He's not old, but he has arthritis and appreciates a helping hand."

She flushed. "You make me sound terrible!"

His pleasant tone had been deceptive. The eyes that met hers were ice-cold and completely unfriendly. "You're about that unappealing, yes," he said bluntly. "I like a woman who can command respect without acting like a shrew or talking down to men. You don't like doors opened for you or concern for your health. Fine. I can assure you that I won't forget again." His jaw clenched. "My Anita was worth ten of you," he added roughly.

"Why didn't you marry her, then?"

"She died," he said, his eyes terrible to look into. He took a slow breath and turned away, weary of the whole thing. "She died," he said again, almost to himself, as he went back toward the truck.

"Mr. Fenton…" she called hesitantly, aware that she'd hit a nerve and felt vaguely ashamed of herself.

He turned and glared at her over the hood of the truck. "I'll phone the manager of the hotel in the morning and have him tell you where to meet me for the next stop on the tour. You can drive yourself from now on."

He got into the truck, slammed the door, and took off in a cloud of dust.

She stared after him with conflicting emotions. It was important to stand on her own two feet, not to be babied or pitied. She'd gone overboard here, though, and she was sorry. He was grieving for his lost love. He must have cared very much. She wondered how the mysterious Anita had died, and why Mr. Fenton looked so tormented when he spoke of her.

She went into the hotel with slow steps, feeling every step she took, hating her weakness and her inability to do anything to correct it. She reached the desk and smiled forcibly as she asked for her key.

The clerk, a personable young woman, handed it to her with an indifferent smile and turned away, pointedly disinterested in the breathless, bedraggled guest before her.

Candy laughed to herself. It was such a contrast from Guy Fenton's quiet concern. She hated having been so hateful to him, when he was only being compassionate. It was just that, over the years, she'd had so much pity and lurid curiosity, and so little love.

When she got to her room, she locked the door and fell onto the bed in a collapsed heap, without even taking her shoes off. A minute later, she was sound asleep.

THE SHOTS WOKE HER. She sat up in bed, her heart hammering at her throat. She had a hand over her chest and she was shaking. More shots, more…

She was out in the open. There were no trees. There was nothing to hide behind. She felt a blow in her chest and touched it with her hand. It came away red, wet with fresh blood. The pain came behind it, wrenching pain. She couldn't breathe….

She threw herself down onto the ground and held her hands over her head. She saw blood. She saw blood everywhere! People were screaming. Children

were screaming. A man in a clown suit went down
with a horrible piercing scream. Beside her, she saw
her father double over and fall, his eyes closed, closed,
closed forever....

Suddenly her eyes opened and she was aware that
she'd been sobbing out loud. She was lying on the
cold floor, on the carpet, doubled up like a frightened
child. She sucked in wind, trying desperately to get
enough air in her lungs to breathe. She dragged herself into a sitting position. She was wet with sweat,
shivering, terrified. All those years ago, she thought,
and the nightmares continued. She shivered once
more, convulsively, and dragged herself back onto
the bed, to lie with open eyes and a throbbing chest.

The nightmare was an old companion, one she'd
managed for a long time. There were, fortunately, not
so many maniacs running loose that her injury was
a common one. But it did appeal to a certain type
of person, who wanted her to recount that horror, to
relive it. She couldn't bear the least reference to her
breathlessness, because of bad memories about the
media, hounding her and the other survivors just after
the tragedy that had taken so many innocent lives that
bright, sunny spring day ten years ago.

She put her face in her hands and wished she could
squeeze her head hard enough to force the memory
out of it forever. Her mother had withdrawn into a
cold, self-contained shell just after her husband's fu-
neral. Forced to assume control of the family ranch or
give it up, she became a businesswoman. She hated
cattle, but she loved the money they earned for her.

Candy was an afterthought, a reminder of her terrible loss. She'd loved her husband more than anything on the face of the earth. Somehow she blamed Candy for it. The distance between mother and daughter had become a gap as wide as an ocean, and there seemed no way to bridge it. Candy's job was a lifesaver, because it got her out of Montana, away from the mother who barely tolerated her.

Mostly she liked her job as a cattle industry publicist. Unlike her mother, she did love cattle and everything connected with them. She'd have enjoyed living on the ranch, but Ida hated the very sight of her and made no attempt to conceal it. It was better for both of them that Candy never went home these days.

She pushed back her damp hair and tried to think about the next day's adventure. They were going to see a rancher named Cy Parks, from all accounts the most unfriendly rancher in Jacobsville, a man with no tact, no tolerance for strangers and more money than he knew what to do with. She was used to difficult men, so this would be just another check on her clipboard. But she was genuinely sorry that she'd been so unfriendly to Guy Fenton, who was only concerned for her. She should tell him about her past and then perhaps they could go from there. He wasn't a bad man. He had a sense of humor and a good brain. She wondered why he wasn't using it. He didn't seem the sort to tie himself for life to managing a feedlot. Surely he could have struck out on his own, started his own business.

She laid her head back on the damp pillow with

a grimace. Only a few more hours to daylight. She had sleeping pills, but she never took them. She hated the very thought of any sort of addiction. She didn't smoke or drink, and she'd never been in love. That required too much trust.

A glance at the bedside clock assured her that she had four hours left to stare at the light patterns on the ceiling or try to sleep. She closed her eyes with a sigh.

GUY FENTON, TRUE to his word, called the motel and left a message for Candy, giving her directions to the Parks ranch and assuring her that he'd be there when she arrived. She was dreading the meeting after the way she'd acted. He probably thought the worst of her after yesterday. She hoped she could undo the damage.

She drove up to the sprawling wood ranch house. The surroundings were well-kept, the white fences were painted, the corrals looked neat and clean, there was a huge barn out back with a fenced pasture on either side of it, and the paved driveway had obviously been landscaped, because there were flowering plants and shrubs and trees everywhere. Either Mr. Parks had inherited this place or he loved flowers. She wondered which.

He came out onto the porch with Guy to meet her, unsmiling and intimidating. She saw at once that none of her former experiences with difficult men had prepared her to deal with this tiger.

"Cy Parks, Candace Marshall," Guy introduced them curtly. "Ms. Marshall is interviewing local

ranchers for a publicity spread in a national magazine to promote new ideas in beef management."

"Great idea," Cy said, but the smile he gave her
wasn't pleasant. "The animal rights activists will use
the platform for protests and the antimeat lobby will
demand equal space for a rebuttal."

Candy's eyebrows lifted at the frontal attack.
"We're trying to promote new methods," she replied.
"Not start a food war."

"It's already started, or don't you watch daytime
television?" Cy drawled coldly.

She let out a slow breath. *"Welll,"* she drawled,
"we could just lie down on the highway voluntarily
and let the other side pave us over."

The corner of his wide mouth jerked, but there was
no friendly light in those cold green eyes, and his lean
face was harder than the tanned leather it resembled.
He was Guy's height, but even slimmer, built like a
rodeo cowboy with a cruel-looking mouth and big
feet. He kept his left hand in his pocket, but with his
right, he gestured toward the nearest pasture.

"If you want to see my new bull, he's that way,"
Cy said shortly. He came down the steps with a slow,
lazy stride and led the way to the fenced area. "He's
already won competitions."

Candy stared through the fence at the enormous
animal. He was breathtaking, for a bull, with his shiny
red coat and eye-catching conformation.

"Nothing to say?" Cy chided.

She shook her head. "I'm lost for words," she replied simply. "He's beautiful."

Cy made a rough sound in his throat, but he didn't take her up on the controversial description.

"I thought you might want to mention your, shall we say unorthodox, pest control methods," Guy prompted.

Cy's black eyebrows jerked under the wide brim of his hat. "I don't like pesticides," he said flatly. "They mess up the groundwater table. I use insects."

"Insects?" Candy had heard of this method, and she began to quote a magazine article she'd read recently about the use of beneficial insects to control pest insects on agricultural land.

"That's exactly where I found out about it," he replied, impressed. "I thought it was worth a try, and couldn't be worse than the stuff we were already using. I was pretty surprised with the results. Now I'm going organic on fertilizer, as well." He nodded toward the heifers in a far pasture, safely removed from his bull. "Shame to waste all that by-product of my growing purebred herd," he added tongue-in-cheek. "Especially considering what city folk spend to buy it in bags. I don't even have to waste plastic."

Candy laughed. Her voice was musical, light, and Guy found himself staring at her. He hadn't heard her laugh, but here was the town's most hostile citizen and he amused her.

Cy didn't smile, but his green eyes did. "You should smile more," he said.

She shrugged. "Everybody should."

He bent his head toward her. "I saw your mother

a few weeks ago at a convention. She's turned to ice, hasn't she?"

Her face was shocked. "Well, yes, I suppose…"

"Can't blame her," he said heavily. He searched Candy's eyes. "But it wasn't your fault."

"Everybody says that," she said shortly, all too aware of Guy's intent scrutiny.

"You should listen," he said shortly.

She nodded. "Now about that bull," she said, changing the subject.

Once on his favorite theme, he was good for several minutes. For a taciturn man, he was eloquent on the subject of that bull and all his good breeding points. He expanded until Candy had all she needed and walked quietly beside him while he showed them around the rest of the compound.

She was ready to leave shortly before Guy. She shook hands with Cy Parks, nodded cautiously toward Guy, got in her rental car and drove back to her motel.

Guy wasn't in such a big hurry. He paused by the fender of his pickup truck and turned toward Cy. "What happened to her?"

"Ask her," he said with customary bluntness.

"I could get more by asking the car she's riding in."

Cy shrugged. "I don't guess it's any real secret. About nine or ten years ago, her dad took her to a fast-food joint for lunch. You know, Dad and his little girl, sharing a meal and talking to each other. As it happened, that particular day the manager had fired an employee for drinking on the job. The guy was using drugs, too, but the manager didn't know that.

So, there's everybody in the fast-food joint, talking and waiting for orders, including Candy and her dad, when this guy they fired comes in with an AK-47 assault rifle and starts shooting."

Guy caught his breath audibly. "Was she hit?"

Cy nodded solemnly. "In the chest. Destroyed one of her lungs and she almost died. They removed the lung. Her dad wasn't so lucky. He took a round in the face. Died instantly. They say that her mother never stopped blaming her for it. It was her idea to go there for lunch, you see."

"And the mother assumed that if she hadn't wanted to go, Candy's father would still be alive."

"Exactly." He stared toward the small dust cloud Candy's car was making in the distance. "She's real touchy on the subject, they say. The media hounded her and her mother right after the shooting. Even now, some enterprising reporter turns up her name and wants to do an update. Her mother sued one of them for trespassing on her ranch and won. She doesn't get bothered much. I imagine Candy does." He shook his head. "I hear that she and her mother barely speak these days. Apparently she's decided that if Mama doesn't want her around, she'll cooperate."

"What's her mother like?"

Cy pursed his lips. "The sort you can't imagine ever getting married. Most men walk wide around her. No inhibitions about speaking her mind, and that mind is sharp as a knife blade. Nothing like Candy, there," he added thoughtfully. "She's all bluff. Underneath, she's marshmallow."

Guy scowled. "How do you know that?"

"I recognize a fellow sufferer," he said, and took his left hand out of his pocket.

Guy's eyebrows jerked, just a little, when he saw it. It wasn't disfigured, but it had very obviously been badly burned. The skin was slick and tight over it.

"Didn't anyone tell you that my Wyoming ranch burned to the ground?" he asked the younger man. "I don't suppose they added that I was in it at the time, with my wife and son?"

Guy felt sick to his stomach. It was painfully obvious that the other two members of the Parks family hadn't survived.

Cy looked at his hand, his jaw taut and his face hard. He put it back in the pocket and looked at Guy with dead eyes. "It took three neighbors to drag me back out of the house. They sat on me until the firemen got inside. It was already too late. I'd gotten home late because of bad weather. There was a thunderstorm while I was finishing up some urgent paperwork in the office on one side of the house. The fire started in the other, where they were both asleep. Later, they said a lightning strike caused the fire." He stared into space with terrible eyes. "My boy was five years…" He stopped, turned away, breathed until his voice was steady again. "I left Wyoming. Couldn't bear the memories. I thought I'd start again, here. Money was no problem, I've always had that. But time doesn't heal, damn it!"

Guy felt the man's pain and understood it. "I was flying my fiancée around the county one afternoon," he said evenly. "I thought I'd impress her with a barrel roll…but I stalled out. The plane went down into some trees and hung there by a thread with the passenger side facedown to the ground. I came to my senses and saw Anita there, hanging onto the seat with her feet dangling." His eyes grew cold. "It must have been a good forty feet to the ground. She was crying, pleading with me not to let her fall. I reached down to catch her, and she let go with one hand to grab mine. She lost her hold." His eyes closed. "I wake up in the night, seeing her face, contorted with fear, hear her voice crying out to me." His eyes opened and he drew in a breath. "I know what hell is. I've lived in it for three years. You don't get over it."

Cy winced. "I'm sorry."

"So am I, for you. But it doesn't help, does it?" he asked on cold laughter. He removed his hat, ran a hand through his hair and put it back on again. "Well, I'll go chase up the publicity lady and carry on."

"Sure."

He lifted a hand and got into the truck. There was really nothing more to be said. But commiseration did ease the sting of things. Just a little.

CHAPTER THREE

GUY FOLLOWED CANDY back to the motel and found her car parked in front of one of the rooms on the end of the complex. He parked his truck beside it, got out and rapped on her door.

She opened the door, looking pale and worn. She wasn't breathing very well, either.

"We can go out to Matt Caldwell's place tomorrow," he said at once. "If you don't mind," he added carefully, trying not to let his concern for her health show too much. "I've got a few things I need to do at the feedlot this afternoon, but if you're determined to carry on...?"

"No, it can...wait." She searched his face. "He told you about me, didn't he?" she added without preamble.

There seemed little reason to hedge. "Yes," he replied, with no trace of expression on his face. He continued as if he hadn't paid much attention to the subject. "I'll phone you in the morning. I've got a client coming to look over his cattle, and he'll want details about our feeding program that I'll have to explain to him. He's a lot like J. D. Langley—he doesn't like feedlots but he's working for a corporation that does. We're expecting him when we open for business, but if he comes later, I may have to let you go to Matt's place alone. If that happens, I'll fax a map over to the motel office and you can pick it up before you leave. His ranch is almost a half hour out of town on some real back roads. Some of them don't even have road signs!"

She was surprised that he didn't mention her past. She relaxed a little. "That will be fine," she said.

He watched her struggle for breath, and she began to cough rather violently. "Have you ever been tested for asthma?" he persisted.

She held a tissue to her mouth while she fought the weakness that was making it hard for her to talk at all. "No."

"Well, you should be," he said bluntly, eyes narrow with concern. "Everybody says asthma makes you wheeze, but it doesn't always. I dated a girl last year who had it real bad, but she didn't wheeze, she just coughed until it sounded like her lungs might come up."

She leaned heavily against the door facing. "Why aren't you still dating her?" she asked.

"I let another woman flirt with me when we went on our first date," he replied. "We didn't have a lot in common, but I felt ashamed. I'm not usually that inconsiderate."

"Did she find somebody else?"

He chuckled. "She married her boss, one of our local doctors. My loss, but I think he was sweet on her from the beginning. He gave me hell about letting her go home alone from the theater."

She searched his eyes quietly. "Why do you get drunk every weekend?" she asked.

He was shocked, and looked it. "Who told you?" he asked impatiently.

"Mr. Gately, while you were looking at the horses," she replied. "He said to stay away from you on weekends, and I asked why."

He rammed his hands in his pockets and looked unapproachable. "My fiancée died in a plane crash. I was flying the plane. I stalled out the engine showing off, and I managed to get it down into the trees without killing us. But the tree we landed in was forty feet off the ground. Her seat belt came loose and she fell out before I could catch her." His eyes darkened with the memory. "I drink so I won't have to see her face as she fell out the door, or hear her scream for me to help her."

She crumpled the tissue in her hand. "I'm so sorry," she said gently. "So very sorry."

"I wouldn't have told you if I hadn't known what happened to you," he replied. "Some people love to hear about violent deaths. Maybe it makes them feel alive. It just makes me feel like getting drunk."

"I can understand that. But she wouldn't have wanted you to mourn that way, would she?"

He hesitated. "No. I don't suppose she would."

"Or live your life alone, either," she persisted. She smiled. "My father was like that, always doing for other people, bringing us little presents, taking care of us. He was much more nurturing than my mother ever was. Of course, now she hates me. I killed him, you see," she added tightly. "I was the one who suggested that we go to that particular place for lunch."

"It could have happened anywhere," he said.

She shrugged. "Sure it could, but it happened there. These days, I spend as little time at home as I can manage. I suppose I'm tired of paying for my sins." She laughed hollowly. "I run. You run. And they're still dead, aren't they?"

Her voice broke on the last word. He couldn't understand why it affected him the way it did, but he couldn't stand there and watch her cry.

He eased her into the motel room and closed the door behind them. He drew her into his arms and held her hard, tight, close against the length of him while his lean hand stroked her soft hair. She'd left it loose today, and it fell to her shoulders like dark silk. It smelled of flowers.

"I don't need..." she began, in just a token protest.

He smoothed the hair back from her face. "You do," he corrected. "So do I. It's human to want comfort."

"Do I?" she asked miserably.

"Yes. And I do, too."

He wrapped her up again and just stood there holding her while she clung to him, more at peace than he'd been in years. He liked the way she felt in his arms, warm and soft and vulnerable.

She sighed after a minute and nestled closer.

"Didn't your mother ever hug you?" he asked.

"Not really. She wasn't affectionate, except with Dad, and that was rare. She still isn't a touching person."

"Neither am I, as a rule." His chest lifted and fell against her. "What a hard little shell you wear, Ms. Marshall," he murmured against her temple.

"I don't want pity."

"Neither do I," he said. "But I could get used to being comforted."

She smiled against his shirt. "So could I."

"Suppose we give up fighting and declare a truce?"

Her heart jumped. "Isn't that cowardice under fire?"

"Not between two old troopers like us."

She smoothed her hand over his soft shirt. "I suppose I could try not to be on the defensive so much if you'll try not to get drunk."

He was still. His eyes went past her head to the big oak tree beside the motel. Absently, he wondered how old it was. "I haven't tried going without alcohol in a long time," he confided. "Even if just on weekends. But I'd have to have an alternative."

Her fingers toyed with a pearl button midway down his chest. "I don't suppose you like fishing."

He lifted his head. "You're kidding, of course."

"Do you or don't you?" she asked, perplexed.

"I won the bass rodeo last year."

Her eyebrows went up and she chuckled. "Only because I wasn't competing with you," she said. "I love to fish for bass!"

A soul mate, he was thinking. He almost said it aloud. "I'll bet you didn't bring your tackle with you."

She grimaced. "I had to fly here. I couldn't carry everything I wanted to."

"I'll kit you out. I've got spinning reels and cane poles, everything from sinkers to hooks to floats. We'll spend Saturday at the lake."

"I'd love to!" She smiled up at him with her soft eyes, and he wondered why he'd ever thought she was cold.

"I'll try to get somebody to substitute for me so I can go with you to Matt's in the morning. About nine suit you? I'll arrange it with him, too."

"That will be fine. Is he like Cy Parks?" she asked, curious.

He shook his head. "Matt's easygoing most of the time, unless he's really mad and then people get out of his way. He likes women. As a rule," he added.

"There's an exception, I gather?"

"Only one." He smiled at her. "I'll see you tomorrow. You might try some strong coffee," he suggested. "They say it helps an asthma attack—if that's what you're having. If you don't get better, call the doctors Coltrain or Dr. Morris. They're all great."

"Okay. Thanks."

He let her go with a sigh. "It's not a weakness to get help when you're sick," he mused. "I just thought I'd mention that."

"I wasn't allowed to be sick at home," she told him. "Some lessons are hard to unlearn."

He searched her wan face. "What a childhood you must have had," he said sadly.

"It was all right, until my dad died."

"I wonder," he mused, unconvinced.

She coughed again, holding the handkerchief to her mouth.

He scowled. "That wheat straw dust gets to you, doesn't it?" he asked with concern. "You need to stay out of enclosed places where it's bad. If you really do have asthma, it's dangerous."

"I have one lung," she said huskily. "It's sensitive to dust, I guess."

He wasn't buying it. "I'll call you tonight, just to make sure you're okay. If it doesn't get better, call the doctor or get to the hospital."

"I will. You don't need to worry."

"Somebody does," he said curtly. "If you're not better in the morning, we might put Matt off until you are. He lives in town, but his ranch is about twenty-five minutes out of town. If you had a life-threatening attack out there, I'd never get you to town in time in the truck."

"Mr. Caldwell has an airplane," she pointed out.

"He has two—a Learjet and a little Cessna Commuter," he replied, "but he's only going to be at the ranch long enough to introduce us to his ranch manager. He's flying himself to Fort Worth in the Learjet for a conference."

"I'll be fine by the morning," she said doggedly. "I know I will." She ruined the stoic image with another choking cough.

"Go drink some coffee, just to humor me, will you?"

She sighed. "Okay."

"Good girl." He bent abruptly and put his mouth gently against hers.

She jumped and a shocked breath pulsed out of her.

He searched her eyes curiously. "You aren't afraid of me, are you?" he asked gently.

"I don't...think so."

Her attitude was surprising. She seemed confident and self-assured, until he came intimately close. She didn't seem to know a lot about men.

"Don't people kiss you, either?" he asked.

"Not a lot."

"Pity," he said, glancing down at her mouth. "You've sure got the mouth for kissing—soft and warm and very sweet."

She put her hand to it, unconsciously. "I don't like sports," she said absently.

"What's that got to do with kissing?"

"Most of the men I meet are married, but the ones who aren't want to take me to football or baseball games. I like fishing."

"I like sports," he mused. "But mostly rodeo and fishing."

"I like rodeo, too."

"See? Two things we have in common, already," he said with a smile. He bent and brushed his mouth against hers again, feeling the same faintly electric sensation as before. He grinned as his lips teased hers. "I could get addicted to this."

She put her hands on his chest. "I can't…breathe very well," she whispered. "I'm sorry."

He lifted his head and stared down at her. "Is that why you don't get involved? You can't get your breath and when you mention it, men think you're giving them the brush-off?"

"How did you know?" she asked, surprised.

"It's the obvious answer to your lack of marriage-able suitors," he said simply. "It certainly isn't due to a lack of looks. Why didn't you tell them you only had one lung?"

She grimaced. "It wouldn't have mattered very much. They wanted a lot more than a few kisses."

"And you didn't."

She shook her head. "I've been dead inside since my father died. The psychologist they sent me to af-terward said it was guilt because he died and I didn't. Maybe it's still that way." She looked up at him. "But regardless of the guilt, I just don't feel that way with most men. Well, I haven't…before."

She was flushing and he knew why. He grinned, feeling ten feet tall. "It's like little electric shocks, isn't it?" he mused.

She smiled shyly. "Sort of."

He pursed his lips. "Care to try for a major light-ning strike?"

She laughed. "Not today."

"Okay." He pushed back a stray strand of her hair, admiring its softness. "I'll see you in the morning, then."

"I'll look forward to it."

He sobered. "So will I." There was an odd little glitter in his eyes. It grew as he looked at her. It was almost as if he had to jerk his eyes away from hers and force himself to move away. In fact, that's exactly how it was. He liked women, and from time to time he was attracted to them. It hadn't been like this. He wanted this woman in ways he'd never wanted any other.

He hesitated as he reached the truck. "I meant it about the doctor," he said with genuine concern. "If that cough doesn't stop, see someone."

"All right." She smiled, waved and closed the door.

He drove away, but not without misgivings. He didn't like the way she looked when that cough racked her. She was fragile, but she didn't realize it or just plain ignored it. She needed someone to take care of her. He smiled at the random thought. That was certainly an outdated notion. Women didn't like being taken care of. They wanted to be independent and strong. But he wondered if they didn't secretly like the idea of being nurtured by someone—not controlled, dominated or smothered, but just…nurtured.

He thought of her as an orchid that needed just the right amount of attention—a growth mixture of bark, a little careful watering now and then—to make it grow. Orchids needed lots of humidity and cool nights. He smiled at the thought of Candy letting him put her in a pot and pour water over her. But it was the sort of thing he wanted, to take care of her and never let her be hurt again. He scowled, because the things he was thinking were very much against his nature.

He was a loner. He'd never thought much about nurturing anything, much less a woman. He couldn't think of Candy any other way, and he'd known her only a matter of days.

It was too soon to be thinking of anything permanent, he assured himself. All the same, it wouldn't hurt to keep an eye on her. He had a feeling that she was going to form a very large part of his future happiness.

BACK IN THE MOTEL, Candy had finally gotten the best of the raging cough by stifling it with a large pot of strong black coffee. She hadn't expected results, despite Guy's assurances about coffee being good for asthma, but apparently he was right. She frowned. If she did have asthma, it was going to complicate her life. Working around ranches and wheat straw dust and grain dust was going to constitute a major challenge, even if there was a reliable treatment for it.

She sipped her coffee and thought about Guy's concern, about the way he took care of her. She was a modern woman, of course she was. But it felt nice, having somebody care what happened to her. Her mother didn't. Nobody had cared what happened to her since her father died. She couldn't help being touched by Guy's concern—and wasn't that an about-face from his first attempts at it, she asked herself wryly.

Later, just before she went to bed, the phone rang. It was Guy, just checking on her. She told him that she was all right and he told her that he'd found someone to handle the visiting cattleman for him. He'd see her in the morning.

He hung up and she held on to the receiver for a long time before she put it down. It wasn't bad, having somebody care about her. It wasn't bad at all.

THE NEXT MORNING dawned bright and beautiful. Candy dressed in a neat beige pantsuit and suede boots for the trip, leaving her hair loose. She felt younger and happier than she had in years. She had a whole new outlook on life because of Guy.

She reviewed her few facts on the Caldwell ranch. It was only one of a dozen pies Matt had his finger in. He was an entrepreneur in the true sense of the word, an empire-builder. If he'd been born a hundred years ago, he'd have been a man like Richard King, who founded the famous King Ranch in southeastern Texas. Matt was an easygoing, pleasant man to most people. She'd heard that he was hell in boots to his enemies. There were always rumors about such a powerful man, and one of them was that he had it in for a female friend of his cousin's and had caused her to lose her job. It was a glaring black mark against a man who was generally known for fair play, and people talked about it. She was a very young woman, at that, not at all the sort of female the handsome tycoon was frequently seen with.

Matt's taste ran to models and Hollywood stars. He had no use for high-powered career women in his private life, although he employed several in executive positions in his various companies. Perhaps that was why the young woman had run afoul of his temper, Candy speculated. She was rumored to be very intelligent and sharp at business.

A rap on the motel door startled her. She went to answer it and found a smiling Guy on the doorstep.

"Ready to go?"

"Oh, yes!" she said brightly. The day had taken a definite turn for the better.

MATT'S SPRAWLING RANCH lay about twenty-five minutes out of town, and it was truly out in the boondocks.

Guy took a road that wasn't identified in any way and flashed a grin at Candy. "I'm afraid even a good map wouldn't have helped much. Matt says he likes being someplace where he's hard to find, but it's hell on people who have to go out here on business."

"He must not like people," she commented.

"He does, in fact, but not when he's in a black mood. That's when he comes out here. He works right alongside his cowhands and the newer ones sometimes don't even realize he's the boss until they see him in a suit and boarding the Learjet. He's just one of the boys."

"How rich is he?" she asked.

He chuckled. "Nobody knows. He owns this ranch and a real estate franchise, two planes, he has property in Australia and Mexico, he's on the board of directors of four companies and on the board of trustees of two universities. In his spare time, he buys and sells cattle." He shook his head. "I've never known a man with so much energy."

"Does he do it to get his mind off something?" she wondered aloud.

"Nobody's ever had the nerve to ask. Matt's very pleasant, but he isn't the sort of man you question."

She bumped along beside him in the truck and something nagged at the back of her mind.

"You said you were flying the plane. Did you own it?" she asked carefully.

He drew in a slow breath. He didn't want to talk about it, but then, she was entitled to know something about him. He glanced at her. "I did. I have an air cargo company."

Her eyes widened. "And you're working for wages at a feedlot?"

"They don't know I own the company," he told her. "I wanted someplace to… I don't know, hide out maybe." He shrugged broad shoulders. "I couldn't cope with the memories there, and I didn't want enough spare time to think. I got the most demanding job I could find. I've been here three years and I like it. My manager is doing great things with the air cargo company. I'm considering making him a full partner."

"Is it a profitable company?"

"I'm not in Matt Caldwell's league," he said. "But I suppose I'm pretty close." He glanced at her and smiled. "I could afford to live high if I liked. I don't. I was too fond of the fast lane. It's what cost me Anita." His face tautened as he stared ahead at the long, winding road. "I'd been on the road all of the day before, and I hadn't slept that night because someone had a party and I was enjoying myself. Anita wanted to go up for a few minutes, so I took her. If I'd had a good night's sleep, I wouldn't have done such a sketchy walk-around and I'd have noticed the problem in the engine before it caused a tragedy. That was when I looked at my life and decided that I was wasting it. I came down here to decide what to do." He shook his head. "It's been three years and I still haven't decided that."

"What do you want to do?" she asked.

His eyes held a faraway look. "I want to settle down and have a family." He saw the expression on her face and chuckled. "I can see that you hadn't considered that answer as a possibility."

"You don't seem the sort of man to want to settle," she said evasively. She twisted her purse in her lap.

"I wasn't, until recently. I'm not that old, but I'm beginning to see down the road further than I used to. I don't want to grow old and die alone."

"Most people don't."

He grinned. "Including you?"

She hesitated. "I'd never really thought about marrying and having a family," she said seriously.

"Because you only have one lung? That shouldn't worry you."

"It might worry a prospective husband," she pointed out. "Most men want a whole woman."

"You're whole, in every way that matters," he said firmly. "With or without two lungs."

She smiled. "Thanks. That was nice. But marriage is a big step."

"Not really. Not if two people have a lot in common and if they're good friends. I've seen some very happy marriages since I moved to Jacobsville. Marriage is what you make of it," he said pensively.

"So they say."

The road dead-ended at a long, winding gravel driveway with a huge black mailbox at the fork which read Caldwell Double C Ranch.

"We're almost there," Guy told her, pulling into the ranch road. "Matt runs some of the prettiest Santa Gertrudis cattle in the state. It's a purebred herd, which means they aren't slaughter cattle. He sells seed bulls and heifers, mostly, and he does a roaring business."

"I like Santa Gerts," she remarked.

"So did my father," he told her. "He worked on the King Ranch. I grew up with cattle and always loved them. I just loved airplanes more. Now I'm caught between the two. That tickles my parents."

"They're still alive?"

He chuckled. "Very. He still works on a ranch, and she's gone into real estate! I go to visit them every few months." He glanced at her. "As I mentioned before, I have a brother in California and a sister in Washington State. She has a little boy about four. Her husband's a lawyer."

"Quite a family," she mused.

"You'd like my family," he told her. "They're just

plain folks, nothing put on or fancy, and they love company."

"My mother screams about uninvited guests," she recalled. "She's not really fond of people unless they come to buy cattle. She's pretty mercenary."

"You aren't."

She laughed. "Thanks for noticing. No, I'll never make a businesswoman. If I had a lot of money, I'd probably give it all away. I'm a sucker for a lost cause."

"That makes two of us. And here we are."

He indicated a sprawling white two-story ranch house with a porch that ran two-thirds of the way around it. There was a porch swing and plenty of chairs and gliders to sit in. The pasture fences near the house were all white, and behind them red-coated cattle grazed on green grass.

"Improved pasture," she murmured, taking notes. "You can always tell by the lush grass."

"Matt's a stickler for improvements. There he is." He nodded toward the front steps, where a tall, darkly handsome man in a suit and a white Stetson was coming down to greet them.

CHAPTER FOUR

MATT CALDWELL WAS ATTRACTIVE, and he had a live-wire personality to go with his lean good looks. He helped Candy from the truck with a charm that immediately captivated her.

"Glad you got here before I had to leave," Matt said, greeting Guy as he came around the truck. "I'm going to have Paddy show you the place. I wish I could, but I'm already late for a meeting in Houston." He glanced at his watch. "I never have a minute to spare these days. I think I need to slow down."

"It wouldn't hurt," Guy chuckled. "Candy Marshall, this is Matt Caldwell."

"Glad to meet you," Candy said with a smile and an extended hand.

Matt shook it warmly. "Publicists are getting neater by the day," he mused. "The last one we had here was twenty-five, unshaven and didn't know a Santa Gert from a Holstein."

"I shaved my beard off just this morning," she said pertly.

Matt chuckled. "Glad to know that you have good personal hygiene," he drawled. "Paddy will show you anything you want to see. If you need to talk to me,

I should be back by tomorrow morning. If that's not soon enough, you can fax me the questions, I'll answer them and fax them back to you." He handed her a business card with Mather Caldwell Enterprises, Inc. in raised black lettering.

"Impressive," she told him.

He chuckled. "Not very." He glanced at Guy with a calculating gleam in his eyes. "If you wanted to give her a bird's-eye view of the ranch, the Cessna Commuter 150's gassed up and ready to fly."

Guy's face went hard just thinking about the small, two-seater plane. It was the type he'd crashed three years ago taking Anita for a ride. "I don't fly anymore."

Matt exchanged a complicated glance with him. "Pity."

"She wants to see cattle on the hoof, anyway."

"I bought a new Santa Gertrudis bull from the King Ranch. Paddy will show him to you. He's a looker." Matt shook hands with them both. "Got to run," he said. "Paddy should be out here any minute. He was with me when you drove up, but he got held up in the office. Have a seat on the porch and wait for him."

"Nice porch," Candy remarked.

He grinned. "I bought the place for the porch. I like to sit out there on warm summer evenings and listen to Rachmaninoff."

He piled into his Mercedes and gunned the engine as he drove out to the small hangar and airstrip that were barely visible in the distance.

"Does he do that often? Offer you his airplane, I mean?" Candy asked when they were comfortably seated in the porch swing.

"Every time he sees me," he said with resignation. "I suppose I'm getting used to it. Which doesn't mean I like it," he added.

She didn't quite know how to answer that. It was a good thing that Paddy Kilgraw chose that moment to come out onto the porch. He was a wizened little man with skin like leather and twinkling blue eyes. He took off his hat, revealing pale red hair on either side of a huge bald spot, and shook hands warmly with them both. He led them out to the barn and Candy got down to business.

Matt's operation was enormous, but it still had the personal touch. He knew each of his bulls by name, and at least two of them were tame. Candy enjoyed the way they nuzzled her hand when she petted them. To her mother, cattle were for slaughter, nothing else. Candy much preferred a ranch that concentrated on keeping them alive, where the owner liked his animals and took proper care of them. Even cantankerous Cy Parks, who did run beef cattle, was concerned for their welfare and never treated them as if they were nothing more than an investment.

But the barn, while neat and clean for such a structure, was filled with wheat straw, and it was strictly an enclosed space. They'd barely entered it when Candy started coughing. She bent over double and couldn't stop.

Guy asked Paddy for a cup of coffee, which the

little man went running to get. Meanwhile, Guy lifted
Candy and carried her out of the barn, to where the
air was less polluted by wheat straw dust. But once
outside, seated on the running board of the truck, she
was still coughing. Tears were running down her face,
which was red as fire.

Paddy appeared with a cup of coffee. "It's cold,
will that do?" he asked quickly.

"Cold is fine. It's the caffeine we want." Guy held
it to her lips, but she was coughing so hard that she
couldn't even drink in between spasms. His face
contorted with fear. He looked up at Paddy from his
kneeling position beside Candy. "I think it's a bad
asthma attack," he said abruptly.

"Has she got an inhaler on her?" Paddy asked.

Guy shook his head worriedly. "She hasn't been
diagnosed by a doctor yet. Damn!"

She bent over again, and this time she was definitely wheezing as she coughed. It was getting worse
by the second and she looked as if she was struggling
to get a single breath of air.

"It's twenty-five minutes to Jacobsville!" Guy said
harshly. "I'll never get her there in time!"

"Take the Commuter," Paddy said. "I've got the
keys in my pocket. Boss said you might like to fly
her while you were here."

Guy's eyes were haunted. "Paddy, I can't!" he bit
off, horror in his expression at the memory of his
last flight.

Paddy put a firm hand on his shoulder. "Her life

depends on it," he reminded the younger man solemnly. "Yes, you can! Here. Go!"

Guy took another look at Candy and groaned. He took the keys from Paddy, put Candy in the truck, swung in beside her and gunned the engine out to the airstrip, with Paddy hanging on in the truck bed.

He pulled the truck to a stop at the hangar. Leaving Candy in the cab of the truck, Guy and Paddy got the little Cessna pulled out onto the apron. Then Guy carried Candy and strapped her into the passenger side. She was barely conscious, her breath rasping as she tried desperately to breathe.

"You'll make it," Paddy said firmly. "I'll phone ahead and have an ambulance and EMTs waiting at the airport in Jacobsville with the necessary equipment. Get going!"

"Thanks, Paddy," Guy called as he ran to get inside the plane.

It had been a long time since he'd flown, but it was like riding a bicycle, it came right back to him. He went over the controls and gauges and switches after he'd fired up the engine. He taxied the little plane out onto the runway and said a silent prayer.

"It's going to be all right, honey," he told Candy in a harsh tone. "Try to hang on. I'll have you to the hospital in no time in this!"

She couldn't manage a reply. She felt as if she were drowning, unable to get even a breath of air. She gripped the edge of the seat, crying silently, terrified, as Guy sent the little aircraft zipping down the runway and suddenly into the air.

He circled and turned the plane toward Jacobsville, thanking God for his skill as a pilot that had made this trip even possible. He could see that Candy was slowly turning blue and losing consciousness.

"Just a little longer, sweetheart," he pleaded above the noise of the engine. "Just a little longer! Please hold on!"

He kept talking to her, soothing her, encouraging her all the way to the Jacobsville airport. He was so preoccupied with her welfare that his horror of flying took a backseat to his concern for Candy. He called the tower and was immediately given clearance to land, which he did, faultlessly. An ambulance pulled onto the tarmac, lights flashing, and came to a halt as he taxied onto the apron and cut the engine.

Seconds later, they had Candy out of the plane and on oxygen. They loaded her into the ambulance, with one EMT and a worried Guy in the back with her. They roared away to the hospital, with Guy holding her hand and praying silently that he wasn't going to lose her, when he'd only just found her.

Her color was better and she was breathing less strenuously when the ambulance pulled up sharply at the emergency entrance. The physician on duty came running out behind the nurses and supervised Candy's entrance.

Guy was gently put to one side while Candy was wheeled right into the emergency room, into a cubicle.

"You can sit here in the waiting area," a nurse told him with a gentle smile. "Don't worry. She's going to be fine."

Easy to say, he thought worriedly. He jammed his hands into the pockets of his jeans and paced, oblivious to the other people also waiting and worrying nearby. He couldn't remember the last time he'd been so upset.

He glanced toward the swinging doors through which Candy had been taken and sighed. She'd looked a little better after the oxygen mask was put into place, but he knew it was going to take more than that to get her back on her feet. He was almost certain that they'd keep her overnight. He hoped they would. She was stubborn and unlikely to follow instructions.

Just when he was contemplating storming the doors, the physician came and motioned him inside.

He pulled him into an empty cubicle and closed the curtain. "Is she your fiancée?" he asked Guy.

He shook his head. "She's a visiting publicist for the cattlemen's association. I was deputized by our local association to escort her around the area ranches."

"Damn!" the doctor muttered.

"Why? What's wrong?"

He glowered. "She's got the worst case of asthma I've come across in years, and she won't believe it. I've got her on a nebulizer now, but she's going to need a primary care physician to evaluate and treat her, or this isn't going to be an isolated incident. She needs to see someone right away. But I can't convince her."

Guy smiled wryly. "Leave it to me," he murmured.

"I think I'm beginning to know how to handle her. Is this a long-standing condition, do you think?"

"Yes, I do. The coughing threw her off. Most people don't associate it with asthma, but while it's not as common as wheezing, it is certainly a symptom. I've prescribed a rescue inhaler for her to carry, and told her that she needs to be on a preventative. Her own doctor can prescribe that."

"She lives in Denver," Guy said. "I'm not sure she goes to a doctor regularly."

"She'd better," the young man said flatly. "She almost got here too late. Another few minutes and it would have been touch and go."

"I figured that," Guy said quietly.

"She owes you her life," he continued.

"She owes me nothing, but I'm going to make sure that she takes care of herself from now on."

"I'm glad to hear it."

"May I see her?"

He smiled and nodded. "Sure. She won't be able to talk. She's very busy."

"Good. She can listen better. I've got a lot to tell her."

The doctor only chuckled. He led the way into a larger cubicle where a worn-looking Candy was inhaling something in a mask that covered part of her face. She glanced at him and looked irritated.

"Asthma," Guy said, plopping down onto a stool nearby. "I told you, didn't I?"

She couldn't speak, but her eyes did. They were eloquent.

"He says you need to see a doctor and get the asthma treated."

She tugged at the mask. "I won't!"

"You will," he replied, putting it firmly back in place. "Committing suicide is not sensible."

She struck the side of the examination couch with her hand.

"I know, you don't want any more complications," he said for her. "But this could have cost you dearly. You have to take precautions, so that it doesn't happen again."

Her eyes seemed to brighten. She shifted and shook her head.

"Hay and wheat and ranches sort of go together," Guy said. "If you're going to spend any time around them, you have to have proper care. I'm going to make sure you get it."

She gave him a look that said him and what army?

He chuckled. "We'll go into that later. Getting easier to breathe?"

She hesitated, and then nodded. She searched his eyes and made a flying motion with her hand. She tugged the mask aside for a second. "I'm sorry…you had to do that. Are you…all right?"

He put the mask back in place again, touched by her concern for him at such a traumatic time for herself. "Yes, I'm all right," he said. "I didn't have time to think about myself and my fears. I was too busy trying to save you. It wasn't as bad as I thought it would be. Of course," he added with a faint smile, "I was pretty preoccupied at the time."

"Thank you," she said in a ghostly, hoarse tone.

"Don't talk. Breathe."

She sighed. "Okay."

The nebulizer took a long time to empty. By the time she'd breathed in the last of the bronchodilator, she was exhausted. But she could get her breath again.

The doctor came back in and reiterated what he'd said about seeing a physician for treatment of her asthma.

He gave her a sample inhaler and a prescription for another, plus another prescription. "This one—" he tapped it "—is for what we call a spacer. It's a more efficient way of delivering the medicine than a pocket inhaler. You're to follow the directions. And as soon as possible, you get treatment. I don't want to see you back in here again in that condition," he added with a smile to soften the words.

"Thank you," she said.

He shrugged. "That's what we're here for." He frowned. "You never knew you had asthma. I find that incredible. Don't you have a family physician?"

"I only go to the clinic when I'm sick," she said shortly. "I don't have a regular doctor."

"Find one," the physician recommended bluntly. "You're a tragedy waiting to happen."

He shook hands with Guy and left them in the cubicle.

Guy helped her to her feet and escorted her to the clerk, where she gave her credit card and address to the woman in charge.

"No insurance, either?" he asked.

She shrugged. "It never seemed necessary."

"You need taking in hand."

She shook her head. "Not tonight. I'm too tired to fight. I want to go back to the motel."

He didn't like that idea at all. He worried about her, being alone at night. "You shouldn't be by yourself," he said uneasily. "I could get a nurse to come and stay with you."

"No!" she said vehemently. "I can take care of myself!"

"Don't get upset," he said firmly. "It won't help matters. It could even bring on another attack."

She drew in a shaky breath. "I'm sorry. It scared me."

"That makes two of us," he confided. "I've never moved so fast in my life." He caught her hand in his and held it tight. "Don't do that again," he added in a strained tone.

She turned to him as they made it into the sunlight. "How do we get to the motel?" she asked worriedly. "And what about your truck?"

"Paddy will take good care of the truck. We have a taxi service here. We can use it," he added with a smile. "Come on. I need to make arrangements to return the plane and then I'll see that you get where you want to go. Eventually," he added under his breath.

CANDY EXPECTED THE cab to take them to the motel, but the address Guy gave the driver wasn't the motel after all. It was a doctor's office.

"Now see here...!" she began.

Her protests didn't cut any ice. He paid the driver and frog-marched her into Drew Morris's waiting room. The receptionist who'd replaced Drew's wife, Kitty, smiled at them.

Guy explained the problem, and the receptionist had them take a seat. But only a couple of minutes later, they were hustled into a cubicle.

Drew Morris came right in. He ignored Candy's protests and examined her with his stethoscope. Seconds later, he wrapped the stethoscope around his neck, sat back on the couch and folded his arms.

"I'm not your physician, but I'll do until you get one. I'm going to give you a prescription for a preventative medicine. You use it along with the inhaler the emergency room doctor gave you."

"How did you know about that?" Candy asked, aghast.

"Guy called me before he called the cab," Drew said nonchalantly. "You use both medicines. If the medicines stop working, for any reason, don't increase the dosage—call me or get to the emergency room. You had a life-threatening episode today. Let it be a warning. You can control asthma, you can't cure it. You have to prevent these attacks."

She gave in gracefully. "Okay," she said. "I'll do what I'm told."

"Have you had problems like this before?"

She nodded. "Quite a bit. I thought it was just a mild allergy. Nobody in my family has any sort of lung problem."

"It doesn't have to be inherited. Some people just

get it—more today than ever before, especially children. It's becoming a major problem, and I'm convinced that pollution has something to do with it."

"What about my job?" she asked miserably. "I love what I do."

"What do you do?" Drew asked.

"I go around to ranches and interview people on their production methods. There's always a grain elevator, a storage silo, a barnful of hay or wheat straw—they're unavoidable."

"Then wear a mask and use your inhalants before you go near those pollutants," Drew said. "No reason you can't keep doing your job. People with asthma have won Olympic medals. It won't get you down unless you let it."

She smiled at him. "You're very encouraging."

"I have to be. My wife, Kitty, is asthmatic."

"How is Kitty?" Guy asked.

He chuckled. "Pregnant," he murmured, and his high cheekbones colored. "We couldn't be happier."

"Congratulations," Guy said. "And thanks for having a look at Candy."

"My pleasure," Drew replied, and not without a noticeable speculation as his gaze went from one of them to the other.

"He seems to know you very well," Candy mentioned when the cab was carrying them back to her motel.

"He does. I used to date his wife, before she was his wife," he said. "I told you about her. She coughed instead of wheezed."

"Oh, yes, I remember." She didn't like the memory. Guy had apparently done a lot of dating locally, despite his grief at losing his fiancée.

"Kitty was sweet and gentle, and I liked her a lot," he continued. "But she loved Drew. I'm glad they made it. He was grieving for his late wife. People around here never thought he'd marry again. I guess Kitty came up on his blind side."

"He's nice."

"Yes, but like all our doctors around here, he's got a temper." He glanced at her pocketbook and leaned forward and told the cabdriver to stop at the nearby pharmacy. "You need to get those filled. We'll wait for them and call a cab when they're filled."

"I could do it tomorrow," Candy began.

"No," he said, leaning over the seat to talk to the cabdriver.

They stopped and got the prescriptions filled and then went on to the motel. Guy left Candy in her room reluctantly and made sure that she had a bucket of ice and some soft drinks before he left, so that she wouldn't have to go out to get them.

"Try to get some rest," he said.

"But we didn't get to see all of Matt's ranch," she protested, frowning. "How will I ever write the story?"

"Matt said he could fax you the answers to any questions you didn't get answered at the ranch," he replied. "I'll explain the situation to him and you can work up some questions. I'll make sure he gets them."

"That's really nice of you," she said.

He smiled down at her, feeling protective and possessive all at once. "This could be habit-forming, too,
you know."

"What could?"

"Taking care of you," he said softly. He bent and
brushed his mouth tenderly against hers. "Lie down
and rest for a while. I'll come back and get you and
take you out to eat, if you're up to it."

She grimaced. "I want to," she said. "But I'm so
tired, Guy."

She did look tired. Her face was drawn and there
were new lines around her mouth and eyes. He traced
one of them lightly.

"Suppose I bring something over to you?" he
asked. "What would you like?"

"Pork lo mein," she said at once.

He grinned. "My favorite. I'll see you about six."

"Okay."

HE FINISHED HIS chores at the feedlot, having had
Paddy drive his truck back to town. He drove Paddy
home and then went to get supper for Candy. He took
the food to the motel. They ate silently and then rented
an action film on the pay per view channel and piled
up together on one of the double beds to watch it.

In no time at all, Candy was curled up against him
sound asleep. He held her that way, marveling at the
wonder of their closeness, at her vulnerability and
his own renewed strength. He hadn't thought seriously about getting involved with anyone since he'd
lost Anita, but Candy had slipped so naturally into

his life that he accepted her presence with no misgivings at all.

He looked down at her with soft, possessive eyes.
He didn't want to go back to the feedlot. He wanted
to stay here with her, all night long. But if he did
that, he'd compromise her. He couldn't risk that. She
might not want commitment so soon. He wondered
about the sanity of getting mixed up with a woman
who lived several states away, but he couldn't talk
himself out of it.

He knew at that moment that she had a hold on
him that no distance, no circumstance, could break.
And he was afraid.

CHAPTER FIVE

GUY BENT AND kissed Candy's closed eyes, brushing his lips against them until they fluttered and lifted.

She looked up at him drowsily, but with absolute trust. Involuntarily, her arms snaked up around his neck and she pulled him down to kiss him slowly, tenderly, on his hard mouth.

He groaned, and she felt him move, so that his body shifted next to hers. The kiss grew in pressure and insistence until one long leg slid right between both of hers and his mouth demanded.

She pushed at his chest, frightened by the sudden lack of breathable air.

His head lifted. He breathed roughly, but he understood without speaking why she'd drawn back. "Sorry," he whispered. His mouth moved to her chin, her neck and into the opening her blouse left. His lean fingers unfastened buttons, so that his mouth could move down past her collarbone and onto even softer flesh.

Her hands picked at his shirt, hesitated, as new sensations lanced through her. She loved the feel of his mouth. She didn't protest as he eased the lacy strap off her shoulder, and his mouth trespassed on flesh that had never known a man's touch before.

She yielded immediately, arching up to meet his lips, pushing the fabric aside to make way for it. She felt his mouth over her hard nipple and its sudden moist pressure made her moan with pleasure.

He lifted his head and looked where his mouth had touched. He traced the firm rise sensually and bent to kiss it once more, lovingly, before he righted the lacy strap and buttoned the blouse again.

Her eyes asked a question.

He smiled and bent to kiss her tenderly. "We have all the time in the world for that," he whispered. "Right now, you're a little wounded bird and I have to take care of you."

Tears stung her eyes. She'd never had tenderness. It was new and overpowering.

He kissed the tears away. "Don't cry," he murmured. "You're going to be fine now. Just fine. Nothing bad is ever going to happen to you as long as I'm around."

She clung to him hard, burying her face in his throat as the tears fell even more hotly.

"Oh, Candy," he murmured huskily. He held her close, rocked her in his arms, until she had her self-control back. Then he got up from the bed and pulled her up beside him, to hold her carefully close.

"Sorry," she murmured on a sob. "I guess I'm tired."

"So am I." He brushed his mouth against her pert

nose. "I'm going back to the feedlot. Can I get you anything before I go?"

She shook her head. She smiled hesitantly. "How about that fishing trip tomorrow?"

He smiled. "I'm game if you are."

"I'll use my medicines," she said without enthusiasm.

"You sure will, or we won't go," he assured her.

She wrinkled her nose at him. "Spoilsport."

"I hate emergency rooms," he said simply. "We have to keep you out of them."

"I'll try."

"Good."

"Thank you for saving my life," she said solemnly. "I know it must have brought back some terrible memories for you, having to fly again."

He wouldn't admit that. He wasn't going to think about it. He only smiled at her, in a vague, pleasant way. "Get some sleep. I'll see you bright and early tomorrow. If you feel like going, we'll go. If not, we'll find some other way to pass the time. Okay?"

She smiled wearily. "Okay."

He left her and went back to the bunkhouse at the feedlot, but he didn't sleep. Over and over again he saw Anita's face. He groaned as he finally just got up and forgot trying to make the memories go away. It was useless.

The next morning, Guy and Candy went fishing on the river, with cane poles and a bait bucket. It was, she muttered, absolutely primitive to try to catch a fish in such a manner.

He only grinned. He'd made a small fire and he had a frying pan heating. He was going to treat her to fresh fish for lunch.

It was a good idea, except that they sat on the riverbank for three hours and at the end of it they had yellow fly bites and mosquito bites, and not one fish between them.

"It must have been this prehistoric fishing gear," Candy remarked with a glowering look. "The fish probably laughed so hard that they sank to the bottom!"

"It isn't prehistoric," he said. "It gives fish a sporting chance."

She waved her hand at the river. "Some sporting chance! And whoever uses worms to catch a self-respecting bass?"

"You just wait until the next bass rodeo, pilgrim," he said with a mocking smile. "And we'll see who can catch fish!"

She grinned at him. The word play was fun. He was fun. She'd smiled and laughed more in the past few days than in her whole recent life. Guy made her feel alive again. He'd knocked the chip off her shoulder about her past and led her into the light. She put down the pole, sighed and stretched lazily.

He watched her covetously. "A woman who likes to fish," he mused, "and who doesn't worry about getting her hands dirty."

"I like to garden, too," she remarked. "I used to plant flowers when I lived at home. Nobody does, now."

He pursed his lips and stared at the ripples on the

river as it ran lazily past the banks. He was thinking about flower beds and a small house to go with them, a house just big enough for two people.

She looked up at him with soft, warm brown eyes. "I've really enjoyed being here," she said. "I'm sorry I have to leave tomorrow."

Reality came crashing down on him. He turned his head and looked at her, and saw Anita's eyes looking back at him. He blinked. "You have to leave?"

She nodded sadly. "I have to write up all these articles and get back to my desk. I expect I've got a month's work piled up there."

"In Denver."

"Yes. In Denver." She pulled in her line and put the pole down beside her. "It's been the most wonderful week I can remember. Thank you for saving my life."

He frowned. He was staring at his line, but he wasn't seeing it. "Couldn't you stay for another week?"

"I couldn't justify the time," she said miserably. "I can't just chuck my job and do what I please. I don't depend on my mother for my livelihood, you know," she added. "I work for my living."

He was more morose than he'd felt in years. He pulled in his own line and curled it around the pole. "I know how that is," he said. "I work for my living, too." He turned his head and looked down at her. He wanted to ask her to stay. He wanted to tell her what he was beginning to feel for her. But he couldn't find the words.

She saw the hesitation and wondered about it. He

got to his feet and gathered the poles silently, placing them back in the truck. He glanced deliberately at his watch.

"I've got another group of cattlemen checking in at the feedlot later," he said, lifting his eyes to hers. "I'd offer you lunch, but I'm not going to have time."

She smiled. "That's okay. I enjoyed the fishing trip. Even though we didn't catch any fish," she added.

He wished he could make some humorous reply, but his heart was heavy and sad. He put out the campfire, gathered up the frying pan and the bottle of vegetable oil and put everything in the truck.

He drove her back to the motel in silence, his whole manner preoccupied and remote.

She got out at the door to her room, hesitating with the passenger door of the truck open. "I don't guess you ever get to Denver?" she asked.

He shook his head. "Not much reason to."

"And this is the only time I've ever been to Jacobsville. I guess they won't send me back."

He searched her face and it hurt him to see the sadness in her dark eyes. He was remembering Anita again, he thought irritably, remembering how it had felt to lose her.

"It's been fun," he said with a forced smile. "I'm glad I got to know you. Keep up with that medicine," he added firmly.

"I'll take care of myself." She hesitated. "You do the same," she added gently.

He hated the concern in her eyes, the softness in

her voice. He didn't want to love someone who was in such a hurry to leave him.

He leaned over and closed the door. "Have a safe trip home," he said. He threw up a hand and gunned the truck out of the parking lot.

Candy stared after him, perplexed. She'd thought they were building toward something, but he seemed anxious to get away from her. She bit her lower lip and turned to go into her room. Amazing how wrong her instincts were lately, she thought as she opened the door and went inside. She seemed to have no judgment whatsoever about men.

Guy, DRIVING FURIOUSLY back to the feedlot, was feeling something similar. He couldn't bring himself to beg her to stay, after all. If her job was so important, then who was he to stop her? Perhaps he'd been too hasty and she didn't want him on any permanent basis. That made him irritable, and the more he thought about it, the more frustrated he got.

By early evening, he was boiling mad. He had supper in the bunkhouse and then drove himself out of town to the most notorious bar in the county and proceeded to drink himself into forgetfulness.

He realized the stupidity of it, so he drank more. In no time at all he was bleary-eyed and spoiling for a fight.

Cy Parks, usually unsociable and rarely seen around town, had stopped by the joint for a beer and saw him. He had a good idea why Guy was there, and he knew just the person to do something about the situation. He walked right back out the door and drove himself to the motel where Candy was staying.

He rapped on the door with his good hand. She came to open it, still wearing jeans and a tank top, with her long hair around her shoulders. She gaped when she realized who was standing at her door.

"Mr. Parks!" she exclaimed. "Did you come to tell me something else about your operation, for the article?" she asked, voicing the most likely reason for his presence here.

He shook his head. "I phoned Justin Ballenger from my car and asked where you were staying." His black eyes glittered, and not just with impatience. He almost looked amused. "I thought you might like to know that Guy Fenton is getting tanked up at the local dive. He looks in the mood to break something. I thought you might like to try your hand at keeping him out of jail."

"Jail?" she exclaimed.

He nodded. "Rumor is that the sheriff won't give him a second chance if he wrecks the bar again."

"Oh, dear," she murmured. She sighed. "Can you drive me out there?"

He nodded again. "That's why I came."

She didn't hesitate. She all but jumped into the passenger seat of his luxury car and fastened her seat belt before he climbed in behind the wheel.

"I made him fly," she said heavily. "I had an asthma attack at the Caldwell place and he had to get me back to town in a hurry, so he had to fly Matt's plane. I brought back all the memories of the girl who died in the plane crash. Poor Guy."

He glanced at her. "Are you sure that's what sent him out to the bar?"

"I can't think of anything else."

He smiled to himself. "Justin says you told him you'll be leaving tomorrow."

"That's right," she said with resignation. "The boss only gave me a week to do these articles. I can't stay any longer."

He didn't reply to that. But his whole look was speculative as he drove. He pulled up at the bar and switched the engine off.

"Want me to go in with you?" he asked.

She glanced at the sheer size of him, and almost said yes. He looked tough, and she knew that having a damaged hand wouldn't save any man who challenged him. But it would be cowardly to take protection in with her, she considered.

"Thanks, but I think I'll go in by myself," she said.

"I'll wait out here, then," he replied. "Just in case."

She smiled. "Thanks."

She got out and walked warily into the bar. There was a hush, nothing like the regular sounds of clinking glasses and conversation and loud music. The band was sitting quietly. The customers were grouped around a pool table. As she watched, a pool cue came up and went down again and there was an ominous cracking sound, followed by a thud and a louder bump.

Following her intuition, she pushed through the crowd. Guy was leaning over a cowboy with a bleed-

ing nose, both big fists curled and a dangerous look
on his face.

She moved right up to him, without hesitation, and
caught one of his big fists in her hands.

He jerked upright and stared at her as if he was
hallucinating.

"Candy?" he rasped.

She nodded. She smiled with more self-confidence
than she felt. "Come on, Guy."

She tugged at his fist until it uncurled and grasped
her soft hand. She smiled shyly at the fascinated au-
dience and tugged again, so that Guy stumbled after
her.

"Don't forget your hat!" a cowboy called, and
sailed Guy's wide-brimmed hat toward them. Candy
caught it.

There were murmurs that grew louder as they
made it to the front door.

Guy took a deep breath of night air on the steps
and almost keeled over. Candy got under his arm to
steady him.

"My God, girl, you shouldn't...be here," he managed to say, curling his arm closer. "Anything could
have happened to you in a joint like this!"

"Mr. Parks said they'd arrest you if you broke it
up again," she said simply. "You rescued me. So now
I'm rescuing you."

He began to chuckle. "Do tell?" he drawled. "Well,
now that you've got me, what are you going to do with
me?" he asked in a sensuous tone.

"If she had any sense, she'd lay a frying pan over

your thick skull," Cy Parks muttered. He moved Candy out of the way and propelled Guy to the car. He shoved him headfirst into the backseat and slammed the door after him.

"We'll drop him off at the feedlot and then I'll take you home. Justin can send somebody for the truck."

"What are you doing here?" Guy asked belligerently. "Did she bring you?"

"Sure," Cy said sarcastically as he cranked the car and pulled it out of the parking lot onto the highway. "She drove my car to my house and tossed me in and forced me to come after you."

Guy blinked. That didn't sound quite right.

"I'm sorry I made you fly," Candy said, leaning over the backseat to look at Guy. "I know that was what did this to you."

"What, flying?" he murmured in some confusion. He pushed back sweaty hair. "Hell, no, it wasn't that."

"Then what was it?" she asked hesitantly.

"You want to go home," he said heavily. He leaned back and closed his eyes, oblivious to the rapt stare of the woman in the front seat. "You want to walk off and leave me. I had a job I was beginning to like, but if I can't have you, I have nothing worth going on for."

Cy exchanged an amused glance with a shocked Candy. "What if she stayed?" Cy asked. "What good is a man who gets stinking drunk every Saturday night?"

"If she stayed I wouldn't have any reason to get drunk every Saturday night," Guy muttered drowsily. "Could get a little house, and she could plant flowers," he murmured on a yawn. "A man would work himself to death for a woman like her. So special…"

He fell asleep.

Candy felt her heart try to climb right out of her body. "He's just drunk," she rationalized.

"It's like truth serum," Cy retorted. "So now you know." He glanced at her. "Still leaving town?"

"Are you kidding?" she asked, wide-eyed. "After a confession like that? I am not! I'm going to be his shadow until he buys me a ring!"

Cy Parks actually threw back his head and laughed.

Guy came to in a big bed that wasn't his own. He opened his eyes and there was a ceiling, but it didn't look like the ceiling in the bunkhouse. He heard soft breathing. Also not his own.

He turned his head, and there, beside him in the bed with just a sheet covering her, was a sleeping Candy Marshall. She was wearing a pink silk gown that covered only certain parts of her exquisite body, and her long dark hair was spread over the white pillow like silk.

He looked down and found that he was still wearing last night's clothing, minus his boots. He cleared his throat and his head began to throb.

"Oh, boy," he groaned when he realized what had happened. The question was, how had he gotten here, in bed with Candy?

She stirred. Her eyes opened, dark velvet, soft and amused and loving.

"What are we doing here in bed together?" he asked dazedly.

"Not much," she drawled.

He chuckled softly and grabbed his head.

"How about some aspirin and coffee?" she asked.

"How about shooting me?" he offered as an alternative.

She climbed out of the bed, graceful and sensuous, and went to plug in the coffeemaker that was provided with the room. She had cups, and she went to her purse and pulled out a bottle of aspirin. Before she shook them out, she paused to use the preventative inhalant Dr. Morris had prescribed.

"Good girl," Guy murmured huskily.

She glanced at him and smiled. "Well, I have to take care of myself so I can take care of you." She brought him the aspirin and a glass of water. "Take those," she directed. "And if you *ever* go into a bar again on Saturday night, I really will lay an iron skillet across your skull!"

"They'll arrest you for spousal abuse," he pointed out.

"Put your money where your mouth is," she challenged.

He chuckled weakly as he swallowed the aspirin. "Okay. Will you marry me, warts and all?"

"We've only known each other a week," she stated. "You might not like me when you get to know me."

"Yes, I will. Will you marry me?"

She smiled. "Sure."

He laughed with pure delight. "Care to come down here and seal the bargain?"

She hesitated. "No, I don't think so. You're in disgrace. First you can get over the hangover and clean yourself up a bit."

He sighed. "I guess I do look pretty raunchy."

She nodded. "And you still smell like a brewery. By the way, I don't drink. Never."

He held up a hand. "I've just reformed. From now on it's coffee, tea or milk. I swear."

"Good man. In that case, we can get married next week. Before Saturday night," she added with a smile.

He opened his eyes wide and studied her with possessiveness. "It wasn't flying at all," he said softly. "It was losing you. I couldn't bear the thought that you were going to go off and leave me. But this time the alcohol didn't work. I've lost my taste for bars and temporary oblivion. If you'll marry me, I won't need temporary oblivion. I'll build you a house where you can plant flowers." His gaze dropped down over her slender body. "We can have children, if it's safe for you."

She beamed. "I'd like that."

"It might be risky."

"We'll go ask Dr. Morris," she assured him. "Since I'm going to be living in Jacobsville, he can be my doctor."

He just stared at her, his heart in his eyes. "I didn't know it could happen like this," he said aloud. "I thought love died and was buried. It isn't."

She smiled brilliantly. "I never even knew what it was. Until now."

He opened his arms and she went down into them, and they lay for a long time just holding each other tightly in the shared wonder of loving.

He lifted his head finally and looked down at the treasure in his arms. "I suppose, if you want to, I can go back to my air cargo company and run it."

"Do you want to?"

He thought about that for a minute before he answered her. "Not really," he said finally. "It was a part of my life that I enjoyed at the time, but there will always be bad memories connected with it." He put his hand over her lips when she started to speak. "I'm not still grieving for Anita," he added quietly. "I'll always miss her a little, and regret the way she died. But I didn't bury my heart with her. I want you and a family and a home of our own. I enjoy managing the feedlot. In many ways, it's a challenge." He grinned. "And if you'd take over publicity for the local cattlemen's association, we'd have a lot more in common."

She beamed. "Would they let me?"

"They'd beg you!" he replied. "Poor old Mrs. Harrison is doing it right now, and she hates every word she writes. She'll make you cakes and pies if you'll take it off her hands."

"In that case, I might enjoy it," she replied.

"And we'd get to work together," he murmured, bending to kiss her gently. He lifted his head. "Oh,

Candy, what did I ever do to deserve someone like you?" he asked huskily. "I do love you so!"

She pulled him down to her. "I love you, too."

NEITHER OF THEM questioned how love could strike so suddenly. They got married and spent their honeymoon in Galveston, going for long walks on the beach and lying in each others' arms enjoying the newness of loving in every possible way.

"My mother wants us to come and visit her when we're back from our honeymoon," she mentioned to Guy after a long, sweet morning of shared ecstasy. She curled closer to him under the single sheet that covered them. "She said she hoped we'd be happy."

"We will be," he mused, stroking her long hair with a gentle hand. "Do you want to go?"

"I think it's time I made my peace with her," she replied. "Maybe I've been as guilty as she has of living in the past. Not anymore," she added, looking up at him with love brimming over in her eyes. "Marriage is fun," she said with a wicked grin.

"Is it, now?" He threw off the sheet and rolled over onto her with a chuckle. "Was that a hint?" he whispered as he began to kiss her.

She slid against him with delight and wrapped a soft, long leg around his muscular one. "A blatant hint," she agreed, gasping as he touched her gently and his mouth settled on her parted lips.

"Anything to oblige," he whispered huskily.

She laughed and gasped, and then clung to him as the lazy rhythm made spirals of ecstasy ripple the length of her body. She closed her eyes and gave in to the pleasure. Love, she thought while she could, was the most indescribable of shared delights.

Outside the window, waves crashed on the beach and seagulls dived and cried in the early-morning sunlight. Somewhere on the boundary of her senses, Candy heard them, but she was so close to heaven that the sound barely registered.

When the stormy delight passed, she held an exhausted Guy to her heart and thought of flower gardens in a future that was suddenly sweet and full of joy. She closed her eyes and smiled as she dreamed.

Guy felt her body go lax. He looked down at her sleeping face with an expression that would have brought tears to her eyes. From a nightmare to this, he was thinking. Candy had made him whole again. She'd chased away the guilt of the past, and the grief, and offered him a new heart to cherish. He knew without a doubt that his drinking days were over. Candy would make his happiness, and he'd make hers.

He settled back down beside her and drew the sheet over them both. In his mind, before he fell asleep, he was already working on plans for that small house where he and Candy would share their lives.

* * * * *

HANK

CHAPTER ONE

SHE WAS THERE AGAIN. Hank Shoeman glared out the window at the figure on the balcony of the ski lodge below. His cabin was on a ridge overlooking the facility, just far enough away to give him the privacy he needed when he was composing. But it wasn't far enough away from the binoculars the slender young woman at the ski lodge was directing toward his living room window.

He shoved his hands into his jeans pockets and glowered at the distant figure. He was used to attention. Leader of the rock group Desperado, and a former linebacker for the Dallas Cowboys, Hank had had his share of adulation from women. In the old days, before his marriage and divorce, it had been flattering and heady to a Texas ranch boy. Now, it was nothing more than a nuisance. He'd had all he wanted of love. And he'd had more than he wanted of star-struck young girls looking for it.

He sighed, the action pulling his silk shirt taut over a hard, impressively muscular chest, and tautening the jeans that outlined powerful long legs and narrow hips. He was thirty-eight, but physically he looked no more than thirty. He had a good body, still fit and athletic. It was his face that frightened people.

He wore a thick beard and a mustache and his dark hair, while scrupulously clean, was unruly and thick around his collar. He wasn't bad-looking, but it was impossible to see that. He liked the camouflage, because it kept all but the most enthusiastic young groupies at bay.

None of the rock group looked much better than Hank with his growth of beard, except for Amanda, of course. The other three male members of the band—Deke and Jack and Johnson—looked as disreputable as Hank did. But Desperado's music won awards, and they were much in demand for public appearances.

The problem with that right now was that Amanda was pregnant. It would be the first child for Amanda and her husband, Quinn Sutton, who lived in Wyoming with his son Elliot. The whole family was anxious because Amanda's pregnancy had been fraught with problems and she'd been forced to take to her bed to prevent a miscarriage. That meant canceled public appearances and vicious rumors that the band was about to break up. It was let people think that, or admit that Amanda was in fierce difficulties with her pregnancy. No one wanted that tidbit of information to get out, and have reporters hounding her. For the moment, they didn't know exactly where in Wyoming she lived. And Hank was here in Colorado, far away from the group's studios—both the one down the hill from Quinn Sutton's ranch in the Tetons, and the one in New York City.

Reporters had hounded him so much that he'd had to escape from the New York studio where the group did some of their recording. It had been impossible to go near Amanda's house, for fear of leading reporters right to her doorstep.

So, this cabin in Colorado was Hank's last resort. He'd come here to work on a new song which he hoped might be a contender for another award. The music had been written, now it was up to Hank to complete the lyrics, but it was slow going. Worrying about Amanda and the future of the group was not conducive to creative effort.

Perhaps he was working too hard, he thought. He needed a break. That woman at the ski lodge was getting on his nerves. If she was a reporter spying on him, he wanted to know it. There had to be some way to get her off his trail and spare Amanda any further media blitz.

He shrugged into his parka and drove to the ski lodge in his white Bronco. The chains made a metallic rhythm on the thick-packed snow covering the road that led to the lodge. Bad weather had plagued the area this January, and there had just been a long period of subzero temperatures and blinding snow, which had made it impossible to ski for the past several days.

When he got to the lodge, it wasn't crowded at all. People who could get out had already gone. Only a handful of hearty, optimistic souls were left in residence, hoping for slightly less arctic temperatures and better skiing when conditions improved.

He walked into the lodge, towering over everyone and attracting a lot of unwanted attention. He went straight to the owner's office.

Mark Jennings got up from his desk and walked around it to shake hands with the visitor.

"What brings you down here, Hank?" he asked with a grin. "Lonesome, are you?"

"I should be so lucky," Hank murmured dryly. "I came down to see which one of your guests is auditioning for the KGB."

Mark's smile faded. "What?"

"You've got a guest with binoculars who spends a lot of time looking in through my living room window," he replied. "I want to know who she is and what she's looking for."

Mark whistled. "I had no idea."

"It's not your job to watch the guests," the other man said, clapping him on the shoulder with a big hand. "Maybe she's a groupie. I'd like to know, in case she's trying to gather material for the wire services. I've had enough publicity just lately."

"I understand. What can I do to help?"

"I thought I'd hang out in the café for a while and see if she turns up for lunch. I'd recognize her. She's wearing a bright blue parka and a matching cap."

Mark frowned. "Doesn't sound familiar, but I don't get out of this office much lately. We don't have a lot of people staying here, though, so she shouldn't be too hard to spot."

"If you don't mind, I'll have a look around."

Mark nodded. "Help yourself. Any chance that

you and the group might sign on next season for entertainment?" he added hopefully.

Hank chuckled. "Ask me again in a few months."

"Don't think I won't!"

Hank shook hands with him and went on into the café, shucking his parka as he walked. It was a bad time to have to hunt down a spy. He was already upset enough about Amanda and the relentless press. Lately his career was playing a bad second to complications of every sort.

He glanced around as he walked into the small café. There were only three women in it. Two of them were drinking coffee at a table overlooking the ski lift. The other was clearing tables. She saw Hank and grinned.

"Hi, Hank," she greeted him, tossing back her blond hair. "Long time no see!"

"I've been busy, Carol," he said with an affectionate smile. She'd been a waitress at Mark's place for several years. There was nothing romantic between them; she was just a friend.

She moved closer, so that they wouldn't be overheard. "Better watch your step down here today," she said confidentially. "One of the women at the side table is a reporter for *Rolling Stone*. I heard her telling the other woman that she'd gotten some juicy gossip about Amanda and that you were in hiding up here. She said she was going to file a really big story with her magazine over her computer modem tonight."

He caught his breath in muted anger and stared at the table intently. One of the women was very petite with short dark hair. The other was a redhead, attractive and full figured. He scowled. "Which is which?" he asked impatiently.

She grimaced. "That's the thing, I couldn't tell. I dropped a plate and I wasn't looking at them when I overheard her. Sorry, Hank. You know most of their reporters, don't you?"

He nodded. "But I don't recognize either of those women. She could be a stringer or even a free-lancer, hoping to find something worth selling to them on a tentative go-ahead."

"I'll bet it's the redhead," she whispered. "She looks like a reporter."

"And I'd bet on the brunette," he remarked as he suddenly registered the color of her jacket. Royal blue. She was the one who'd been spying on him with the binoculars.

"Could be," Carol replied. "I wish I could be more help. Heard from the rest of the group?"

He shook his head. "We're all taking a rest from public appearances."

"I guess you need one! Give everyone my best, won't you?"

"Sure."

He watched the women from the next room, staying out of sight for a minute, before leaving the lodge. He was easily recognizable these days, with all the media attention, and he couldn't afford to give that reporter a shot at him.

He was going to have to do something, but what? If she filed that story, reporters were going to swarm

Amanda like ducks on bugs. He couldn't have that. Her pregnancy had been one big secret so far, ever since she started to show and the band cut short their tour. They were still recording, but no one knew why they'd left the road so quickly. Where Amanda was, on Quinn Sutton's ranch, no one was likely to be able to get near her. Quinn was a formidable bodyguard, and he loved his pretty blond wife to distraction even if they'd gotten off to one of the world's worst starts.

He leaned against the hood of the Bronco, ignoring the sudden snow flurries and folded his arms over his chest while he tried to decide on a course of action. How was he going to prevent the reporter from filing her story? All sorts of wild ideas occurred to him, the first being that he could cut the telephone wires.

"Great solution," he murmured to himself. "You should try writing fiction."

As he turned over possible solutions to his problem, lo and behold, the brunette came walking out the front door of the ski lodge with a camera and binoculars around her neck and a backpack over one shoulder. She came down the steps and started around the Bronco and Hank when the perfect solution presented itself to him on a silver platter.

Without thinking about consequences, jail terms or FBI intervention, he suddenly walked behind her, picked her up bodily and slid her into the Bronco past the steering wheel. Before she could get over the shock, he had the vehicle headed up the mountain.

Poppy O'Brien stared at him with wide dark eyes full of shock. "Either I'm still asleep and dreaming or I'm being kidnapped by a grizzly bear," she said suddenly.

"I'm not a grizzly bear."

"You look like a grizzly bear."

He didn't look at her. "Insults won't do you any good."

"Listen, I have terrible diseases…" she began, using a ploy she'd heard on a television talk show.

"Don't flatter yourself," he remarked with a speaking glance. "I don't seduce midgets."

"Midgets?" Her dark eyes widened. "I'm five foot five!"

He shrugged. "Okay. So you're a tall midget. You're still too small for a man my size."

She looked at him fully then. His head almost touched the roof of the Bronco. He was huge; not fat, but well built and powerful looking. "Are you one of those wild-eyed mountain men who kidnap hikers?"

He shook his head.

"Hopelessly lonely and desperate for companionship?"

He smiled reluctantly. "Not a chance."

"Then would you like to tell me why you've kidnapped me?"

"No."

She leaned back against the seat. He looked sane, but one could never tell. She studied him with curiosity and just a little apprehension. "What are you going to do with me?" she asked again.

"I don't know."

"That's reassuring."

"I won't hurt you."

"That's even more reassuring." She frowned as she studied him. "You look familiar."

"Everyone says that."

"Have you ever worn a wide-brimmed hat and asked people not to start forest fires?"

He did chuckle then. "Not lately."

"I'm on my way to look for a lost dog. I promised."

"He'll come home."

She glared at him. "After I've found the dog, I have to pack. I'm leaving tomorrow," she informed him.

"Fat chance."

She took in a sharp breath. "Now you listen here, Tarzan of the Snow Country, what you're doing is a federal offense. You could be arrested. You could go to jail."

"Why?"

"Because you're kidnapping me!"

"I'm doing no such thing," he returned, pulling up into the driveway of the cabin. "I'm extending my hospitality to a ski lodge guest who was lost in the mountains."

"I am not lost!" she stormed. "I was at the ski lodge, right in front of the ski lodge…!"

"You looked lost to me. It's snowing. Very hard, too," he remarked as he got out of the truck. In fact, it was worse than snow. It looked like the beginnings of a blizzard. "Come on. Let's get inside."

She folded her arms. "I am not leaving the truck," she informed him bluntly.

"It isn't a truck. It's a four-wheel-drive vehicle."

She lifted her chin. "Oh, details, details! I am not...ohh!"

In the middle of her impassioned resistance, he picked her up and carried her to the cabin.

She was too shocked to resist. She'd been independent most of her life, and at twenty-six she was used to being on her own. She was attractive, and she knew it, but she was also intelligent and studious, traits that didn't endear her to suitors. Her choice of career had made it impossible for her to carry on any sort of affair. She'd spent years in school with midterms and final exams always hanging over her head, with lab after lab eating up her free time. The only people she spent time with were fellow students. The curriculum required for a science degree was so much more difficult than that required for a liberal arts degree that it often seemed she did nothing but study.

And then after graduation, there was the apprenticeship, and that required all sorts of odd hours that none of the other partners wanted. She was the one who spent weekends and holidays and nights at work. Two boyfriends had quickly given her up for women who had nine-to-five day jobs and were geared to nights on the town.

None of that had prepared her for being swept off her feet, literally, by a blue-eyed grizzly bear.

The sheer power and size of his body had her as spellbound as a young girl. She lay in his huge arms like a statue, gaping up at him as he balanced her easily on one knee while he unlocked the cabin door.

He caught that rapt stare and laughed mirthlessly.
He was used to the look. His ex-wife had found him
fascinating at first. Afterward, it was his best friend
and the man's bank account that fascinated her. The
divorce was inevitable, with all the time Hank spent
on the road. His best friend had probably been inevitable, too. Hank was powerful and talented, but he
wasn't handsome. His best friend was. He'd given in
to the divorce without a protest, and the parting had
been amicable—on the surface, at least. He'd settled
a nice amount of money on her. She was grateful. He
was alone, as usual. He'd gone home afterward to
the Texas ranch that his father and five brothers still
owned. It had been comforting there, but he never had
fit in. The only horse big enough for him to ride was
a Percheron and he'd never been able to spin a rope.
He often thought that his brothers despaired of him.

He put the woman down and closed the door, lock-
ing it and pocketing the key. Then he took a good,
long look at her. She was attractive, pert and pretty
and a little irritated. Her dark eyes glared up at him
fearlessly.

"You can't keep me here," she informed him.

"Why not?"

"Because I have responsibilities. I have a job. I
need a telephone right now, as a matter of fact, so
that I can tell someone I'm not looking for that dog."

"Dream on," he said pleasantly. "Can you cook?"

Her eyebrows lifted. "Cook what?"

"Anything."

He was stripping off his parka as he spoke. Her

eyes drifted over a magnificent body in jeans and a well-fitting, long-sleeved red shirt. He could have graced a magazine cover. He was perfectly proportioned and huge. He made her feel like a child as he towered over her.

"I can cook toast," she said absently. "How tall are you?"

"Six foot five," he said.

"You must eat like a horse."

He shrugged. "I use up a lot of calories."

She was still staring at him, fascinated. "Who are you?"

He laughed without humor and his blue eyes began to glitter. "Pull the other one."

"I beg your pardon?"

"You might as well get comfortable," he informed her. "You're going to be here for several days."

"I am not. I'll walk back to the lodge."

"Not in that you won't," he said, gesturing toward the window, where snow was coming down outside at a frightening rate.

She gnawed on her lower lip, a nervous habit that often resulted in a sore mouth. "Oh dear," she said uneasily, more worried about the possibility of losing her job than of being sequestered here with a madman.

"You'll be perfectly safe here," he said, mistaking her apprehension. "I won't attack you."

"Oh dear, oh dear," she repeated again. "They'll think I'm having too good a time to come back. They'll think I'm not serious about my job. They didn't really want me in the beginning because they thought I was too young. They'll use this as an excuse to find someone to replace me."

"No doubt," he said irritably. "But what does it matter? You'll find another job."

She glared at him. "Not like this one, I won't!"

"Pays good, does it?" he asked, thinking that reporters always seemed to get a high rate of pay for selling out people's private lives for public consumption.

"Very good," she retorted, "with excellent chances for advancement."

"Too bad."

"You have no right to keep me here," she informed him.

"You had no right to spy on me," he returned.

Her face stiffened. "I beg your pardon?"

"You've had those damned binoculars trained up here for the past few days," he said shortly. "Spying on me."

"Spying…and why, pray tell, would I want to spy on you? Do you think I'm so desperate for a man that I have to peek through windows to get a glimpse of one?"

"You don't need to play games with me," he said coolly. "I'm not likely to be taken in by you. I'm an old hand at fending off groupies."

"This is unreal," she snapped. "Things like this don't happen except in books and movies! Men don't go around kidnapping women unless it's a desert and they're wearing long sheets!"

"Sorry," he said. "I didn't have a sheet handy."

"And what do you mean, calling me a groupie?" She put her hands on her slim hips and glowered up at him with flashing dark eyes.

"Why were you spying on me?"

"Spying…!" She threw up her hands. "I was watching a bald eagle," she said shortly. "They've just released a pair of them ten miles north of the ski lodge, as part of a federal repopulation program. I'd come to see them."

"Oh, my God, tell me you're not one of those animal-loving fanatics!"

"If there were more of us in the world, it wouldn't be in such a mess."

He looked angry as he studied her. "They tried repopulating wolves up north. The damned things are eating lambs and calves all over the mountains, and the people who released them went back home to their apartment buildings."

He said it with such sarcasm and contempt that she almost took a step backward. But she was made of sterner stuff. "Nature exists largely on a system of checks and balances. You've overlooked the fact that without predators, prey multiplies. If you don't be-lieve that, look at Australia where the rabbits hadn't enough natural enemies and overran the country."

"Well then, why don't we ship them some of our leftover wolves?" he asked smugly.

"Show me a wolf who can survive in the desert and it might be a good idea."

"You hotshot animal lovers might consider cross-breeding a wolf with a camel. I hear they're doing some fantastic genetic experiments in labs all over the country."

"To produce healthier animals and disease-resistant strains of plants."

"Hybrids," he scoffed. "Hybrids are sterile, aren't they?"

"I don't deal in experiments," she informed him hotly. "I wouldn't know."

"They turned loose two eagles. Isn't that an experiment?"

She was losing ground. "Why have you brought me here?" She tried again for an answer.

"I'm a lonely man," he said sarcastically. "I don't have any company up here, and I can't get girls. So periodically, I stake out the ski lodge and appropriate their overflow." He lifted an expressive hand. "Think of it as repopulating my bachelor environment with healthy new specimens. That should appeal to someone like you. And think of all the juicy material you can use later."

"Material? Use? For what?"

"Cut it out," he said carelessly. "We both know what you do for a living. I heard it all from Carol at the lodge."

"Carol? Oh, the blond waitress." She sighed. "Well, I guess it doesn't matter if you know, does it? I mean, I wasn't exactly hiding it from anyone."

"Just as I thought. Now. How about something to eat?" He indicated the window. "It's highly doubtful that you could go anywhere right now even if I was willing to let you leave. Which I'm not."

She pursed her full lips and stared up at him curiously. "When the snow clears, I'm heading out," she informed him sweetly. "Or you'll find yourself in jail the minute I can get to a telephone."

"Threats are only useful when you can enforce them."

"And you think I can't?"

"I think that by the time you leave, you won't need any." He was hopeful that he could convince her not to bother Amanda. He was persuasive when he tried to be, and if she liked animals, she had to have a soft center. Knowing the enemy was half the battle. He didn't think he was in for any surprises with her.

CHAPTER TWO

"WHAT'S YOUR NAME?" he asked as he fried bacon.

"Poppy O'Brien," she replied. "And yours?"

He chuckled. She was a game player, all right. "Call me Hank."

"Hank what?"

He glanced toward her with an insolent smile. "Just Hank," he said with faint challenge.

She joined him in the kitchen. "Have it your way. I suppose if I'd kidnapped someone I wouldn't want to give them my real name, either." She started opening cabinets.

"What are you doing?" he demanded. It irritated him that she felt free to rifle through his kitchen.

"I'm going to make biscuits. Unless you think you can."

"I can make biscuits," he said defensively.

"A lot of people can. But can you eat them?" she asked.

He hesitated. After a minute, he paused in his own chore and produced vegetable shortening, flour, milk and a big bowl. "Go for it."

She rolled up the sleeves of her blue sweater and

proceeded to make drop biscuits. He'd finished with the bacon and was working on beating eggs in a bowl.

"They'll be cold by the time the biscuits get done if you cook them now," she said pointedly.

He didn't argue. He finished beating the eggs, covered the bowl and put them in the refrigerator. Then he perched himself on the edge of the big table and watched her pat the biscuits into a pan and dab milk onto the tops.

"You do that as if it's a regular thing with you," he commented.

"It is," she said. "I've been feeding myself for a long time. Eating out is expensive. I cook a lot."

"Do you cook for someone?" he probed.

She smiled as she put the biscuits into the oven she'd already had him preheat. "Yes. For myself."

He stuck his hands into his pockets and stared her down.

She lifted a shoulder. "I don't have time for that sort of thing," she said. "I work nights and weekends and holidays. Before I got this job, I was in school."

High school, he figured, by the look of her. She seemed very young. She wasn't hard on the eyes at all, with that trim figure and her big dark eyes and soft oval face. She had a vulnerable manner that appealed to his masculinity. His wife had been a take-charge sort of woman, very businesslike and intelligent, but with hard edges that he could never smooth. She liked being a real-estate executive and she had no thoughts of being a housewife and mother. She didn't like children. She did enjoy pretty clothes and parties, though.

His best friend was taking her to a lot of those, he heard.

Poppy glanced at him and saw the expression that narrowed his deep blue eyes. "Do you have someone to cook for?" she asked bluntly. If he could ask questions, so could she.

"I was married," he said flatly. "She took up with my best friend and divorced me. I wasn't home enough to suit her."

"I'm sorry."

"Don't be. It was a friendly divorce. We weren't compatible." He looked down at his hand-tooled leather boots. "I wanted kids. I have a bunch of brothers back home."

She leaned back against the pine counter and folded her arms across her chest. "I don't have any family left. My mother died when I was born and my father was killed in an airplane crash four years ago."

"Are you an only child?"

She nodded. "It's a good thing I was goal-oriented and self-sufficient, I guess," she confessed. "I threw myself into studying and got over it in time."

"How did you manage to support yourself while you got through high school?" he asked curiously.

"High school?" Her eyes widened. "I was in college." She laughed. "How old do you think I am?"

"Eighteen. Maybe nineteen."

She grinned. "Thanks. I'm twenty-six."

His heavy brows drew together. "Hell!"

"I am. I have a degree."

"In what—"

The thunderous, crashing sound outside cut him off. He rushed to the window and looked out. Snow had come off the mountain above the lodge in a small avalanche, taking down telephone lines and power lines.

"Good thing Mark's got emergency generators," he murmured. "So have I. But those telephone lines are well and truly out until this weather clears a little."

"Do you have a phone?" she asked from beside him.

He looked at her. "No. I've been using the phone at the lodge. I hate telephones. Unlisted numbers are a farce—there's no such thing. You ought to know that."

She wondered how he did know that her private line was flooded with calls from people at two in the morning whose problems couldn't wait until the office opened.

She laughed. "Well, yes, I do know."

He glanced back out the window. "The lodge is okay, at least. I met a guy in the ski patrol this morning when I went out for supplies. He said they'd checked the slopes earlier and there was no threat. I wonder what caused the avalanche?"

"People skiing outside the safe boundary, a gunshot from an irresponsible hunter, God knows." She grimaced. "I hope that poor dog got found."

"Marshmallow heart," he accused. "The only dog I know of around here is a stray who hangs around the lodge for handouts. He belongs to a retired Austrian skier who lives about a half mile over the hill. That dog knows these mountains better than any human being, and he doesn't get lost. Somebody was pulling your leg." One eye narrowed. "Who sent you out?"

She frowned. "It was one of the younger ski instructors, the one they call Eric. He said that he'd start from the other end of the trail and we'd meet in the middle at some little cabin…" She stopped. "Why are you laughing?"

"Eric Bayer," he said, nodding. "They call him St. Bernard, because he's pulled that lost-dog stunt so many times with pretty young tourists. That cabin is almost a shrine to his prowess as a lover."

She flushed to her hairline. He watched, smiling.

"Where do you come from?" he asked lazily.

"Sioux City, Iowa," she said. "Why?"

"It figures." He moved back into the kitchen just in time to remove the biscuits before they burned. They looked light and fluffy and they were just tanned enough to be tempting. "Nice," he pronounced.

"Thanks." She got butter from the refrigerator while he scrambled the eggs. She made coffee and when the eggs were ready, she poured it into two thick mugs and put them on the small, square kitchen table.

"Forks," he said, handing her one. "I don't fuss with table settings when I'm alone here."

"Ah," she said. "So you're not usually alone?"

"Only when I'm working." He raised his fork and took a mouthful of scrambled egg. "And you should know," he added mockingly, "because *Rolling Stone* prints something about every visit I make here."

Her eyebrows arched. "Rolling Stone? They're a

rock group, aren't they? I thought they were in England. Do they have a newsletter?"

"You do that amazingly well," he remarked.

"Do what?"

"The innocent look," he replied, finishing his eggs before he started on the biscuits. "I wish I had some jam. I ate the last of it yesterday and forgot to get more."

"Too bad. What was that about looking innocent?"

"Eat your lunch before it gets cold. These are great biscuits!"

They must have been, he was on his fourth one. She smiled. "Breakfast for lunch," she remarked. "I can't wait to see what you eat for the evening meal."

"Cereal, usually," he remarked. "Or sandwiches. I don't cook much when I'm working. If I get a yen for breakfast in the middle of the day, I have it," he added firmly.

She smiled. "I wasn't complaining. I love breakfast."

Her easy acceptance of the odd meal put him at ease. He finished eating and sat back with the coffee mug in one huge hand and looked at her. She was small. Not tiny, but small, and beautifully proportioned. He liked her soft complexion and those big brown eyes. She had a pretty mouth, too, very full and sweet-looking.

"I feel I should tell you that I know karate."

His eyebrows lifted. "Do you, really?"

She nodded.

He smiled lazily. "Do you really think it would do you any good against someone my size?" he asked gently.

She looked him over. "You ruined it."

"Ruined what?"

"I was going to tell you that I knew karate and several *other* Japanese words."

It took a minute to sink in. When it did, he began to laugh.

She smiled, too. "And to answer that, no, I don't think it would do me a bit of good against someone your size. Even if I knew how to use it." She finished her coffee and put the mug down. "Why did you think I was spying on you?"

"You kept looking in my living room window."

"The eagle was sitting on the top limb of one of those aspen trees behind your house."

He let out a soft whistle. "There really was an eagle?"

"Two of them," she amended. "Beautiful eagles. They're huge birds. I'd never seen any up close before. I thought they were small, but they aren't, and they have pale golden eyes."

"I've seen eagles," he replied. "I spend a lot of time here and in Wyoming."

"I'd love to see Wyoming," she remarked. "I've always wanted to go to Cheyenne during the rodeo season."

"Don't you animal lovers consider rodeo a cruel sport?" he taunted.

"I'm not a fanatic," she said pointedly. "And I know

better than some people how well treated most rodeo stock is. My dad used to handle bulls for the bull-riding events, back in Oklahoma."

"I thought you said you were from Sioux City."

"I live there now. I grew up outside Oklahoma City." She touched the rim of the coffee cup. "Where are you from?"

She was laying it on thick, but he was too tired to question her. He'd been up late for the better part of a week trying to write lyrics that just wouldn't come. "I'm from Texas, up near Dallas."

"Around the cross-timbers country?" She smiled at his surprise. "I've been through there a time or two with Dad, when he went to rodeos."

"It's pretty country. So is this."

The portable generator made a noise and he glared toward the back of the house. "Damn that thing," he muttered. "I knew I should have replaced it. If it goes out, we'll freeze and starve to death in here."

"Hardly," she said. "There's plenty of cut wood out front and you have a fireplace. I know how to cook on a fireplace."

"Good thing," he muttered. "I sure as hell don't."

"I gather that there's no way out of here except down the mountain we just came up?"

He nodded.

She looked out at the blinding snow and rubbed her arms. "You still haven't told me why you brought me up here."

"Does it matter now?" he asked. "You can't leave, anyway. From the looks of that snow, we're going to be cabin-bound for a few days until they can get the snowplows in."

"Well, yes, I think it does matter," she replied. "After all, nobody's ever tried to kidnap me before. I'd like to know what I've done."

"Why do you insist on playing games with me?" he muttered. "I know who you are!"

"Yes, you've already said so."

"Then you know what you've done," he said. "You threatened to call in a story that would damage several careers and possibly cost a woman her child."

"Call in a story." She repeated it again, staring blankly at him. "Call it in to whom? And how would I, since the only things I know how to fill out are medical reports?"

"Medical reports?"

She glowered at him. "Yes, medical reports, prescriptions, medicines, that sort of thing. I have a degree. I'm in practice. That's why I need to be back home, before I lose the partnership I've worked so hard to get!"

"You're a doctor?" he bellowed.

"Yes. Dr. O'Brien!"

He slapped his hand over his forehead. "Oh, God, I got the wrong one!"

"Wrong one. Am I to gather that you meant to kidnap some other poor woman?"

"Yes!" he said impatiently. He ran his hand through his bushy, thick hair. "Damn! Damn, damn, damn, she's probably halfway to New York by now with a heaving bosom full of unsubstantiated facts!"

"She, who?" Poppy demanded.

"That damn reporter!"

"The girl I was sitting with when you came in? But she isn't due to leave for two more days. She's meeting her fiancé in Salt Lake City and then they're going on to Los Angeles."

"She is?"

"That's what she said."

He leaned forward. "This is important. Did she say anything to you about Amanda Sutton?"

"I don't remember any names," she said. "She was talking about a singer who'd vanished from sight and the breakup of a big rock group."

"Which rock group?" he asked.

She grimaced. "Sorry," she said apologetically. "I don't keep up with pop music. I like classical and opera."

He stared at her, long and hard.

"You needn't look like that," she muttered, sweeping back the fall of hair that dropped onto her brow. "There isn't one thing wrong with symphonies and opera!"

"I didn't know that anyone in the world still listened to them." From his perspective, rock music was all that existed. He spent all his time with people who composed it or played it.

"I see," she returned. "You're one of those MTV fanatics who think that music without a volcanic beat isn't worth listening to."

"I didn't say that."

"I am so *tired* of skeletal men in sprayed-on leather

pants wearing guitars for jockey shorts, with their hairy chests hanging out!"

He couldn't hold back the laughter. It overflowed like the avalanche that had brought half a ridge down a few minutes before. "You're priceless."

"Well, aren't you tired of it, really?" she persisted. "Don't you think that there's a place in the world for historical music, beautiful music?"

He sobered quickly. He didn't know how to answer that. It had been a long time since he'd listened to anything classical, and he'd certainly never thought of it in that way. "Historical music?" he asked.

"Yes." She began to smile. "It's like talking to someone who lived a century, two centuries ago. You play the notes they wrote and hear them, just as they heard them. History comes alive in that moment, when you reproduce sounds that were heard in another time."

His heart leapt in his chest. He thought about the history she'd mentioned. Then her wording came back to him.

"You said you play the notes...do you play?"

"Piano," she said. "A little. I only had lessons for five years, and I'm not gifted. But I do love music."

His face softened under its thick covering of hair. "But not rock music," he persisted.

"So much of it is noise," she said. "After you listen to it for a while, it all blurs into steel guitars. But, once in a while, another sort of song sticks its head out and a few people find magic in it." She mentioned one of his songs, one of Desperado's songs. "There

were a lot of flutes in it," she recalled, closing her eyes
and smiling as she remembered it. "Beyond it was a
high, sweet voice that enunciated every word. And
the words were poetry." Her eyes opened, dark and
soft with memory. "It was exceptional. But it wasn't
their usual sort of music, either. The announcer said
so. He said the composer did the song on a dare and
didn't even want it included on the album, but the
other members of the group insisted."

That was true. Hank had been certain that no one
would like the soft, folksy song he'd written. And
to his amazement, it had won a Grammy. He'd let
Amanda accept it for him, he recalled, because he
was too embarrassed to take credit for it publicly.
"Did you see the video?"

She shook her head. "I've never had time to watch
videos. I just listen to the radio when I'm driving."

Incredible. She loved his music and she didn't even
know who he was. He wasn't sure if he was insulted
or amused. It was the only song of that sort that he'd
ever written and he'd sworn that he'd never do another one. A lot of the music critics hadn't liked it. He
was trying to break out of the mold and they didn't
want to let him. It was a kind of musical typecasting.

"Do you remember the group the reporter was
talking about?" he asked, returning to his earlier
question.

"She told me, but I was watching the eagle out
the window," she confessed sheepishly, and with a
grin. "I'm afraid I wasn't listening. She was alone and
wanted to talk, and I was the only other person handy

when she came in. She was friendly and I didn't mind sharing the table. It was just that the eagle came pretty close to the window…"

"You really do like animals." He chuckled.

"I guess so. I was forever bringing home birds with broken wings and once I found a little snake with its tail cut off by a lawnmower. I couldn't stand to watch things suffer and not try to help."

His blue eyes searched her dark ones for longer than he meant to. She stared back, and he saw the color flood her cheeks. That amused him deep inside and he began to smile.

Poppy felt her heart race. He didn't seem to be dangerous or a threat to her in any physical way, but that smile made her feel warm all over. She hadn't been at a disadvantage, except when he'd carried her inside the cabin. Now she wondered if she shouldn't have fought a little harder for her freedom. He was very big and powerful, and if he wanted to, he could…

"You're amazingly easy to read," he remarked gently. "There's nothing to be nervous about. I don't force women. It's the other way around."

She didn't quite believe him. He had a fantastic physique, but he looked like a grizzly bear. She couldn't imagine him being beset by women.

"Are you rich?" she asked.

His eyes narrowed and the smile faded. "Meaning that I'd have to be rich to attract a woman?" he drawled with muted anger.

He hadn't moved or threatened, but the look in his eyes made her uncomfortable. "I didn't say that."

"Yes, you did."

"I didn't mean to insult you. It's just that you're, well, you're…bushy."

His lips compressed. "Bushy?"

"You look like a grizzly bear!"

"A lot of men wear beards and mustaches!"

"Most of them have some skin on their faces that shows, too!"

He moved away from the window and took a step toward her. She took a step back.

"There's no need to start stalking me," she protested, looking him right in the eye. She stopped. "I won't run. You can't make me run. I'm not afraid of you."

She acted like a woman confronting an attack dog. It would have amused him if he'd been a little less insulted.

"I haven't had to chase women in ten years," he said through his teeth, and kept coming. "They chase me. They hound me. I can't even check into a hotel without having someone search the room. I could have a woman twice a day if I felt like it, and I wouldn't have to pay them for it. I turn down more proposals in a week than you've probably had in your lifetime. But you think I look like a grizzly bear and no woman would want me unless I was rich."

She held up a hand, nervous of him now. "I didn't say that at all," she began soothingly. She came up against something hard, and realized that he'd edged her back against a wall. "Now, see here," she said firmly, "this isn't any way to win an argument, with sheer brute force."

"Isn't that what you think I'd need to get a woman?"

"I didn't mean it," she assured him. She tried to edge past him, but he put an arm that was like a small tree trunk past her on one side and another on the other side and trapped her.

"What makes you think you're qualified to judge?" he continued irritably. "You're almost thin. There's nothing to you. You act as if you've spent your life buried in books. What do you know about men?"

"I date," she said shortly. "In fact, I can go out anytime I like!" And she could, with one of her partner's sons, who seemed to have six hands and used every one of them the time she'd been crazy enough to go to a movie with him. He'd have taken her out again if she liked, but she wouldn't go to the front door with him!

"How much do you have to pay him?" he mocked.

When that sank in, she drew in an angry breath, forgot her embarrassment and fear and raised her hand sharply toward his hairy cheek.

He caught it with depressing ease and pressed it against the side of his face. The hair that grew on it was surprisingly soft, when it looked like steel wool.

"You don't know much about men's egos, do you?" he asked, bending. "If you don't learn one other thing, you'd better learn right now that insults have consequences. And I'm just the man to show you how many!"

She started to defend herself, and before she could get a single word out, his lips had opened and fitted themselves exactly to the shape of her soft, shocked mouth.

CHAPTER THREE

IT HADN'T OCCURRED to her that a human grizzly bear would be so good at kissing. He wasn't clumsy or brutal. He was slow and almost tender. Even the huge hands that slid around her waist and brought her lazily against him were all but comforting.

He nibbled at her upper lip where it clung stubbornly to her lower one. "It won't hurt," he breathed softly. "Give in."

"I won't…"

The parting of her lips gave him the advantage he'd been looking for. He eased them open under his with a pressure that was so slow and arousing that she stood, stunned, in his embrace.

He towered over her. At close range, he was even larger than he'd seemed at first. His big hands spread over her back, almost covering both her shoulder blades, and he smiled against her shocked gasp. His teeth gently worried her lower lip while his tongue trailed over it, and she thought dizzily that she'd never known such an experienced caress from the few, the *very* few, men she'd dated.

He felt her stiffen and lifted his head. The blue eyes that searched her dark ones were wise and perceptive. His hand came up and traced the soft color that overlaid one high cheekbone.

"You taste of coffee," he murmured.

It was beginning to dawn on her that he might not be lying about his success with women. And she didn't think it was because he was rich. Not anymore.

He didn't see fear in her face, or experience. He saw a charming lack of it. His big thumb smoothed over her lips and her body seemed to leap into his at the sensation he produced.

"Nothing to say, Poppy?" he asked.

She shook her head, her eyes unblinking as they sought his for reassurance.

"You're perfectly safe," he replied, answering the look. "I'm not a rake, even if I do fit the picture of a kidnapper. But I had noble motives."

"You're…very big, aren't you?" she faltered.

"Compared to you," he agreed. His eyes narrowed as he studied her. She did look very small in his arms. He looked down to her breasts, pressed against his shirt. She barely came up to his chin and she had a fragile build. If he made love to her, it would be touch and go, because she was so much smaller. He scowled.

"What's wrong?" she asked curiously.

He met her eyes. "I was thinking about how careful I'd have to be with you in bed," he said absently.

She flushed and pushed at him. "You'd be lucky!" she raged.

He smiled at her ruffled fury and let her go. "Wouldn't I, though?" he agreed lazily. Her red face told him things she wouldn't. "You're very delicately built. I've deliberately limited myself to tall, buxom women because I'm so big. Do you know, I can't even let myself get into fistfights unless I can find another man my size?"

She studied him, under the spell of a hateful attraction. Her heart was still racing. His shirt was open at the neck and there was a dark, thick nest of hair in it. She wondered what he looked like under his clothes and could have choked on her own curiosity.

"You never told me what you do," she said, diverting her eyes to his face.

"I used to play professional football," he volunteered.

She frowned, searching his features. "I'm sorry. I don't watch it. I'm not much of a sports fan."

"It figures. It was a long time ago."

That explained how he could afford this nice cabin in such a luxury area of the state. He'd probably made a fortune in professional sports and saved a lot of it. It would explain the women, too. All at once, it bothered her to think of him with women.

She wrapped her arms over her breasts. "How long will that last, do you think?" she asked, nodding toward the snowstorm.

"A couple of days," he said. "I'll get you back to the lodge as soon as I can, I promise." He sighed heavily, wondering where that reporter was, and if she'd managed to get out. "I fouled this up really good," he muttered. "Poor Amanda. She'll never forgive me if they get to her."

Amanda? She frowned. "Have I missed something?"

"Probably." He turned away. "I'll check on that generator. I don't have a television here, but there's a piano and plenty of books. You ought to be able to amuse yourself."

"Thanks."

He paused as he shouldered into his parka and looked at her. "If you don't get back to your job, they won't really fire you, will they?"

"I don't know." It worried her. She interpreted his expression and smiled ruefully. "Don't worry. I'd be stuck at the lodge anyway, even if you hadn't kidnapped me, wouldn't I?"

That seemed to lessen the guilt she read on his face. "Maybe. Maybe not. I'm sorry. I'll make it up to you, if I can. I should have made sure before I acted."

"What were you going to do with that reporter?" she asked.

"I was going to keep her here until I could warn Amanda," he said. "She's not having an easy time of it and all the wire services are after the story. I thought I was safe here, but they can track you down anywhere."

Amanda must be his girlfriend, because he was trying so hard to protect her from the press. She wondered why. "Is she married?" she asked involuntarily.

"Yes," he said solemnly. "I'll be back in a minute."

So that was it, she thought as he left the cabin. He was in love with a married woman and the newspapers were after him. He must be somebody very

famous in sports to attract so much media attention
even if he didn't play football anymore. She wished
she'd paid more attention to sports. He was probably
very famous and she'd go home without even knowing his name. She thought whimsically of selling her
story to the tabloids— "I was kidnapped by a football
star…" But of course she couldn't do that, because
she didn't even know his full name.

She wandered out of the huge living room and
down the hall. There were two bedrooms, one with a
huge, king-size bed and the other with a normal bed.
They were nicely decorated and furnished, and each
had its own bathroom. Farther down was a room with
all sorts of electronic equipment, including speakers
and recorders and wires and microphones, a huge
keyboard, an electric guitar and a piano. She stood
in the doorway, fascinated.

After a minute, she approached the piano, drawn
by the name on it. She knew that name very well;
it was the sort of instrument even a minor pianist
dreamed of being able to afford. It must be his hobby,
playing, and he must be very rich to be able to buy
something so astronomically expensive to indulge
that hobby on.

Her fingers touched the keys and trembled. It was
in perfect tune. She sat down on the bench, remembering when she was a child how she'd dreamed night
after night of owning a piano. But there had been no
money for that sort of luxury. She'd played on other
people's pianos when she was invited, and along the
way she'd picked up some instruction. Eventually,

when her father died, she was left with a huge insurance policy that she hadn't even wanted; she'd wanted her parent back. But the money had put her through college, bought her a small, inexpensive piano and lessons to go with it. And it had made it possible for her to make her own way in the world. She didn't earn a lot just now, but if she could continue in the partnership—if they didn't fire her—she had prospects.

She put her trembling hands on the keyboard, thinking that if she'd had the opportunity to study as a child, she might have made music her life.

She closed her eyes and began to play the *Moonlight Sonata,* softly at first, and then with more power and pleasure and emotion than she'd ever felt before. This magnificent instrument was all hers to enjoy, and enjoy it she did. When the last chord died into the stillness, she came back to her surroundings with a jolt as she realized that she wasn't alone in the room.

She turned around. Hank was there, leaning against the doorway, something in his eyes that she couldn't grasp. He wasn't smiling. His face was somber and oddly drawn.

"I'm sorry!" she stammered, rising quickly to her feet. "I didn't mean to presume…"

"Why aren't you playing professionally?" he asked surprisingly.

She stared at him blankly. "I chose medicine instead of music."

"A noble choice, but you have a gift. Didn't you know?"

She looked around her, embarrassed. "You play, too, I guess? Is it a hobby?"

He smiled to himself. "You might say that."

"I've never thought of a football player as a musician," she said quietly. "It's…surprising."

"Some people think so. I'm too damned big for most hobbies. At least music fits me."

She smiled gently and turned her attention back to the piano. She touched it with loving fingers. "She's lovely, isn't she?" The wonder in her voice was evident. "A real lady."

He was touched and delighted by her unconscious reverence. "That's what I call her," he remarked. "Odd that you'd think the same way, isn't it?"

"I guess a lot of people love music."

"Yes. Even football players."

She laughed self-consciously, because he sounded bitter. "Did that sting? I'm sorry. I didn't mean to sound disparaging. I've never known anybody in sports before. I know a little about baseball, and once I met a minor-league baseball player."

"The thrill of your life?"

"Oh, no, getting my degree was that." She glanced at him uneasily. Some people were immediately hostile when she mentioned her extensive education.

He lifted a bushy eyebrow. "Fitting me for a mold?" he mused. "Will you faint if I tell you that I have a degree of my own?"

Her eyes brightened. "Really?"

"I'm a music major," he said.

"I'll bet that gave the sports announcers something

to talk about during games—" She stopped dead. Things she'd read and heard on television, bits and pieces were coming back to her. She didn't follow sports, but there was one sports figure who'd confounded the critics and the fans when he suddenly dropped out of professional football to found of all things a rock group. He'd only had a mustache then, not a full beard and long hair besides. She'd seen his photograph in the paper, and she'd seen an interview on television.

"Oh, my God," she said in a whisper.

"Put it together, did we?" he mused, smiling. "Go ahead."

"Desperado," she said. "You played for the Dallas Cowboys and quit after the best season you'd ever had to go into music. Everybody thought you were crazy. Then you won a Grammy…"

"Several Grammies," he said, correcting her.

"Several. Amanda is your lead singer," she added, remembering that tidbit. "She's beautiful. But…didn't she marry?"

He chuckled. "Yes. She married a poor Wyoming rancher and she's very, very pregnant and Quinn Sutton is beside himself with worry. She's not having an easy time. We're trying to protect her from the press and it hasn't been easy. We're all afraid that word is going to get out about her problems with the pregnancy and she's going to be covered up by the press."

"We?"

"The group," he said. "She's very special to all of us, although she and Quinn are deeply in love."

"Are you in love with her?" she asked bluntly.

"I was, in the old days," he said easily. "We all were. She's beautiful and talented. But now she's kind of like a kid sister that we try to take care of. I'd do anything to protect her. Even," he added ruefully, "kidnap a reporter."

"That would have been terribly intelligent," she said sarcastically. "What a story it would make!"

"I didn't say I was thinking clearly," he muttered darkly. "I had to act fast, before she could file that story. And look what a great job I did!"

"Anybody can make a mistake. But she doesn't know about Amanda, you know," she added. "She knew that you were here and she was going to tell her office that a man at the lodge said you were about to get engaged to someone you met here. *That's* the hot scoop she had."

He leaned back against the door and laughed delightedly. "Good God!"

"So it doesn't really matter if she gets to a phone, does it?"

"No." He groaned and ran a hand through his thick hair. "Hell, I could have saved myself all this trouble!"

"Not to mention saving me a little," she said irritably.

He looked surprised. "I saved you from St. Bernard."

Her lips protruded. "I don't need saving from a man like that. He had lips like a lizard."

He chuckled. "Did he?"

She closed the lid on the piano. "He wasn't my type at all."

He moved closer and raised the lid. "What is your type?" he asked as he ran his elegant fingers over the keyboard.

"I'll know the minute I find him," she assured him.

He lifted his head and looked into her dark eyes. "You don't like rock music, you said."

"I don't listen to it," she confessed. "Except that one song that I told you about."

"Yes. This one."

He sat down at the piano and began to play it, softly, smoothly, his eyes seeking hers.

"It was you," she said slowly.

He nodded. "Amanda sang it. I don't have a lead voice, only one good enough to second the rest of them. But I can write music. None of them can."

She came to stand just behind him, with a soft hand on his shoulder as he increased the tempo.

"I meant it to be a rock song. Amanda made me slow it down. They ganged up on me and made me put it on the album. I didn't want to."

"Why?"

"Because it's intimate," he said shortly. "It's part of me, when I do something like this. There are things I don't want to share with the world."

"You should share music like this, though," she replied. "It's exquisite."

He smiled at her. "But you like opera. And historical music."

Her fingers became unconsciously caressing on his shoulder. "Yes. But this is beautiful."

He finished the piece and lifted his hands from the keyboard. She hadn't moved.

He reached up and smoothed his fingers over her hand before he lifted it to his mouth.

He swiveled around and caught her by the hips, his eyes darkening, narrowing as they looked up at her.

She felt him move before she saw him. He drew her to him and eased her to her knees between his outstretched legs. Then he framed her face in his big hands and bent to kiss her with slow, tender hunger. She started to protest, but he stayed the instinctive backward movement of her head and kept kissing her, until she gave in to him and slid her arms around his neck.

It wasn't until his hand trespassed onto her soft breast that she stiffened and caught his fingers.

He lifted his head and looked at her flushed face as she fought with his invading hand. There was something very calculating about his expression.

"You're…analyzing me," she accused.

"You aren't used to a man's hand on your breast," he commented, watching her gasp. "You're twenty-six, right? Then why haven't you had a man, Poppy?"

"For heaven's sake!" She pushed at him and he let her go. She scrambled to her feet, pushing back her hair, and stared unseeing out the window while she fought for composure.

He joined her at the window, leaning idly against

the window frame with his big hands in his pockets. "Are you physically or emotionally scarred in some way?"

She shook her head.

"Then, why?"

She frowned. "What do you mean, why?"

"Why haven't you slept with anyone yet?"

He seemed to think it was a matter of course, that women had the same freedom that men did and should enjoy it.

"Well, I don't respect men who sleep around just because they want to satisfy a fleeting physical hunger. Why should I want to be that way myself?"

He frowned. "Everyone sleeps around."

"Bull," she said, raising her hand when he started to speak. "And don't quote me statistics. Statistics depend on whom you interview. If you ask two hundred people in New York City what they think of a free sexual life-style, and then you ask the same question of two hundred people in a small town in Iowa, you're going to get a heck of a different set of statistics!"

His big shoulders moved. "I hadn't thought about it that way. But the times are changing."

She only smiled.

"Don't tell me," he chided gently. "You're going to save yourself for the man you marry."

"Of course I am," she said matter-of-factly.

He threw up his hands. "Lunacy," he muttered. "You don't know what you're missing."

"Sure I do. I'm missing all those exciting risks, including the one that can kill you." She pursed her lips as she studied him. "And if we're going to get so personal, how much of a swinger are you?"

"I'm not," he replied, shocked. "Only an idiot sleeps around these days!"

She burst out laughing.

He liked the way she laughed, even the way she lost her temper. "Want to draw straws to see who gets to cook supper?"

She traced his face with soft eyes. "I'll do it, if you'll tell me what you like. Not cereal," she added.

"Steak and baked potatoes and salad, then," he said.

"I like steak, too."

"Two of each for me," he added. "I have to get enough protein."

"I'll bet you're expensive to feed," she remarked.

"Yes. But I'm rich," he added with a meaningful glance.

"I take it all back, what I said about buying women for yourself," she told him pertly.

"Oh?"

The expression on his face was only faintly threatening, but she left him with the piano, just the same.

THEY SHARED MEALS and conversation for two days. He didn't come near her in any sexual way, although she caught his gaze on her. He wasn't feeling well. His skin was flushed and he had a terrible cough. He'd been out working on that generator her first day at the cabin, and he hadn't really been dressed properly for the cold and the vicious snow. He'd caught a cold and it had gone into his chest. She was worried now, because he was obviously feverish and there was no telephone, no way to get him to a hospital. When he went to bed, he refused to take even an aspirin.

She went to bed in the guest room, reluctantly, hoping that he'd be better the next day even when she knew in her gut that he wouldn't.

The third morning, he didn't get up. If only she had access to her supplies back at the clinic in Sioux City, she could have used enough antibiotic to do him some good. As it was, she could only hope that he had a virus or the flu and not pneumonia. If it was a bacterial pneumonia, he could die if help didn't come in time.

She went into his bedroom to check on him, and had to force her legs to carry her the rest of the way. He'd thrashed his way out of the covers and he was lying there totally nude on top of the sheet and blanket. Her embarrassed eyes couldn't leave him. She'd never seen a man in such a condition before. He was beautiful without his clothing, tanned all over, with just enough body hair to make him attractive to the sight and not enough to make him repulsive. It was all on his chest and flat stomach, black and curling hair that ran over his broad chest in a wedge and down over the ripple of powerful muscles to his flat stomach and powerful thighs. Her eyes lingered there with curiosity and fascination and a little fear. She didn't need anyone to tell her that this man was physically exceptional.

He groaned and his eyes opened. He was flushed with fever, his lips dry, his body lifting as he coughed and grimaced from the pain.

"I've picked up that damned bug my band had," he said hoarsely. "Getting chilled working on the generator must have pushed me over the edge." He sat up, realized his condition and with a rueful smile, jerked the sheet over his hips. "Sorry. I must have kicked off the covers. But then, you're a doctor. I don't suppose you're easily shocked by a man's body."

She wasn't about to answer that.

He lay back and coughed again. She moved a little closer, grimacing. "We're going to have a problem if you get worse. Your medicine cabinet is inadequate and I don't have my bag. I don't even have the right medicines or enough of them. The best I'm going to be able to do is mix up a folk remedy for cough and give you aspirin for fever."

"I don't need nursing," he told her.

"Of course not," she agreed. "Oh dear, oh dear."

He closed his eyes, too weary to talk anymore, and fell asleep. She spent the rest of the day sitting by his bedside in a chair, trying to keep his fever down with aspirin and his cough at bay with a mixture of honey, lemon and whiskey. Amazingly the cough remedy seemed to do some good. But the fever didn't go down, despite the aspirin.

The generator was holding, thank God, so it was warm in the cabin. She had to get that fever down. He did at least have a thermometer, but what it reg-

istered was hardly reassuring. A high fever could
burn up the very cells of the body. She had to stop it.

She got a basin of warm water and a washcloth and
towel. With a deep breath as she gathered her nerve,
she turned the covers back.

He lay quietly until she began to bathe him, then
he groaned harshly and opened his eyes. "What are
you doing?" he asked in a weak, raspy tone.

"Trying to get the fever down," she said. "I'm
sorry, really I am. But this is the only way I know.
The aspirin is only holding it at bay. It's very high.
I'll try not to let you get chilled in the process."

"Stroke of luck, kidnapping you," he said with wan
humor. "And they say you can't find a doctor when
you need one."

She winced, but his eyes had closed again and he
didn't see it. She kept on sponging him down, drying
him with the towel as she went and feeling his skin
slowly begin to cool.

It wouldn't have been so complicated if his body
hadn't started reacting to the motion of the washcloth
against areas that were normally hidden to the eyes.

He groaned again when she reached his flat stomach and his eyes opened as his powerful body suddenly reacted helplessly—and visibly—to her touch.

She drew her hand back at once and blushed to
the roots of her hair. The terrible thing was that she
couldn't drag her eyes away. She was paralyzed by
the forbidden sight, fascinated and shocked.

"It's all right, Poppy," he said huskily. "Don't be

embarrassed. It's a natural reaction, even if it seems shocking to you."

Her wide eyes sought his for reassurance.

"Go ahead," he said gently. "Don't worry about it. We'll both ignore it. Okay?"

She hesitated for a minute, but as the shock wore off, she began to weigh her embarrassment against his state of health. "Sorry," she said as she continued, working her way down his powerful legs.

"You're a doctor," he murmured, but he was watching her narrowly. "Aren't you?"

"Well, yes. Sort of."

His eyebrows lifted. "Sort of?"

She cleared her throat as she finished sponging him down and gently pulled the cover up to his waist, averting her eyes as she did so. "Yes. I am a doctor. I have a degree and a diploma to prove it. But…"

"But?"

"Well… I'm not exactly the sort of doctor you think I am." She put the basin and cloth on the floor by the bed.

"What sort are you?" he persisted.

She bit her lower lip and looked at him guiltily. "I'm a veterinarian," she confessed.

CHAPTER FOUR

"You're a what!"

"Please lie down, and don't get excited," she pleaded, pushing him gently back against the pillows. "And it's all right, really, I did have two years of premed, so I'm not a dunce about human anatomy."

"I don't believe this," he groaned, throwing a big arm across his eyes. "My God, I'm being treated by a vet!"

"I'm a good vet," she muttered. "I haven't lost a patient yet. And you shouldn't complain about being treated by a vet, if you insist on looking like a grizzly bear!"

She got up from the bed and walked out with the basin and cloth and towel, fuming. He acted as if she were guilty of malpractice, and she'd been nursing him all night long!

He must have thought about that, because when she went back into the bedroom, he was more subdued.

"I'm sorry," he said shortly. "It was a shock, that's all. I don't guess you slept all night, did you?"

"I slept in the chair there," she said. "I was nervous about leaving you with such a high fever."

"Thanks."

"I'd have done the same for any sick animal," she replied.

"Rub it in," he said with a wan smile.

She smiled at him. "I'd love to."

He was barely strong enough to glower at her. "What if you catch this stuff?"

"Then I guess you'll have to look after me, if the blizzard doesn't stop," she informed him.

He lifted an eyebrow and let his eyes work their way up and down her slender body with a speaking glance. "I'd get to sponge you down, then, huh?" He smiled wickedly. "What a thrill."

She flushed. "You stop that! I didn't enjoy it!"

"Didn't you? I thought you were familiar with a man's anatomy until I saw that scarlet blush. I wondered if you were going to faint." His blue eyes narrowed. "You haven't seen a naked male like this before, have you?"

She moved restlessly. "I've seen lots of naked male dogs," she said defiantly.

He chuckled, stifling a cough. "It's not quite the same thing."

She could have agreed wholeheartedly with that, but she wasn't going to. She pushed back her hair with a weary hand. "If you'll be all right for a few minutes, I'll heat up some soup."

"You're tired. Why don't we both sleep for a little while, and then you can worry about food."

"Are you sure?"

"I'm sure. I don't feel half as bad as I did last night.

Go on. Grab a couple of hours' sleep. I'll wake you if I need you."

"How will I hear you?" she asked worriedly. "The guest room is down the hall...."

"Curl up beside me, if you're concerned about that. It's a big bed."

She wasn't sure, and it showed.

"Don't be silly," he said gently. "I'm too sick to be a threat."

He was. She gave in, smiling shyly as she went around to the other side of the bed and lay down, all too aware of the expanse of his hair-roughened chest, the length of his powerful body. He was really huge this close and she'd never been more aware of her lack of stature. Of course, beside him, a six-foot woman would seem small. She curled up under the covers and stifled a yawn.

"Don't you want to put on something less constraining?" he said. "I won't look."

She smiled. "I'm too tired even to do that. I could sleep for...a week...." Her voice trailed off. She was out like a light.

It was dark when she woke up. A night-light was on and Hank was snoring gently beside her. He'd knocked the covers off again, but it was chilly now. She got up and went around the bed to replace them, pulling them up over his chest and tucking them over him. He looked younger when he was asleep, relaxed and unstressed. She wondered what he was like when he wasn't upset or sick. She'd probably never have the chance to find out, because he was famous and she was a nobody in the veterinary practice back home. It would be something to remember, though, that she'd known someone like him, even briefly. Under normal circumstances, she was certain that they'd never have met at all.

She went into the kitchen and heated some soup. He must be hungry. He was a huge man. He needed nourishment.

She carried the bowl of soup back into the bedroom and put it on the bedside table before she shook him awake.

"Let me take your temperature first, then I'll feed you," she said, sitting beside him on the bed. She put the thermometer under his tongue and he watched her while she timed it. It beeped just as she'd counted off a minute.

"It's down!" she said, delighted.

"Of course it's down, it was only a virus," he muttered.

"How can you be so sure?"

"Damned if I know. I'm not a vet," he said, drawling out the word.

"I still know more about medicine than you do," she said curtly, reaching for the soup.

"The hell you do. I've had more operations and been in more emergency rooms than you'll ever see over the years."

With all sorts of football injuries, no doubt, she thought, but she didn't argue. He was obviously feeling better and spoiling for a fight.

"Eat," she demanded, holding a spoon of chicken noodle soup to his firm lips.

"I hate chicken soup."

"It's made with real chickens," she said coaxingly.

"Prove it."

She put the spoonful back into the bowl and searched until she found a tiny cube and produced it for him to see. "There!"

"Right. A square chicken. A microscopic square chicken."

"You really must feel better," she said pointedly. "You're being very unpleasant."

"I have a reputation for being very unpleasant," he informed her. "Ask the group."

"You're one of them. They wouldn't admit it. They'd lie for you. They wouldn't want your adoring public to know what a bad man you really were."

"Point taken." He laid back against the propped pillows with a sigh. "Okay. Go ahead. Feed me."

She did, liking the power it gave her. She smiled, enjoying herself. She'd never had anyone to take care of, because her father had never been sick. She took care of animals but it really wasn't the same.

He was enjoying her tender ministrations, too, and hating to admit it. "I'll be back on my feet by tomorrow," he said. "So don't get too fond of this routine."

"God forbid," she agreed.

But he let her feed him the entire bowl of soup, and the warm feeling it gave him wasn't just from the temperature of the liquid. Afterward, he stretched and then relaxed with a long sigh. "God, I'm weak.

I feel as if I don't have enough strength to get up."
He smiled grimly. "But I've got to, for a minute." He
threw back the cover, ignoring her flush, and got to
his feet. He staggered a little, and she forgot her dis-
comfort in the rush of concern she felt.

She got under his powerful arm and helped support him.

"Thanks," he said, starting toward the bathroom.
"I feel like I've been clotheslined."

"I guess you do. I'm sorry you're sick."

His arm tightened. "You'd better be glad of it," he
said grimly as he noticed her shyly appreciative eyes
on his body. "I like having you look at me like this.
I like it too damn much."

She felt pulsing heat run through her body, and
quickly averted her eyes. "I'm not looking," she said
at once.

"Of course you're looking. You can't help it. I fas-
cinate you, don't I?"

She glared up at him. "I'll find you some shorts."

"I won't wear them," he returned with a cool smile.
"I'm not changing the habit of a lifetime to satisfy
some prudish animal doctor."

"I am not a prude!"

"Right."

She refused to notice his amused expression. She
helped him to the bathroom door, waited until he
called her and then helped him back to bed, averting
her eyes while she tugged the sheet up to his waist.

He sighed, his chest rattling a little. He propped

himself up on the pillows and coughed, reaching for a tissue.

"It's a productive cough, at least," she said to herself. "That's a blessing. And if the fever's dropping, hopefully, it's a viral bronchitis and not pneumo-nia."

He lifted an eyebrow. "Well, you sound professional enough."

"Medicine is medicine," she said pointedly. "Of course, the anatomical structure is a bit different and the pharmacology certainly is, but ways to treat illnesses are basically the same."

He didn't feel like arguing. He yawned widely. "I'm so tired," he said softly. "So tired. I feel as if I haven't had any rest in years."

"From what you've said, I wonder if you've had any rest at all," she remarked. "Perhaps being stuck up here is a godsend."

"I wouldn't say that," he murmured. "The only good thing about it is that reporter doesn't know about Amanda. God forbid that she should cause trouble. Most of that magazine's reporters are top-notch."

"She doesn't work for a magazine," she recalled. "She said she was trying to sell a story that would get her foot in the door. But she was also on the trail of some sports star who was supposed to be hiding out in the Tetons up in Wyoming."

"A hopeful," he said, relieved.

"She was pretty optimistic. And very ambitious."

He fingered the sheet. "Something you should know about."

"I only want to work in a partnership and not have

to do all the rough jobs and odd hours," she said wistfully. "I was lucky to get the partnership at all. There are four of us in the practice, but I'm the junior one. So until I prove myself, I can't really expect much free time."

"It sounds to me as if they're the lucky ones," he muttered. "Are they all men?"

She nodded. "All older than me, too. I'm just out of college and full of new ideas, new theories and treatments and they think I'm a hotshot so they won't listen."

"You probably make them feel threatened," he said pointedly. "And as to who's the lucky one, I think it's the other partners, not you. They're getting all the benefits and none of the unpleasant work."

"I could hardly open my own practice fresh out of school," she began.

"Why not? Plenty of people do!"

"I'm not rich," she said. She went to the window and looked out. The snow was still coming down without a break in sight in the sky. "I barely had enough money in the bank to finish school, and part of it was done on government student loans. I have a lot to pay back. That doesn't leave much over for furnishing an office."

"I see."

She shrugged and turned back with a smile. "I don't mind working my way up from the bottom. Everybody has to start somewhere. You did."

It was a nicely disguised question. He adjusted the pillows and leaned back again. "I started as a second guitarist for a group that got lost at the bottom of the pop charts. Eventually I worked up to helping do backup work for some of the better musicians. That's how I met Amanda Sutton—she was Amanda Corrie Callaway back then," he added with a smile. "She and I started working together on a project, along with another guy in the band, and we discovered that Amanda had a voice like an angel. It didn't take us long to put an act together, add a drummer and a second guitarist, and audition for a record company." He shook his head remembering. "We made it on the first try. Amazing, that, when some people take years just to get a record company executive to listen to them."

"Didn't it help that you'd been a football star?"

"Not in music," he replied with a rueful smile. "I was a nobody like the rest of the group until our first hit."

"Why the name Desperado?" she asked.

"You've never seen a group shot of us, I gather?"

She smiled apologetically. "Sorry."

"Look in the top drawer of the desk over there against the wall." He pointed toward it.

She opened it and there was a photograph of four men and a woman.

"Now do you need to ask why?" He chuckled.

"Not really." They were a frightening bunch, the men all heavily bearded and mustached with unruly hair, and they looked really tough. Amanda was a striking contrast, with her long blond hair and dark eyes and beautiful face.

"We've been lucky. Now, of course, we may really have to stop performing. It all depends on how Amanda is doing." He looked briefly worried. "I hope she's all right. I can't even telephone to ask how she is. At least I know Quinn won't let anything happen to her. He's a wild man where Amanda is concerned."

She thought about having someone that concerned for her welfare and wondered how it would feel. Her father had cared about her, but no one else had since he died. She'd been very much alone in the world.

She picked up the soup bowl, but her mind not at all on what she was doing.

He didn't understand the sadness in her face. He reached out and caught her wrist. "What's wrong?" he asked softly.

She shrugged. "I was wondering what it would be like to have someone worry that much about me," she said, and then laughed.

He let go of her wrist. He'd been wondering the same thing. His lean hand smoothed over the bedcover. "I want a bath. Do you suppose you could run some water for me?"

"You're very weak," she cautioned. "And what if you get chilled?"

"It's warm in here. Come on. I can't stand being grungy."

"Grungy?"

He chuckled. "Maybe there's a better word for it somewhere."

"If you get stuck in the tub, how will I ever get you out?" she asked worriedly, measuring him with her eyes. "Heavens, I couldn't begin to lift you!"

"That's a fact. But I wouldn't risk it if I didn't think I could cope. Humor me."

"All right. But if you drown," she advised, "I'm not taking the rap for it."

She went into the bathroom and filled the tub with warm water. It was a Jacuzzi, luxurious and spotless, and she envied him. Her guest bedroom had a nice shower, which she'd used the night before, but nothing like this. She put soap and lotions and towels close to hand and went to help him out of bed and across the tub.

"It's big," he declared as he lowered himself into it. "Why don't you strip off and come in with me?"

She chuckled, trying not to let her faint, remaining embarrassment show. She'd grown used to the sight of his body, although it still intimidated her a bit. "I might fall and break my leg. Where would we be then?"

He stretched his big arms over the sides. "Just as well, I suppose." He sighed, letting his gaze wash over her like warm water. "You aren't the type, are you?"

"What type?"

"For brief interludes," he said seriously. "You're a forever-after girl, despite the fact that forever-after doesn't exist anymore."

"It could, if two people loved each other enough," she said.

"My wife and I loved each other, when we married," he said. "We thought it would last forever." He smiled cynically. "It lasted for a while, then we burned out."

She chewed on her lower lip and frowned a little. "Oh."

"I learned one thing from it. Marriage requires more than a mutual fever. You need common interests, backgrounds, and you need to be friends as well as lovers. That's trite, but it's true."

"It's a hard combination to find," she said.

"People don't have time to look for it anymore." He picked up the cloth and soap and lathered his arms and chest slowly.

"I'd better go..."

"Don't be silly. Sit down."

She perched herself on a chair by the bench that contained a hair blower and electric razor, along with a rack of lotions and powders. She folded her hands together on her jean-clad legs and tried not to look uncomfortable.

"In the old days, people lived in small communities and everyone knew everyone," he said while he bathed. "Now we're all so busy trying to support ourselves that we move around like migrating birds. We don't stay in one place long enough to get to know people."

"Your singer, Amanda. How did she meet her husband?"

He chuckled. "They got snowbound together up in Wyoming," he said. "And he was the ultimate misogynist. He hated Amanda on sight. But she's feisty and she has a kind heart. It was only a matter of time until they fell in love. Unfortunately that happened before he found out who she really was. He went all noble, because he was poor and she was famous. So for her own good, he threw her out. She left and her plane crashed on the way to L.A."

She caught her breath. "He must have been devastated."

"Half out of his mind," Hank replied, remembering the band's nightmare trip back to Wyoming. They'd all left on the bus because Hank and the boys didn't like airplanes. But Amanda had insisted on flying. Hank had felt responsible because he hadn't pushed harder to get her to come with them. "Quinn skied down an unpatrolled ridge into the valley to get her— only a handful of men in the country could have made that run, but he was an Olympic contender in downhill in his younger days. Hell of a trip it was. He found her badly concussed, damn near dead, and he had to have another man ski down to help tow her out of the valley on a litter to a waiting helicopter. There was too much wind for the chopper to land where the crash occurred. As it was, they barely made it in time. Three days after the doctor pronounced her on the mend, they got married, right there in the hospital."

"My goodness!"

"They'd been married for two years when she got pregnant," he recalled. "They were both over the moon about it, but she's a lot more fragile than she looks. It's been a rough pregnancy and she's had to have constant medical care. We'd more or less given up touring when she first married, but we had one commitment we couldn't break, for a charity in New York. She barely got through it and Quinn put his foot down, hard. He's kept her home since then. He won't even let her do recording sessions now. The rumor is that we're breaking up the group."

"Are you?"

He finished bathing his legs. "I don't know." He looked at her. "The band wouldn't be the same without Amanda. No singer could replace her."

"I don't suppose so," she agreed gently. "But I'm sure the baby is the most important thing to her right now."

He nodded. There was a bitter look on his face that she didn't miss.

"Why didn't your wife want a child?"

He glared at her. "That's none of your business."

He sounded fierce, but she overlooked the bad temper because of the sadness in his blue eyes. "I'm sorry. I didn't mean to pry."

He paused long enough to wash his hair and rinse it before he said anything else. "She said that I wasn't cut out to be a parent," he said shortly. "That I wasn't home enough or patient enough. And besides that, she didn't want a child who might grow up to look like me."

Her eyes lingered on his broad shoulders and chest, on the power and strength of his tanned, hair-roughed skin. "What's wrong with you?" she asked dreamily.

He caught his breath as the surge of desire shot through him like a bolt of lightning.

She saw the tautness of his face and grimaced. "I keep putting my foot in it, don't I?" she said miserably. "Honestly, you make me feel like a babbling adolescent!"

"That isn't how you make me feel," he said with grim humor. "What she meant," he explained, "was that I've got a thick neck and an oversize body and a face that only a mother could love. She said with her luck, she'd have a little girl with a big nose and feet like a duck."

"What a cruel thing to say," she replied, wounded for him. "I expect you'd have a very pretty little girl with blue eyes and brown hair. Except that if you have four brothers, it's a lot more likely that you'd have a little boy."

"So I've heard." He let his narrowed eyes sweep over her. "You're very delicately built," he said quietly. "Slender hips, small breasts, almost a foot shorter than I am. We'd have a hard time just making love, much less having a child together."

She couldn't believe he'd said that. She just looked at him, flustered.

"You know everything there is to know about me, physically." He continued in that same quiet, gentle voice. "But it's one thing to look, and another to consider the problem of intimacy." His eyes narrowed more. "I'll bet you're as small as I am big," he said insinuatingly.

She jumped up from the chair, red faced and shocked. "How dare you!"

"Tell me you haven't thought about how we'd fit together in my bed," he challenged, and he wasn't smiling.

Her fists clenched at her sides. "You can't talk to me like this!"

He searched her outraged eyes with curiosity and faint tenderness. "Another first, hmm?" he mused. "And you're a vet. How did you survive labs?"

"Half the people in my class were women," she informed him. "We forced the men to respect us enough not to make sexist remarks."

"I'm not making sexist remarks," he argued. "I'm indulging in a little sexual logic." He pursed his lips and held her eyes relentlessly. "If I'm very careful, we might try," he said gently.

"Try what?"

"And I can use something. There won't be any risk."

She clenched both fists tighter. "You can stop right there. I'm not sleeping with you!"

He smiled without malice. "You will," he replied. "Eventually."

"I won't be here eventually. The minute the snow lets up and the snowplow clears the roads, I'm getting out of here!"

"I've never been to Sioux City," he remarked conversationally. "But you're an old-fashioned girl, so I guess I'll have to chase you for a while, won't I?"

"You don't need to start thinking that you'll wear me down. You won't. I have no inclination whatsoever, at all, to…to…"

He stood up slowly in the middle of her tirade, turned off the Jacuzzi and stepped out onto the mat. She couldn't take her eyes off him. It must be some deep-seated weakness, she decided, some character flaw that made her into a blatant Peeping Tom.

And it was worse than ever when he reacted to her appreciative eyes and laughed about it.

She groaned as she pulled a huge bath sheet from the heated towel bar and handed it to him.

He ignored the bath sheet. His hand shot around her wrist and jerked, pulling her completely against his wet body. Even in his weakened condition, he was alarmingly strong.

She started to struggle, the sheet dropping to the floor, but he clamped a big hand around her waist and held her firmly to him, groaning in pleasure as her hips moved sharply in her efforts to escape.

She subsided at once, made breathless by the huge body so intimately close to her. He was so tall that she felt the insistent pressure of him, not against her hips but against her midriff. She caught onto him to keep from reeling, and the feel of that thick mat of hair under her hands paralyzed her with curious pleasure.

"Shrimp," he accused at her temple.

"Giant," she taunted.

His hands swept over her back, burning hot through her thin cotton blouse, flattening her breasts against his diaphragm.

"We don't even fit together like a normal man and woman," he remarked as he looked down at her. "We're like Mutt and Jeff."

But it felt right. It felt as natural as breathing to stand close against his aroused body and be at home.

She laid her cheek against his damp chest and just stood there, letting him hold her close, while she tried to deal with the unfamiliar feelings that were over-whelming her. It felt like more than physical attraction. It felt like…love.

CHAPTER FIVE

"I'M OUT OF my mind," he said pleasantly. "I must be, even to consider such a thing with a midget like you. We'd be totally incompatible in bed."

She closed her eyes and relaxed against him, feeling him tauten in response. "No, we wouldn't. I studied anatomy. I'd have to be a foot shorter than I am to be worried. A woman's body is very elastic."

"Is yours elastic enough to accommodate mine?" he asked quietly.

She lifted her head and looked up into his blue, blue eyes. She felt the hunger all through her, burning and hot. "I think so," she said involuntarily.

His jaw clenched as he searched her face. "Then, let me."

She swallowed. Her fingers went up to touch his hair-roughened face. His lips were the only bit of skin visible below his cheekbones and his blue eyes. "I can't."

He scowled. "Those damned old-fashioned ideas again! This is the nineties, for God's sake!"

"I know." She traced his hard mouth and wanted so much to lie in his arms and learn what it was to love. But it wasn't what she wanted. "I'm not emotionally strong enough for brief affairs. That's why I don't have them. I really do want a home and children, Hank. I want my husband to be the first. If that's outdated, I'm sorry. I don't feel inferior or out of step just because I put a high value on my chastity. I hope the man I marry will feel the same way about his body."

His hands loosened. "In other words, you don't want a permissive man for a husband."

She lowered her eyes to his broad chest. "I suppose a lot of women think a man like that can reform, that he can be faithful. But if he's had a hundred women, he's already proven that he can't. He sees sex as an itch to scratch. He'll probably always consider it that casual, so he'll feel free to sleep around after he marries. And it will probably surprise him if his wife objects."

His big hands smoothed up and down her arms. "I guess I've given you the impression that I'm that way with women."

She looked up. "Yes."

He took a slow breath and smiled tenderly. "You don't think I might one day value a woman enough to become faithful rather than risk losing her?"

"I don't know you," she said solemnly.

"No. You really don't." He hesitated for another minute, but then he let her go and bent to pick up the bath sheet she'd dropped.

She moved away while he dried himself, finding a robe hanging behind the door that she handed to him when he was through. He put it on without a protest and let her help him back to the bedroom.

"Your hair is still damp," she said.

"It dries fast. Don't bother about the blower." He started toward the bed, but she diverted him into the chair.

"I want to change the sheets first. You'll be more comfortable."

He smiled. "Thanks."

"Where are they?"

He told her where to look and sat like a lamb while she remade the bed and then helped him out of his robe and into the bed.

"Are you all right?" she asked, because he looked so tired.

"I'm just weak. I think I may sleep for a while."

"That would be the best thing for you. Do you need anything?"

He shook his head. He studied her blouse for a long time, and she wondered why until she looked down and flushed. It had gotten so damp while she was standing against him that it had become see-through, and she wasn't wearing anything under it because her bra and the clothes she'd put on yesterday were in the load of laundry she'd started earlier.

Her arms came up over her body and she looked at him defensively.

"They're very pretty," he said with quiet reverence, and no mockery.

"Marshmallows," she muttered with self-contempt.

"Stop that," he said sharply. "I don't like big women."

Her eyebrows lifted. "All men do…"

"Not me," he repeated. "You're perfect just the way you are."

He eased her inferiority complex quite a lot, because he obviously wasn't lying about the way he felt. She managed a self-conscious smile. "Thanks."

He arched his arms behind his head and shifted with an oddly sensuous movement of his body. His eyes cut into hers, faintly glittering. "Open your blouse and come down beside me. I'll put my mouth on them and show you ten different ways to moan."

She flushed, jumping to her feet. "No doubt you could. I'm grass green that way. But I wouldn't thank you for reducing me to that condition, even if a dozen other women have."

She walked toward the door and heard him mutter under his breath.

"I haven't had a hundred women," he said angrily.

"Oh, sure." She laughed as she put her hand on the doorknob.

"I've had one. My wife. And she left me impotent."

The shock that tore through her spun her around to face him. He wasn't joking. It was all there, in his drawn face, his bitter eyes, even in the taut line of his mouth.

"But you're not impotent!" she blurted.

"Not with you," he said, chuckling softly. "You can't imagine what a shock it was to find out. I've been putting off women for years because I was sure that I couldn't perform in bed."

She leaned back against the door. Her legs felt

weak. "You weren't married for very long, though, were you?"

"Six years," he told her. "Before that, I gave everything in me to football. I lived in the gym. I had no interest in seducing scores of women, however prudish that sounds. I was like you, bristling with idealism and romance. I saved myself for the right woman. Except she wasn't the right woman," he said shortly. "We burned each other up in bed, but we had nothing to talk about in broad daylight."

"Did she…know?"

"No," he replied. "Because by the time we decided to get married, I discovered that I was one in a line. She'd had one lover after another until I came along, and never wanted to marry any of them. She said that she didn't think she could ever be faithful to one man, but I was certain that she could. More fool me," he added bitterly. "Amusing, isn't it, that you know already that permissive people find it difficult to be faithful, and I had to learn it the hard way."

"I wasn't in love," she reminded him. "You were."

"I should have known. Permissive people don't seem to make faithful lovers."

"But if she was like that," she began, moving closer to the bed, "experienced, I mean…how did you become impotent?"

"I stopped being able to want her after she had her third extramarital affair," he said honestly. "And without a lifetime of experience behind me, I thought that meant that I was permanently demanned. So I didn't try."

She saw him quite suddenly in a different light. Not as a playboy of the music world, but as an intense, deeply emotional man who felt things right down to his soul.

"Feeling sorry for me, Poppy?" he taunted as she paused by the bed.

"Oh, no. I'm feeling sorry for her," she said. "How sad to have someone love you so much and to be able to feel nothing in return."

"She's happy. She has a husband who doesn't require faithfulness, and plenty of money to spend."

"That wouldn't make me happy."

He smiled. "What would?"

"Being loved. Having a home. Having children. I'd still practice, of course. I guess I'd have to marry a man who was willing to sacrifice a little so that I could, but I'd make sure he never regretted it."

"Do you have hang-ups about sex?" he asked curiously.

"Just about having it before I get married," she replied, and grinned at him. "Deep-seated principles aren't easily uprooted."

"People shouldn't try to uproot them," he replied. "I'm sorry about that. It was a delicious surprise to find myself so quickly capable with you. I wanted to explore it." He shrugged. "But I shouldn't have put pressure on you."

"I want to," she said sincerely. "I'll bet you're a wonderful lover. But I want it all, the white wedding gown, the wedding night, the honeymoon... I'm greedy."

He smiled. "Don't sound as if you're apologizing for it. You're a breath of fresh air to a cynic like me." He frowned quizzically at her. "Has it occurred to you that in a few days we've become as intimate as a married couple except in one respect?"

"We still don't know each other."

"You'd be surprised at what I know about you," he remarked gently. "You like to go barefoot on the carpet. You're neat, but not fanatical about it. You like to cook, but you don't like to clean up. You're intellectual so no situation comedies for you. You like nature specials and news and politics and music. You have a kind heart and you like animals and children, but underneath all that is a passionate nature held under very tight control." His eyes narrowed on her body. "You'll be a demanding lover, little Poppy, and some lucky man will probably find you next to insatiable in bed."

She lifted both eyebrows. "Stop that."

"I wish it was going to be me," he replied. "But I've already messed up one marriage by leaping in with my eyes closed after a one-week courtship. I'm not going to do it twice in one lifetime."

"Neither would I, although you didn't ask."

"Sit down." He pulled her down on the bed and drew her hand to his chest, holding it there. "I'm on the road six months out of the year, recording and making business deals, doing interviews and talk shows and working with underprivileged inner-city kids. It's a project of mine, finding volunteers to work with them once a week to help keep them out of trouble," he added with a grin. "When I'm home, and home is Texas, I compose to the exclusion of everything else. Sometimes I go for a whole day without eating, because I'm so wrapped up in my work that I forget to cook." He smoothed his thumb over the back of her hand. "I'd make a lousy husband. In fact, I did. I can't really blame her—"

"I can." She interrupted him. "If you love someone, you accept it all, the separations, the good times, the bad times, the illnesses. It's all part of marriage."

"You've already had the illness part," he mused.

"I'd have done that for anyone," she protested.

"You did it for me, though," he replied. "Blushing all the way. You don't do it so much anymore, though," he added amusedly. "You're getting used to me, aren't you?"

"You're very nice, when you forget to grumble."

"I have my faults. A quick temper is the worst of them. But I don't drink or gamble, and when I'm not working, I'm fairly easy to get along with." He searched her eyes. "Why are you called Poppy?"

"My father told me that my mother loved flowers," she recalled. "But he added that when I was born, the first thing she thought of was a poem about poppies growing in Flanders Fields where the veterans of World War I were buried. She went into the hospital to have me on Veterans Day and they were selling Buddy Poppies…." She smiled.

"Muddled, but I get the idea," he said. "My name is Henry, but everyone called me Hank from the time I was in grammar school."

"It's a nice name."

"So is yours." He drew her hand to his lips and kissed it softly. "Thank you for taking care of me."

The gentle caress was thrilling. She smiled. "It was very educational."

One blue eye narrowed. "Just don't start experimenting with men who aren't sick," he said.

Her eyebrows went up.

He laughed and let go of her hand. "Now I know I must be delirious with fever."

"I guess so," she murmured dryly. "I'll finish the wash then clean up the kitchen while you nap."

"You don't have to do that," he said gently.

"We both need some clean clothes. It's no trouble."

"Thanks, then."

She shrugged, smiled and went back to her chores. All the while she was thinking about Hank and how easily they seemed to fall into living together. Not that it was the normal sort of living together, she reminded herself.

But it was exciting all the same, and there was a closeness here that she'd never known. She liked just being with Hank, listening to his deep voice as he talked. He was intelligent and kind, and not at all the unprincipled rounder she'd thought he was. She thought of him in a totally different light now, and she knew that she was going to miss him terribly when the weather broke enough to let them out of this cabin.

She tried to put it out of her mind while she did the chores. She was beginning to feel very much at home here. The views were spectacular and she enjoyed the solitude. It would have been the ideal place to live, with the right man.

It occurred to her that Hank was the right man, the one she'd been looking for all her life. But it was impossible. You couldn't fall in love in four days, not the sort of love you needed to get married. Besides, Hank had a failed marriage behind him and he didn't want to risk a second. All that would have been left for them was an affair, which she couldn't accept.

She finished the washing and put the clothes into the dryer, wondering how it was going to be when she got back home. Probably she'd put this adventure into perspective and forget about it in a few months. Of course she would.

HANK SLEPT FOR the rest of the afternoon, while Poppy amused herself with the piano, lowering the volume to keep from disturbing the man in the master bedroom. The song he was working on was lying on the table beside the piano. She glanced over the tune and began to pick it out, slowly, smiling as the beautiful melody met her ears.

He didn't have more than a few words on paper, rhyming words mostly and not in any sort of order. Love, he'd written, when the feeling stirred fluttered like a…and he'd crossed out two words that didn't quite rhyme with it.

"A bright redbird," she mumbled, "playing in the snow."

"That's it!"

She jumped and caught her breath. Hank was leaning against the doorframe in his bathrobe. His blue eyes were glimmering, and he was laughing.

"I couldn't get the rhyme or any sort of reason to go with those words," he explained. "But that's it, that's exactly it…!"

He moved to the piano and slid onto the bench beside her. He played the song with a deep bass beat that emphasized the sweetness of the high melody.

"Love when the feeling stirred, fluttered like a redbird, playing in the snow," he sang in his deep, soft voice, looking at her and grinning. "Flew like an arrow through the sky, higher than a redbird flies, left me all aglow."

Only words, she thought, but when the music was put with them, major and minor chords intermixing, when he sang the words, when the deep, throbbing counterrhythm caught her up—it was going to be a hit. She knew it and felt goose bumps rise on her arms at the power and beauty of it.

"You feel it, too, don't you?" he asked, stopping. "It's good, isn't it? Really good."

"The best yet," she had to agree. "Who did the music?"

One corner of his mouth tugged up just a fraction of an inch and she laughed. "Silly question," she murmured. "Sorry."

"It will take some more work, but that's the melody." He chuckled. "Imagine that, I'd been sitting in here for a solid week trying to come up with something, anything…and all I needed was a veterinarian to point me in the right direction." He grinned at her. "I suppose you treat birds, too, don't you?"

She nodded. "Parrots and canaries and parakeets, for lung infections. Birds are mostly lung, you know." She searched his face. "You shouldn't be up. It's too soon."

"I heard you playing my song," he explained. "I had to come and see what you thought of it."

"I think it's great."

He smiled. "Thanks." She was slowly touching the keys again and some soft sadness in her face touched him. "What's wrong?" he asked.

She looked up. "The snow's stopped."

He looked out the window. He hadn't noticed. He got up from the bench and walked to stare out the other window down at the road. It had stopped, and the sun had come out. "Great skiing weather now," he murmured. "The snowplows will dig us out by tomorrow." He stuck his hands into the pockets of his robe. "You'll be free."

What an odd way to put it. "I don't plan to rush out and file kidnapping charges against you," she said pointedly.

He turned. "That wasn't how I meant it, although I will apologize handsomely for kidnapping you by mistake." His eyes swept over her very slowly, almost possessively. "I suppose you'll be rushing back to your practice."

"I need to."

"What if you don't have a job to go back to?" he persisted seriously.

She blew out a soft breath. "Well, I suppose they'll repossess my car and my apartment first..."

"Is there somewhere else you could work, if you had to?"

"Of course!" she said, laughing. "Sioux City isn't that small. There are other practices. I could find something, but it wouldn't be as a partner. I'd have to start at the bottom again."

"Honey, I don't think you've realized that you're at the bottom right now."

The endearment made her heart race. She dropped her eyes before he could read the pleasure it gave her.

"Sorry. That slipped out," he said, teasing.

"Oh, I liked it," she replied. "Nobody ever called me honey except the mailman, and he was seventy."

He burst out laughing. "I'll have to make up for that. You can't leave until morning, anyway, not unless they get those roads cleared early."

"I wouldn't leave until you were well, regardless," she said, surprised at his assumption that she couldn't wait to get out.

His face smoothed. All expression went out of it. "I see."

"You needn't look shocked," she said. "You'd do it for me."

"Yes, I would." He began to realize how much he'd do for her. Under different circumstances, they might have had a real beginning. But it was the wrong time, the wrong place, and he was still afraid of the risk.

"It's been an experience I'll never forget," she said

absently. "I'll listen to your tapes from now on. I suppose I was a bit of a musical snob."

"Maybe I was, too. I think I'll buy an opera tape or two."

She smiled. "That's nice. You might try Puccini."

"Is he that Italian singer?" he asked.

"He's the composer. He's dead. But Domingo and Pavorotti sing the operas he wrote. My favorite opera is *Turandot*."

"Turandot." He smiled back. "I'll remember."

She got up from the piano. "How about something to eat?"

"You took the words right out of my mouth!"

She went into the kitchen and made potato pancakes and steak and biscuits with a side salad. When she went to call Hank, he was out of bed and dressed in jeans and a green pullover shirt. Despite that overshadowing growth of hair that covered his face, concealing its shape, he looked wonderful to Poppy.

"Are you sure you feel like eating at the table?" she asked worriedly.

"Yes. I'm still a little weak, but I'm on the mend." He smiled. "Doesn't it show?"

She nodded. "I guess it does."

They ate at the small table in the kitchen. His appetite was much better, and he was only coughing occasionally now. He ate heartily. Considering the speed of his recovery, it didn't take much guesswork to tell that overall, he was in great shape.

"How did you learn to cook like this?" he asked.

"From my dad. He was a chef. He really was good

at it, too. He taught me how to make pastries and sauces. I enjoy cooking."

"It shows. This is delicious."

"Thank you!"

They were silent until they finished eating. They drank their second cup of coffee at the kitchen table, and Hank stared into his mug pensively.

"You're brooding, aren't you?" she asked.

He nodded. He looked up into her eyes and held them for a long, static moment. "I haven't had anyone around me, close like this, for a long time. You've grown on me, Poppy," he mused half-humorously. "I'm going to miss you."

She smiled back, a little sadly. "I'm going to miss you, too. I haven't had anyone to look after or care about since my dad died. It's been lonely for me."

He turned the coffee mug idly on the table's glossy surface. "Then suppose we keep in touch," he suggested without looking at her.

Her heart leapt. "Oh, that would…" She calmed her tone. "That would be nice. I'd like that."

He smiled at her. "So would I. I'll give you the address here and in Texas. Write to me when you get back."

"Are you terrible about answering letters?" she asked.

He shook his head. "I'm very good about it, in fact. I answer most of my own fan mail with the help of a secretary."

"I see."

"No, you don't." He corrected her, interpreting her

expression accurately. "I don't leave her to do the answering, I dictate the replies. And I won't let anyone answer your letters. I'll do it myself."

Her stiff posture relaxed. "Then I'll write."

"And don't assume that if you don't hear back immediately that I've forgotten you or that I'm ignoring you," he added. "I'm on the road a lot, I told you. It may take a week or two, sometimes longer, for my mail to catch up with me."

"I'll remember," she promised.

He reached out and covered her soft hand with his big one. "One more thing," he said gently, coaxing her eyes up to meet his. "Find another job."

She gaped at him. "My job is my business."

"Your job is a joke," he returned. "They're using you, sweetheart, dangling the idea of a partnership so that they can get someone to take over the jobs they don't want. There won't be any partnership. One day they'll find someone more useful and you'll be out on your ear, perhaps at the most inconvenient time."

"You're very cynical," she remarked.

He nodded. "I'm an expert on people who use other people," he told her. "I've been used a time or two myself."

She wiggled her eyebrows. "Can I have three guesses about how they did it?"

He glowered at her. "I'm serious."

She finished her coffee. "Okay. I'll think about it."

"You do that."

She got up and put the dishes in the dishwasher. "Is there anything else that needs doing?"

"Yes." He came up behind her and slipped his lean arms around her, hugging her back against him. "I need to be ravished."

She laughed with pure delight. "I'm not up to your weight," she reminded him, looking up over her shoulder with sparkling dark eyes. "And besides, I'd never be able to overpower you."

"I'll help."

She shook her head. "No. I expect that you're as addictive as caffeine. One taste of you wouldn't be enough. I'd get withdrawal symptoms."

He chuckled and hugged her closer for a minute. "So would I. And I'm probably still a little contagious," he added with a sheepish grin as he let her go. "No matter," he mused, watching her. "When I'm well and truly back on my feet, I'll come calling. Then, look out."

The soft warning kept her going, all through the rest of the day, and through the anguish of the parting the next morning, when he had to take her to the ski lodge and leave her with barely more than an affectionate hug.

She worried about him all the way to the airport on the lodge's shuttle bus, because even though the snowplows had been along, the roads were still treacherous. But as the shuttle passed the road to his cabin, she saw that his Bronco was safely parked at the door and smoke was coming out of the fireplace. He'd made it home, and hopefully, he'd be fine. She settled back into her seat, trying not to cry. It was amazing, she thought, how five days in Colorado had altered the rest of her life. Her last thought as they left the snow-covered valley behind was how would she survive until she saw Hank again?

CHAPTER SIX

POPPY BEGAN TO realize very quickly after her return to Sioux City, Iowa, that Hank had been right about her supposed partnership. The vets with whom she worked seemed to have plenty of free time and yet they made three times her salary. She was always the one to work nights and weekends and holidays, and whenever the weather was particularly bad, it was Poppy who had to go out on large-animal calls. That could be very difficult indeed when she was asked to deliver a calf or a foal, or treat a mean-tempered bull for a cut.

She had bruises all over her, a bad cold and there was no mention of an increased salary or a partnership two months later. She was getting fed up. And not only with the veterinary practice.

She'd written twice to Hank. So far, there hadn't been even a postcard in reply. On one of the music talk shows, which she'd started watching, there had been one tidbit about Amanda Sutton being in a hospital in Wyoming awaiting the birth of her first child and some more rumors about the breakup of her group, Desperado. But that was all the news there had been. Remembering how fond Hank was of Amanda,

Poppy hoped she was all right and that her child had been born healthy.

She tried very hard to remember what Hank had said about not being upset if she didn't hear from him right away. But when two months rolled into three, she began to put the past in perspective. The time she'd spent with Hank had been a five-day interlude and nothing serious had really happened, except for a few kisses. He'd told her he wanted nothing less than another marriage, so what had she expected? Perhaps he'd decided that even friendship with her was too much of a risk, and he'd withdrawn.

She couldn't blame him. He hadn't had an easy time of it where women were concerned. But the last thing on her mind had been trapping him into a relationship he didn't want. When she thought about it, it seemed likely that he'd had his share of ambitious women stalking him because he was rich and famous. She wasn't like that, but he wouldn't know. He didn't know her at all. Apparently he didn't want to.

Poppy tried to put him out of her mind, but his new song, "Redbird," had just been released on an album along with several other newly recorded tracks. It meant that Amanda had to be working again, because her sweet, clear soprano could be heard above the deep bass voices of her group. The song that Poppy had given him the inspiration for was as beautiful as it had sounded in the cabin, and it was a surprise to find that her first name was mentioned in the dedication of the album, jointly to Carlton Wayne Sutton—very obviously the new baby—and herself. She tingled all

over at the thought that Hank had remembered her
even that well. She was a nobody, after all, hardly his
sort of woman. The terrible thing was that she had no
close girlfriends, no one to share the thrill with. She
mentioned it to a clerk in the nearby record shop, but
he only smiled and agreed that it was a great honor.
She was sure that he didn't believe her.

Her stamina was giving out. Despite her youth,
the practice was really getting her down. Eventually
she couldn't take it anymore and she went looking
for another job.

She found it in a very small practice in a town
twenty miles outside Sioux City, in a farming community. The elderly veterinarian there had one young
partner but needed someone to take care of the office
while the two of them were out on large-animal calls.
Poppy wasn't overly eager, but she was pleasant and
had qualifications that they liked.

"What about experience?" Dr. Joiner, the elder
partner, asked gently.

"I'm working for a group practice in Sioux City,"
she explained, "but I have to do all the large-animal
calls and work nights and holidays and weekends."
She smiled sheepishly. "I'm sorry. I suppose that
sounds as if I'm lazy. I'm not, and it is a great opportunity to learn how a practice works. But I'm so
tired," she concluded helplessly.

Dr. Joiner exchanged a speaking glance with his
young partner, Dr. Helman. "It isn't quite so busy
here," he explained. "But we have enough work for

three people. The thing is, I can't offer you a partnership. You'd be a salaried employee and nothing more."

"Oh, that's all right," Poppy said, relieved. "I don't think I've got enough stamina for another partnership."

Dr. Joiner chuckled. "Dr. O'Brien, you're a peach. I'll be happy to have you aboard. When can you start?"

She explained that she'd have to give two weeks' notice, and that she'd make sure she got a reference from her partners. She thanked Dr. Joiner again, smiled at Dr. Helman and set off to her office with a lighter heart.

THE PARTNERS WEREN'T surprised when she announced her resignation, and they gave her a good recommendation as well. They apparently expected that no junior partner was going to last very long with what was expected of her or him. But they were interviewing other new graduates the last few days Poppy worked for them. She couldn't even warn the excited prospective employees. They'd have to find out the truth the same harsh way she had. But it would teach them a good lesson. Heaven knew, she'd learned hers.

She kept her apartment. It was only a twenty-five-minute drive to the new office, and she'd have to have time to look for a new place to live that was closer, if her new job worked out.

The job itself, after the long, strenuous practice she'd left, was wonderfully uncomplicated and enjoyable. She didn't have to work every weekend. The other vets alternated with her. Each one was on call a different night, so she didn't have to work every night, either. Holidays were shared. It was heavenly and the odd thing was that she made just as much money as she'd made in the practice. She felt at home after just one week on the job. She decided that moving closer was a pretty safe bet, considering how well they all worked together.

She found a room in a nice, comfortable boarding house and paid a week's rent in advance. Then she went to pack up her things and have them moved to her new home.

It didn't take long, because she didn't have much. She made two trips in her car and was just packing it for the third time when the telephone rang inside. It was supposed to be disconnected already, so she ignored it. The last few calls had been salespeople doing promotions. She couldn't imagine who might be looking for her, short of her old partners. Certainly, she knew, it wouldn't be Hank Shoeman. It had been over four and a half months and he'd surely forgotten all about her by now. She'd faced that fact, without much enthusiasm, because her memories of him were sweet.

She settled in her new apartment in the boarding house and got more comfortable in her job over the next week. She'd just finished examining and inoculating a three-month-old poodle puppy when she heard the waiting-room door open. She was alone in the office, because it was just after hours and the receptionist had gone home. Drs. Joiner and Helman were out on calls.

"I'll only be a minute!" she called out. She finished with the poodle, assured the owner that he was in excellent health and that he'd be automatically notified when to bring the dog back for his next round of shots.

He thanked her and she smiled happily as she watched him leave. She finished writing up the chart and went out into the waiting room, hoping that it was going to be something uncomplicated so that she could go home and eat.

She opened the outer office door with her professional smile, and stopped there, frozen in place.

The man looked familiar, and not familiar. He was wearing a gray suit. His hair was conventionally cut. He had a mustache, nothing more. The rest of his lean, handsome face was clean-shaven, and except for a couple of thin scars and a crooked nose, it was an appealing face. Blue eyes twinkled out of it as he studied her in her neat white lab coat.

"Nice," he said pleasantly. "You haven't lost a pound, have you? And I gather that this new job doesn't require your life's blood."

"Hank?" she asked uncertainly.

He nodded.

"Your hair...your beard," she began.

"I'm changing my image," he explained. "I'm tired of looking like a refugee from a cave."

"You look very nice," she said.

"So do you. How about supper?"

"There aren't any restaurants around here," she told him. Her heart was beating madly. "You didn't answer my letters."

"It's a long story," he said. "I'll tell you everything you want to know. But for now, I'd enjoy a good meal. I've spent two days tracking you down and except for breakfast at the hotel and a couple of sandwiches, I'm running on empty."

"There are lots of restaurants in Sioux City," she said.

"Then we'll go there. Do you need to stop by your apartment first?"

She shook her head, bemused by the sight of him. He looked unspeakably elegant and sexy. She wanted to throw herself into his arms and tell him to forget about explanations, it was enough that he was here. But she couldn't do it. He was probably on his way to or from Texas and had only stopped in because he wondered what had happened to her. It wasn't a proposal or a proposition; it was just a visit. She had to remember that and not let her imagination run away with her.

She took off her lab coat and slid her arms into the deep pink cotton jacket she wore over her pale pink blouse. She took time to run a brush through her hair and refreshen her makeup before she rejoined Hank in the outer office.

"I have to lock up," she explained, and took time to do that, too. When the lock was secure and checked, and the burglar alarm set, she walked with Hank to his car. But she stopped short when she saw it, and her uplifted face was wary and a little scared.

He reached down and took her hand, holding it tightly in his. "It's all right," he said gently.

The driver came around, smiling, and opened the door of the big white stretch limousine for them. Hank helped Poppy inside and slid in next to her. The driver closed them in and went around to get behind the wheel.

Hank had already told him where to go. He took off without a word, and Hank closed the curtains between front and back and turned on the interior light.

Poppy's expression fascinated him. She looked at everything, explored the CD deck, the television, the well-stocked bar, the telephone...

"Six people could ride in here," she remarked, smoothing her hand over the burgundy leather seat.

"Six people usually do," he replied, stretching out lazily to study her. "Like it?"

She grinned. "I love it. I only wish I had a friend that I could brag about it to."

"Surely you have one or two."

She shook her head. "I don't make long-lasting friends that easily. Only casual ones. My best friend married years ago, and we lost touch."

He crossed one long leg over the other. "Did you see the song on the charts?"

"Yes! It was great! Thank you for the dedication."

He waved her thanks away. "Thanks for the help. Everyone loved it, especially Amanda."

"How is she?"

"Blooming," he said with a smile. "She and Quinn and Eliott are all moonstruck over that baby. They take him everywhere, even to recording sessions with the group." His eyes were sad and faintly wistful. "I've always envied them that closeness. Now I envy them the baby."

"The album was dedicated to him, too," she recalled.

"He's a good-looking kid," he said. "Even cries with rhythm. We're all going to buy him a set of drums when he's two."

"Do they still hang people in Wyoming?" she asked meaningfully.

He got the joke at once and chuckled. "Quinn might just do that to me." He locked his hands behind his head, pulling his suit coat pleasantly taut over the powerful muscles of his chest and arms while he looked at her. "I've been tying up loose ends, settling business affairs, getting recording contracts and publicity tours finalized. I'm free for the next two months."

"You're not in town on business, then?" she asked conversationally.

His blue eyes narrowed. "You know why I'm in town, Poppy."

Her heart jumped but her face gave nothing away. "Actually I don't. I wrote you two letters, neither of which was ever answered. There wasn't a telephone call or any communication for months. You don't ignore people for almost half a year and then just drop by as if you saw them yesterday."

"You're mad." He sighed. "Yes, I was afraid you would be. I kept trying to put down what I felt on paper, and failing miserably. I couldn't boil it down to a telephone call, either. Just when I thought I'd fly out here, something kept coming up. It's been a long five months, honey. The longest five months of my life. But I'm here now, and you're going to have hell getting rid of me."

"Don't you have contractual obligations to fulfill?" she asked.

He shook his head, slowly. "That's why it took me so long to come after you. I didn't want any interruptions."

She shifted back against the leather seat. "I won't have an affair with you, so if that's why you came, I'll save you the time."

He began to smile. "Have you forgotten what a low boiling point you have with me?"

"Yes," she said uncomfortably. "And that should bother you. One more groupie might be more than you could take."

"Not if she was you," he said pointedly. "I'd love having you throw yourself at me and hang on for dear life."

"Why?"

"That's something we'll talk about for the next few days." He stretched again and yawned. "I haven't slept. You're a hard woman to track down. Eventually I phoned every single veterinarian's office in the city. Do you know how many there are?"

"I have a fairly good idea," she replied, shocked.

"Couldn't you have had your secretary or someone do that for you?"

"Why, no," he said, surprised at the question. "It wouldn't have occurred to me to trust something so important to another person."

She flushed. "You'd forgotten all about me, surely? I've seen some of the photos on your other albums. You attract beautiful women."

"Beauty isn't everything," he replied. "And sometimes it isn't anything at all. You're beautiful to me, Poppy, because you have the kindest heart of any woman I've ever known. I've never had anyone want to take care of me when I was sick until you came along. And under those circumstances, too, when I'd practically kidnapped you. You'd have been perfectly justified in walking out and leaving me there to cough myself to death."

"I couldn't have done that," she protested.

"Not even if you'd hated me. Yes, I know. But I don't think you hated me, Poppy," he mused, watching her like a hawk. "In fact, I think you felt something quite different on that last day we spent together."

"Compassion," she said abruptly.

"Compassion." He smiled. "Is that all I get?"

"What do you want?"

He leaned forward with his hands clasped loosely over his long legs. "I want you to love me, Poppy," he drawled deeply. "I want you to become so obsessed with me that you grow pale if I'm out of your sight for an hour. I want you to hate women who look at me or touch me. I want you to ache for me in your bed at night, and go hungry for the feel of me in your arms."

She already felt that way. She wasn't telling him so, however. She cleared her throat. "Well!"

"And before you start raging at me about indecent proposals before dinner," he added slowly, "I want a hell of a lot more than one night with you."

Her eyebrows levered up. "An affair is still..."

"I want a baby, Poppy," he said in a deep, soft whisper. "I want a son of my own, so that I don't have to stand over Amanda and Quinn and covet theirs."

Her body reacted to the statement in an unexpected way, so that she had to fold her arms over her breasts to keep him from noticing.

He noticed anyway, and his eyes gleamed with feeling. "You want it, too, don't you?" he said coaxingly. "A home, a husband, a family of your own. Maybe a few pets to look after, too."

"My job..."

"Whatever," he said easily. "If you want to keep on practicing, that's all right with me. It will give you and the kids something to do when I'm out of town."

Her heart was racing wildly in her chest. He looked sane. Perhaps he had a fever again.

"I'm not crazy," he explained. "I'm just lonely. So are you. So if we get married and make a family together, neither of us will ever have to be lonely again."

"There are plenty of women who would be willing..."

"I want you," he said simply. "You can't imagine how empty my cabin has been since you left." He laughed, but without mirth. "All my life I've been self-sufficient, independent. Women have chased me for years, before and after my marriage. But here you come, spend less than a week in residence, and you're living with me still, here and here." He touched his head and his heart. "I can't get rid of you. And believe me, I tried. I tried for five months."

She glared at him. "Maybe I had more success at it than you did," she taunted.

"Maybe you didn't."

He reached across the space that separated them and lifted her body right into his arms.

"Now, you see here…!"

His mouth hit hers while she was getting the last word out. He wasn't brutal or rough, but the action was amazingly effective. She went under without a protest. Her arms went around his neck and she lifted to the slow, soft caress of his hands even as her mouth opened to accept the deep, hard thrust of his tongue inside it.

Her legs trembled where they lay over his. He drew her closer and deepened the kiss even more, held it until he felt her begin to shudder. His hand smoothed up over her thighs, her flat stomach, her breasts. She moaned.

"You got over me, right?" he whispered against her mouth. "It's really noticeable, how completely you've gotten over me. Open your mouth again…"

She barely heard him above the wild throb of her heart. She clung to him while one kiss led to another, each more arousing than the one before. He turned her so that her hips pressed deeply into his own, so that his arousal was suddenly blatantly threatening. But she wasn't afraid.

"You're so small," he groaned as he let his mouth slide onto her throat. "Too small!"

She kissed his cheek, his temple, his closed eyelids with quick, warm lips. "I'll fit you," she promised. "I'll fit you like a glove."

"Poppy," he groaned again in anguish.

"Do stop worrying," she whispered as she found his mouth. "I love you."

"No more than I love you," he whispered back, holding her closer. "Are you going to marry me, complications and all?"

"I don't seem to have any choice. How else can I protect you from scores of sex-crazed beautiful women?"

He chuckled and kissed her again, murmuring his agreement against her soft, welcoming mouth.

AND THEY WERE MARRIED, six months to the day after Hank had abducted Poppy to his mountain cabin. The whole group of Desperado was there as witnesses in the small Wyoming church where Amanda had married Quinn Sutton several years before. They spoke their vows and exchanged rings. The look Hank gave his new bride would have melted snow, but fortunately it was summer.

"Where are you going for your honeymoon?" Amanda asked them when they'd changed and were ready to get into the limousine.

"That's our secret." Hank chuckled. He kissed Amanda's cheek, and the baby's, and shook hands with Quinn Sutton and Elliot.

"Well, write when you get time," Quinn asked. "Let us know you're okay."

"I'll do that. Take care of each other. We'll be in touch."

The Suttons all stood close together, waving until Poppy and Hank were out of sight.

"They're a very special couple, aren't they?" Poppy asked, sliding as close to Hank as she could get.

"A very special family," he agreed. "We're going to be one, too. I'll prove that to you tonight," he said, his voice deepening, lowering. There had been nothing more than kisses all during the time they waited for their wedding day. Now the time had come for all the secrets to be unveiled for Poppy and she was as excited as she was apprehensive. She loved him. That had to be enough, she reminded herself. She slid her small hand into his big one and snuggled close.

But she was less comfortable after they ate a leisurely supper and cleared away the dishes. Her disquiet showed on her face, too.

He tossed aside the dishcloth and pulled her gently in front of him. "Weddings are traumatic at best," he said quietly. "We can wait until you're rested and feel more like a new experience."

She nibbled at the skin on her lower lip. "I'm not usually so cowardly," she began.

He took her face in his big hands and tilted it up

to his tender eyes. "I don't have anything that you haven't already seen," he reminded her.

"But I do," she said miserably. She plucked at his shirt. "And I'm grass green and inhibited...!"

"And five minutes from now, you won't know your own name," he whispered as his mouth searched for her lips and opened on them.

Actually it took less time than that for him to reduce her to insensibility. Her desire for him matched his for her, and by the time he carried her into the bedroom, she was fighting her way to his bare chest through the confining shirts that separated them.

"Slowly," he whispered as he put her down and slid onto the bed beside her. "Slowly, darling, we have all the time in the world. Nice and easy, now. Let's not rush."

She was shivering with new sensations, new expectations, but he gentled her until she lay drowsily in his big arms and let him undress them. She didn't have the will to protest or the sense to be embarrassed as he studied her pink nudity with covetous, possessive eyes. His hands were slow and thorough, like his warm mouth. He aroused her and excited her, and when she was whimpering softly with the overwhelming pleasure of his ardor, he moved into total possession.

She stiffened a little and gasped, but his mouth savored hers, and pressed reassuring kisses over her closed eyelids as he coaxed her into accepting the raw intimacy of his body.

"You are...very much a virgin," he whispered

against her trembling lips, and he smiled. "Is it all right? Am I hurting you?"

"No," she managed to say. Her nails dug into his shoulders as he moved again, very tenderly.

"It stings, doesn't it?"

"Yes."

"Only a little farther," he said half to himself, and his mouth crushed down hard on hers, his tongue shooting deeply into her mouth. The action shocked her so much that she relaxed and allowed him complete and total access to the soft warmth of her body.

She cried out, surprised, because it was the most profound experience of her entire life. Her eyes opened wide and she looked straight into his.

"Yes," he whispered huskily. "It's a miracle, isn't it? Man and woman, fitting together so closely, so completely, that they form one person." He kissed her damp face gently as he began to move, each tender shift of his body bringing a sudden, sharp pleasure that lifted her to him in delight. "Feel the rhythm and move with me," he coaxed, smiling as she began to match him. "Think of it as composing a symphony, making music...that's it. Hard now, baby. Cut loose and move to the beat. Move hard. Real hard...!"

She lost control of herself completely then and although she heard his urgent whispers, she seemed outside her body, watching it dance to his tune, contort and convulse with pleasure that seemed to feed on itself. Finally there was a hot burst of it that made her cry out against the unbearable sensations deep within her body. She buried her face against his throat and moaned endlessly as it went through her in waves. Somewhere in the heat of it, she heard him, felt him, as he joined her in that surreal existence with a hard shudder that arched his powerful body down roughly against hers.

Minutes later, the dazzling heat and color began to fade away and she found tears falling down her cheeks.

"It stopped," she whispered miserably.

He rolled onto his side and gathered her very close. "We'll get it back again when we've rested." He kissed her gently. "For a first time, it was fairly volcanic, wasn't it?" he mused. He laughed delightedly. "And we fit, don't we?"

"Oh, yes." She nuzzled closer, shivering with pleasure and love. "Hank..."

His mouth slid over hers. "We've just said all there is to say, and we never spoke a word," he whispered into her mouth. "I'm glad you waited for me, Poppy. I wish that I'd been able to wait for you, all my life."

She hugged him closer. "I'll settle for the rest of our lives," she said gently, "and everything that's ahead of us."

His big arms folded her close. "Love, then. Years and years of it."

She smiled against his chest. "And children to share it with."

"Yes." He tugged the cover over them, because it was chilly at night this high up in the mountains. "I'm glad I didn't apologize for abducting you," he murmured. "It was the only sensible thing I've done in the past few years."

"All the same, you can't abduct anyone else, ever."

"Oh, I'm reformed," he promised her with a grin. "The only thing I expect to abduct in the future is a piano now and again, so that I can compose an occasional song."

Her eyes fell to his mouth. "I particularly like the way you compose in bed. Would you like to try a new theme? Something on the order of a blues tune?"

He rolled over, smoothing her body against his in the growing darkness. "I think I can manage that." He chuckled. "How about you?"

She whispered that she had no doubts at all; about that, or about the future with him. It was going to be wonderful. And she told him that, too.

* * * * *

"Now, I know the circumstances aren't ideal, but I'm looking forward to working with you."

She appeared to struggle, like she was thinking how to formulate her words. "I wish I was working with you by choice and not circumstance. Not that I would choose to," she said with a chuckle.

"I hear you. If it weren't for this situation, we would still be throwing daggers at each other during leadership meetings."

"Put yourself in my shoes. If you were going through this, how would you feel?" she asked, rubbing her toe into the carpet. "Honest answer."

"I'm not as brave as you are, and I have more pride than common sense."

She blushed and averted her eyes. "I would have resigned if I didn't have a mother and sister to consider. Pride is secondary to priority."

He felt ashamed and got to his feet. He went over to her. "You're right. I'm thinking like a single man. If I were married or had other responsibilities, I'd do what I'd have to and keep my job. I was hoping that Irene—" He stopped, unsure of the etiquette of bringing another woman into the conversation.

"No need to stop on my account. I know you had—have—a life."

Lynx wasn't about to talk about Irene, no matter how cool Shanna claimed she was with it. "I'm ready to fall in love, get married and install the white picket fence."

"How do you know you're ready?" she asked.

He rubbed his chin. "I'm at the brink of where I want to be professionally. I want someone to share my success with me."

"I get it," she said, doing that half-bite thing with her lip again.

Don't miss
Rivals at Love Creek
by Michelle Lindo-Rice,
available July 2022 wherever
Harlequin Special Edition books and ebooks are sold.

Harlequin.com

Love Harlequin romance?

DISCOVER.

Be the first to find out about promotions, news and exclusive content!

f Facebook.com/HarlequinBooks

y Twitter.com/HarlequinBooks

O Instagram.com/HarlequinBooks

P Pinterest.com/HarlequinBooks

You Tube YouTube.com/HarlequinBooks

ReaderService.com

EXPLORE.

Sign up for the Harlequin e-newsletter and download a free book from any series at **TryHarlequin.com**

CONNECT.

Join our Harlequin community to share your thoughts and connect with other romance readers!
Facebook.com/groups/HarlequinConnection